A Shadow in the Yard

By the same author

Acts of Subversion

A Shadow in the the Yard

Liz McManus

WARD
RIVER
PRESS

This novel is entirely a work of fiction. The names, characters and incidents portrayed in it are the work of the author's imagination. Any resemblance to actual persons, living or dead, events or localities is entirely coincidental.

Published 2015
by Poolbeg Press Ltd
123 Grange Hill, Baldoyle
Dublin 13, Ireland
www.wardriverpress.com

1

A catalogue record for this book is available from the British Library.

ISBN 978-178199-9363

Printed and bound by CPI Group (UK) Ltd, Croydon, CR0 4YY

www.poolbeg.com

ABOUT THE AUTHOR

Liz McManus was born in Montreal, Canada, and lives in Ireland. She is a novelist and short fiction writer. Her awards include Listowel, Irish PEN and the Hennessy Award for New Irish Writing. Her first novel, *Acts of Subversion*, was shortlisted for the Aer Lingus/*Irish Times* award. She has also been a newspaper columnist. She has an MPhil, with Distinction, in Creative Writing (TCD 2012). Residencies include the Tyrone Guthrie Centre at Annaghmakerrig and the Heinrich Böll cottage on Achill Island. She was a TD for County Wicklow for eighteen years and a Minister of State for Housing and Urban Renewal in the Rainbow Government 1994/97. She chaired the National Taskforce of the Needs of the Travelling Community and the Monitoring Group on UN Resolution 1325. Currently she is the chairperson of the board of the Irish Writers' Centre. She trained and worked as an architect for a number of years in Derry, Galway and Dublin. She lives at 1 Martello Terrace, Bray – one of the childhood homes of James Joyce.

For Sean with love

MOSAIC

A man may objectively inherit
a role in history,
reluctantly or with devotion,
soldier, functionary, rebel,
engaging himself as an instrument
of required stability or urgent change.

But the bystanders accidentally involved,
the child on an errand run over by the army truck,
the young woman strayed into the line of fire,
the elderly person beside the wall when it fell
are marginalia only,
normally excluded from documents.

History is selective. Give us instead
the whole mosaic, the tesserae,
that we may judge if a period indeed
has a pattern and is not merely
a handful of coloured stones in the dust.

John Hewitt

PART ONE

WINTER 1970
INISHOWEN, COUNTY DONEGAL

Tom

Strictly speaking, it was his dog Liadh that found the body.

During the night a storm rolled in from the Atlantic. It howled around the house, bouncing twigs off the roof-slates and breaking branches from the walnut tree in the garden. With a tinkling exuberance, the dilapidated greenhouse collapsed in on itself. The next morning brought a brilliance that graced the fields with an unseasonal warmth. In the distance Lough Swilly, a sullen pewter colour, went quiet.

The dog had been restless all night and growling in her sleep. As soon as it was light, Tom Mundy took her out for a walk. Now that he was old, he found that, once he woke up, he couldn't get back to sleep no matter how hard he tried. He got out of bed and made a cup of tea before putting the dog into the boot of the car and driving to the forest. With her at his side he walked along the track in his even, loping stride. The evidence of storm damage was everywhere: his boots sinking in the waterlogged ground; a

3

broken fence; a fallen tree splayed across the path, its roots upended in a vaguely prurient display. He clambered over it with care. Liadh bounded out of the undergrowth, her night worries forgotten, and jumped around him as he straightened up.

'Bad dog,' he pushed her away, 'shoo, shoo . . .' and yet he was glad of her company. He was grateful too, that there was enough life in his aged bones to get him out walking in the early-morning air.

High with rain, the river thundered beyond the trees. Its song was a rambling commentary that accompanied him as he wound his way up the hill. When he was a child he'd been told about a man and a boy who had tried to cross that river when it was in full spate, before there was a bridge. Their bodies had been found at the mouth of the river where it emptied into the sea. Afterwards, the forestry men had built a bridge and, from then on, local people could cross in safety. It was a well-built timber bridge that had withstood the worst of weather. All the same, it had been a terrible storm, powerful enough to destroy any bridge. He thought . . . better to be sure . . .

Beneath his tweed cap his bony face looked indestructible. As the forest fell away behind him, he walked out into a landscape of scoured rock and whin.

His instinct had been correct.

Below him the bridge lay skewed towards one side of the river. It was broken up like matchwood. The long beams protruded out of the water and the cross-braces were smashed. Some timbers were caught in among the rocks, others had been swept along on the current. One end of the bridge was still held fast to its foundation while, at the other side, there was a cascade of rocks and stones left behind where it had broken free in the storm.

Loose stones gave way under his feet as he scrambled

down to get a closer look. Liadh, her tail up, passed him. She leapt into the river and disappeared among the rocks. He whistled. There was no answer.

'Bad dog!' he grumbled as he grabbed onto the end of the bridge that was still fixed to the ground. Where was she?

Liadh barked: a clear whistle-like call. Then again, for a second time, as if she had something to tell him. The dog scampered back to jump around him while the man stared across the river at the bundle of clothing caught up in the pile of rocks. Again the dog lunged forward. Shouting obscenities, the man pulled her back and thrashed her with his stick.

'Stay!' he shouted. The dog slunk off to crouch down on the grass.

Suddenly exhausted, the old man staggered on the wet ground. Behind his closed eyes, he saw scattered figures moving forward in a line as they beat the heather and peered under rocks and prodded pools of bog-water with sticks. Nature had succeeded, he thought, where the gardaí and the local people had failed. The thought broke him. His knees crumpled as a tide, foul as acid, rushed up from his stomach and spewed onto the grass.

'Shoo, shoo . . .' the man whimpered, more to himself than to the dog. His head in his hands, he knelt down and a long wail rose from somewhere deep inside. 'O Sacred Heart of Jesus, give me strength,' he prayed. 'O Mary, Mother of Christ, forgive me!'

He blessed himself and struggled up to stand on the bank. Then he waded through the water, until he was close enough to see her bloated hand, half-eaten by fish, the cuff of a red cardigan and, where her face had once been, a spongy mass of flesh already torn away from her skull. He knew at once that it was the girl in his photograph. Unmistakable.

His young neighbour, Rosaleen McAvady.

Rosaleen

1

The car was stuffy but I didn't dare open the window because I couldn't trust the two small children in the back. In a flash they'd stick their heads out and God knows what would happen next. They were so young – just six and four years old. I envisaged their slender bodies curving up into the air and flying away out of my grasp, so we sat in the heat and waited for the lights to change.

'Red, red, *greeeeen*!'

The children's chorus subsided when the car moved off. The boy drummed his feet into the back of my seat while the girl looked dreamily out the window. Aoife and Conor. My children. Sometimes they were like visitors from Mars, invading my planet, taking over my life.

'*Stop that!*' I said to myself and to Conor. He stopped kicking. I softened. 'So what was your favourite subject today?'

'We did art and we did painting,' said Aoife.

'And what about you, Conor?' I smiled into the rear-view mirror.

No reply.

'What was your favourite subject at school today?'

Again the drumming feet found the small of my back through the seat.

'Lunch is my fav'rite!' he shouted, his face pink with exertion.

Every time I drove this way home, my spirit lifted at the bend in the road, at the point where the view opened out across the watery expanse of Lough Swilly and, beyond it, towards Scotland – with the clouds swaggering across the sky and birds skimming the surface of the estuary.

The gateposts looked shabby in the sunshine. I took note of the never-ending inventory of household management that existed in my head. Today, the painting of gateposts, tomorrow, the dismantling of a house. '*No*,' I muttered.

When the car stopped, two sweaty little bodies leapt out and ran into the kitchen through the scullery, jettisoning schoolbags as they went. The scullery was cool and smelt of something embalmed. The stone slab floor and slatted shelves were what I wanted. What I still want, I told myself. I heard a deep sigh as if it came from someone else, not, as it did, from somewhere inside me.

All right, look forward, what's next? I asked as I emptied plastic bags of food onto the kitchen table. Dinner, I replied. A tin clattered across the floor. I bent to pick it up and felt a twinge in my stomach. God, it cannot be . . . I'm just late, I told myself. All the same, there was that night when we were tiddly after the Engineers' Annual Dinner Dance in the City Hotel and I forgot. Dourly the kitchen stared at me. The Belfast sink, propped up on bricks, overflowed with unwashed dishes and, under it, a plastic bucket full of rubbish begged me to take it outside. Above the lead pipe-work and crumbling plaster, a beam of sunshine was alive with motes of dust. No clue to be found here except a new damp spot at skirting level which I added to the inventory.

For once Kevin arrived home early, his car grinding up the stones on the driveway. As always, he went first to the sitting room where the children were stretched on the floor.

'*Wanderly Wagon*, silly!' they shouted at their father when he asked in faux innocence what they were watching.

Kevin was built to last. He was dark-haired and had broad shoulders and a barrel chest. It didn't bother him that he was going bald and his belly was starting to spread over his trouser waistband like custard over a piecrust. He was comfortable with himself. His enemies, of whom there weren't many, might have called him smug. Most people responded to his air of authority with a sense of relief that someone was in charge and I, too, warmed to the web of reassurance that he spun around me. It made me feel loved.

'I like to see you bending down to the oven . . .' He came up beside me and patted my behind.

I straightened up and looked sourly at him but I didn't say anything. What was there to say? One drunken night and I'd pay the price, not him. Before I knew better, I used to think you could get pregnant from kissing, and when a boy kissed me at a church hop I spent a fortnight afterwards in a state of panic. I told myself now that it was pointless to worry and that one slip-up was negligible, statistically speaking, but that was no comfort at all.

'That's a great welcome for a man home from the fields,' Kevin said without rancour. 'Mmmm, but that dinner smells good.'

Over our meal we talked while the children fidgeted and

played with their food. Kevin and I could talk for hours without necessarily saying very much. He talked work and often I just listened. Without leaving my own kitchen, I had shared countless site visits with him and had many a stand-off with builders and clients who pulled him in different directions. There were estimated radiator sizes and valve reductions with which I was intimately familiar, although I'd never actually seen them.

'Is that what he said, really?'

'The bastard actually said it to my face.'

'Kevin, *shhhhhhh*!'

'Sorry, kids. I meant the bad man said it.'

I listened contentedly – content that I was not out there trying to fathom the complexities of a building site. How I had ever got onto one in the first place was a mystery in itself. A studious girlhood, good exam results, five years in UCD and an inscribed parchment to show off at the end of it – none of this had made me an architect. When I had started work, I quickly learnt that you can fool a lot of people without fooling yourself, so I worked at a drawing board, talked the office vernacular and spent a lot of time keeping my head down.

Kevin rescued me and I was grateful for that. Yes, and grateful too for the route my life had taken since: to Inishowen and family and home. I had wanted so much to buy the house overlooking the estuary that, finally, Kevin had acquiesced to my pleading. He had been very serious and grown up about it. Against his better judgement, he had said, but – all the same – I got my way. It was a plain, two-storeyed farmhouse with an overgrown garden and a view of the lough. To one side was a small enclosed yard. After living in the house for more than three years, its rough, white-washed walls and mossy slates could still lift my heart, even though the task of its renovation weighed me down.

'Twenty years it will take to get this place right and you'll be pancrocked by the end of it,' Mammy had said when we had brought her to see the house. *After the sacrifices she had made to get me through college,* her unsaid comment. Although she never complained, I still felt guilty, but I was glad she approved of Kevin, whom she considered to be a good catch.

'Why couldn't you have got yourselves a new house?' she grumbled.

'We'll manage,' I said lightly. I was too excited to argue.

That day when the auctioneer had unlocked the door and let us into the stale, gloomy rooms for the first time and opened up the shutters to a flood of light and a wide view of water, fields and mountains, I had been captivated.

It did not take long before Kevin and I, children wandering in a wild wood, found ourselves in an alien world of rising damp and creeping wet rot.

'Are you going out?' Kevin asked.

'I told you,' I answered. 'The swop sale.'

Darkness had crept into the sitting room where he sat with the newspaper on his knees. The lamp beside his shirtsleeved arm formed a warm pool of light. Upstairs the children whispered loudly to each other across the landing.

'Go to sleep!' I was putting on my coat and practically running out the door.

'Hey,' he shouted, 'hey!'

I turned back.

'Don't be late, Rosaleen. Remember Mass in the morning is early.'

I'd forgotten the Anniversary Mass for his mother – my mother-in-law – a world of difference between the two. Mrs McAvady had been a fierce woman who spent her last days gasping for a cigarette in a hospital bed. After she

11

died, we found a stash of twenty Carrolls No. 1 in the bedside locker. That night, in the hospital, the nurse on duty had given a wry smile. 'Vonnie was wild stubborn,' she said.

Vonnie . . . I'd never heard my mother-in-law called by a diminutive name before. I didn't even know what to call her until the children came. After that it was easy. Granny McAvady had a magisterial sound which suited her better than her actual name. She had been christened Veronica after the patron saint of laundry workers. An appropriate name. Granny McAvady loved dirty laundry – other people's, that is. She gathered in gossip and spent her time relaying the scandals of the parish on the phone to a friend or into a relative's ear.

'Otherwise,' a malicious glint in her eye, her knuckles white on the arms of her wheelchair, she asked, 'what pleasure is left to me?'

She was like an old horse gone lame. Tough. Tied. Trapped. On her seventy-fifth birthday the family gathered in her house for the party. A cake was cut and we sang 'Happy Birthday'. She blew out the candles and then munched her way through pink icing and soft sponge cake. Glasses of sherry for the women and bottles of stout for the men were brought out.

As the company became more animated, the old woman's deafness isolated her. Pursing her lips, she sat hunched in her wheelchair. At a momentary lull in the conversation she seized her opportunity with a roar.

'Who's in charge of *those* two?'

All eyes turned on the children who were running through the crowd, squealing with excitement. A blushing young mother, a cousin of Kevin's, stepped forward. Ignoring their protestations, she grabbed the children by the hand and led them out of the room, shutting the door behind her. As the sound of the children's howls faded, the old lady bent her head onto her chest, lit a cigarette and sat back happily into her wheelchair.

'The Mass, yes, of course. I hadn't forgotten.'

'Hey!' Kevin said again, gently this time, and proffered his cheek.

I bent down over him. I knew my lips must be cold on his skin. I could sense the blood coursing through his veins, rich and buoyant.

Heavily, he placed his hand on mine. 'Don't be late.'

Outside there was still light in the sky. The lough had settled down for the night and the trees were blackening on the roadside. I had two bags of clothes in the back seat which I had collected for the swop sale, although the purpose of the event had little to do with trade in garments and everything to do with trading experiences, stories, gossip.

At Laura's house the connecting doors between the living room and the kitchen had been opened and there were young women everywhere, sifting through piles of garments. Some of them were half-undressed and shrieking with excitement as they tried on each other's clothes.

Fingers appeared above the crowd and waved shiny red nails. 'Welcome to the cattle mart!' Laura extricated herself from the crowd. She took the bags from my hands and emptied them onto a chair. 'Bring on your expensive mistakes! Hmmm,' she said, rummaging, 'I see you didn't bring the green trouser suit.'

'Over my dead body.' I grinned at her.

'Pity, it would look so much better on me.'

'Bitch!'

'Oooooh!'

She disappeared into the kitchen and returned with two glasses of wine.

She slipped one to me and nodded at the crowd, 'Watch out, Rosy, or they'll all want a glass.'

Laura had grown up in Derry. When she was nineteen, she'd had to get married. She and Cathal had gone to England straight after the wedding. A year later they came back with the baby and moved into a bungalow in Letterkenny. When we were young she had spent a term in the same boarding school as me. Funnily enough, we weren't great friends then. She was in the Pass stream; I was an Honours pupil. She played camogie while I watched on the sidelines and cringed whenever anyone got the bang of a stick. Later we found ourselves sharing the common ground of motherhood and hardly a day passed without us talking. She had grey eyes and the red hair of a tinker and talked as if she was in a hurry, which she was in a way, always running on about how when the children were hardy she'd be able to do what she wanted. What that was was never specified but, still, the ambition was there burning her up inside.

'I like the colour,' I said and nodded at the fingernails. I loved Laura. *The day isn't complete until we meet.* Sounds like a song, I thought, like a love song. Through the hurly-burly of children she was my other. She was another mother.

'Thanks. It's a work in progress. I've still my toes to do. So how're you doing?' She looked at me and her smile faded. She saw the trouble in my face, even though I thought my trouble was so deep that it couldn't show.

'I'm okay,' I muttered.

'Come on, Rosy, you're so shallow I can see through you.'

'Thanks for nothing.'

She took my arm and led me towards a window. Our reflections conspired blackly in the glass and I thought of the drive home in the dark. Was I desperate to come here or desperate to get away from there?

'Now tell me,' she said, lowering her voice.

Automatically I did the same.

'I'm late,' I whispered. 'I can't be but I am.' Tears trickled in my throat. I came here, I wanted to say, because I can't bear to be there.

'All right,' she said slowly. 'Well, you won't die from it. At least not any more.'

I gnawed on my lip.

'Have you told Kevin?'

'No.'

'Good.'

'Doesn't make any difference,' I sighed. 'He'll know soon enough.'

'But what do *you* want?'

Why was she asking me that? It wasn't as if I had a choice.

'You do have a choice, you know.' Deliberately Laura turned her back on the room and faced the window.

I turned away too and gazed out at the front garden with its solitary cherry tree and scuffed-up lawn.

'I don't know what you mean,' I said. 'If I'm up the pole, that's it.'

'Not necessarily.'

I felt cold, as if my heart had stopped beating, and yet I could feel it pounding under my ribs. *No!* I wanted to say but my mouth was as dry as dust. Determined not to listen, I made to walk away but her hand on my arm was gentle, insistent.

'You could go to England,' she murmured in my ear.

Jesus, had she gone mad? How could she even think of such a thing?

'Stop it, Laura.' I turned to face her but she was unrepentant.

'Only wish *I'd* gone when I had the chance.'

'Don't even *say* such a thing!'

'Keep your hair on. Sure, the dear knows, you wouldn't be the first one from here, or the last.'

'What do you mean?' I couldn't resist asking.

'If *she* could do it . . .'

Aghast, I looked at Laura. She nodded towards to a group of women huddled over teacups and slices of cake.

'I don't get it. Who is *she*?'

'Gillian. Over there at the counter.'

I saw a pale girl with lank shoulder-length hair, the kind of hair you find spilling out of an old mattress. She looked exhausted, her back slouched against the kitchen counter as she pulled on a cigarette.

'Are you crazy?'

Laura giggled. 'The one you're looking at is Sheila O'Rourke. She's just had a baby. I'm talking about that one – Gillian.' She indicated a woman who was talking animatedly and waving her hand elegantly to emphasize a point she was making. Gillian wore a well-fitting jacket with Chanel-style trimming and round earrings that glinted as she moved. Gillian looked perfectly normal. In fact, she looked fabulous.

'She went over last year and no-one knew. She's not even married.'

I wasn't sure that I could believe Laura.

'Oh God, Laura,' I said. '*Oh my God . . .*'

Laura looked at me. Imperceptibly she began to shake her head. Then I was shaking my head. We were like puppets, the two of us, with our mute, wobbling faces.

'So what do you want?' she asked.

I flinched. Even in different circumstances I had difficulty answering that question. I did what was required and drew happiness where I found it, out of the nooks and hollows of my life, but it still felt as if I was living in a cosy, protective fog.

'My advice,' she whispered, 'is to say nothing to no-one. Kevin or anyone. Just in case.'

Then she encompassed me in her arms and her hair smelt chokingly of meadowsweet.

2

The next morning I waited for Kevin outside the church door. He was coming from the office over the Border, in Derry where he worked. I had dropped the children to school and arrived before him but I was content to wait. The newly built church at Burt was one of the wonders of my small world. I loved the fluidity of its circular form, its granite cobbles, its battened walls, its copper roof sweeping up to a conical spire, the careful assembly of stone, glass, metal and wood. It was a sacred monument that was simultaneously Christian and pagan. Although its form was unequivocally modern, the inspiration for the church sprang from an ancient source. High above it, on the mountain, a prehistoric ring fort, An Grianán Aileach, had the watchful air of a parent brooding over its offspring.

When Kevin arrived we went into the church together.

Under the bellied roof a circular band of stained glass glowed in brilliant colours.

'This church is so beautiful,' I whispered as we sat in a pew. 'It makes up for me being a lousy architect.'

'Aye,' he said, 'you and a few more I can think of.'

A priest emerged from a door and went onto the altar. He opened his arms in a call to prayer. I pressed my face into my hands and the space behind my eyelids was filled with an ominous presence: a wall of stone loomed out of a pale sky. Startled, I opened my eyes to the glow of the priest's vestments, the tabernacle at the altar, the flickering red lamp. In my ears the responses of the congregation to the priest's prayers sounded puny and thin. We made up a small number of people scattered across the pews: daily communicants and a few there to honour Veronica McAvady's memory but already, only a year after her death, that number was shrinking.

'*And who is my neighbour?*' the priest read from the Gospel of St Luke 10.29. '*Jesus answering said, "A man was going down from Jerusalem to Jericho and he fell among robbers, which stripped him of his raiment and wounded him and departed leaving him half dead. And by chance there came down a certain priest that way and when he saw him he passed by on the other side. And likewise a Levite when he was at the place came and looked on him and passed by on the other side. But a certain Samaritan as he journeyed came where he was and when he saw him he had compassion on him."*'

When he had finished reading, the priest lifted the Bible and kissed it. It was a sign. With a clatter the congregation sat back in the pews and waited.

In his sermon Father Cullen omitted any mention of the parable's pitiless priest. He spoke about our neighbours who were close to us and yet who were at one remove because they were living across the Border and how they needed our prayers, especially now that there was the threat of trouble in the air and how God would listen if we prayed and how nothing was solved by violence and unrest. Property and lives must be respected. This was the Word of the Lord.

Property and lives . . . in that order, I wondered, but I was hardly listening to what he was saying, even when Veronica McAvady's name was mentioned. I had an anxiety of my own gnawing inside me. Was it a sin to ask God to take away a pregnancy? If Father Cullen knew what I was thinking, no doubt he would send me out of the church in disgrace.

Beside me, Kevin shifted on his knees. He had a meeting at noon and he would never be late for a meeting because, he always maintained, that would be discourteous.

I followed him up the aisle to take Communion. As we shuffled forward I wondered if God would send me to hell for my bad thoughts.

The Mass came to a sudden end and the priest slipped away into the sacristy as discreetly as he had emerged.

Outside, the day was bright and rich with sounds: birds chattering, cars revving up, people. Kevin and I stood and waited for his sisters to come out of the church. I slipped off my headscarf and spread it awkwardly like an apron in front of me to prevent my knees being seen. Kevin liked me in miniskirts but his sister Maureen didn't approve of them, particularly at Mass.

Maureen was the elder of the two sisters: a big woman, like her mother had been, plain as a horse, with a thatch of wiry hair and bony, awkward hands. When she came out of the church and joined us on the grass, she squinted up at the copper roof of the church.

'I have to say I think it's a shame they didn't build a

proper church,' she said. 'This one looks like one of those Chinese things.'

'A pagoda?' Beside her, Kevin's younger sister, Sheena, winked at me.

She was the pert, bright-eyed wife of the assistant bank manager in Lifford. She was competitive at everything she turned her hand to: golf, knitting, amateur dramatics, the Irish Countrywomen's Association. Over the years, she had managed to fall out with a lot of people but now she had on her best smile for the Mass-goer who had stopped to shake hands with Kevin.

Sheena turned to me. 'I suppose *you* like it.'

'What?'

'Our new church.' she said, waving her hand. 'All this.'

'Yes, I do,' I said defensively.

'Well, so do I. Actually, I love it.' The sound of Sheena's laughter was like ice cubes rattling in a glass of gin and tonic.

Appropriately so, I thought. When she wanted to, Sheena could really put them away.

'I'm not sure *why* I love it,' she said, 'but it makes me feel welcome.'

Unexpectedly she dug her elbow into my arm and the scarf fluttered out of my grasp. I stooped to pick it up but Maureen was in ahead of me. The big-boned woman was nimbler than she looked. She picked up the scarf and ran it through her fingers before handing it over.

'Pretty material,' she said and then, with a pointed glance at my bare legs, 'Mind you don't catch cold.'

To my relief Kevin interrupted and said he had to get back to work. The three of them walked on ahead. I hung back and watched them go. I had never noticed the resemblance before: each of them with the same long broad back and short legs, as they moved together towards the car park.

Only my faithful Morris Minor was waiting for me when I got there. I swear it had a face. That car had a frisky look to its bonnet and headlights.

'So,' it demanded to know, 'what *do* you want?'

What I wanted to do was to run away. There was an urgency about my need to escape as I clambered over a style and hurried through the gorse. Out on the mountain the wind roared in my ears: a balmy wind playing around me as I walked. Under my feet, the ground was early-summer dry, crackling with tiny shoots and wild flowers. Maybe, I thought, I should get a puppy. With a new baby, I scoffed, was I nuts? The summit rose up ahead and I lost sight of the ring fort but I kept making my way up towards it. By nature, I am dogged. One step after the other. That's all it takes.

You do have a choice. Laura's voice intruded into the blowy air. The future was crowding me in and I felt as if I were suffocating. I stopped to draw breath and looked down at the church below me. I'd be thirty-three when that child was four. When he was ten, I'd be thirty-nine. I would be *ancient!* And yet the trouble I had was small compared to some. In Belfast there were people abandoning their homes out of terror of their neighbours while I stood amidst the gorse and heather and viewed the scenery. Inside me, a cluster of cells full of promise. *Nothing more . . .* Dinky cars travelled on the road below through fields that were dotted with houses; a watery swathe spread out on either side of Inch Island as the sea pulsated on its tide.

'I have a choice.' I said the words aloud, tasting each one on my tongue as if it were flavoured with danger.

I started to climb again, in my stride now, happy suddenly, as the sunlight chased shadows across the heather.

The majestic structure edged above the rim of mountain

as I approached. The stronghold of Aileach: a circular wall of boulders enclosing a grassy bowl. Was it my imagination or did the temperature drop when I bent my head to pass through the narrow entrance? As I walked under the lintel, I paced the thickness of the wall, the way I used to do as a child.

Inside the ring fort, there were concentric terraces with narrow steps and, against the limestone, the grass glowed green. As I looked up at the dome of blue sky, the colour was so intense it made my eyes water; the silence so deep my ears flattened. I sat down, leaning my back against a stone step.

Are you afraid? Laura's voice came out of nowhere. Yet again, in my head, I was re-running our conversation from the night before.

'It's selfish and wrong.'

'Are you a selfish person?'

'Well, I don't think so.'

'Exactly, I don't think you are either. Other women make this choice all the time. In England it's legal, clean and above board.'

'But it's killing a child, Laura. I mean it's murder!'

She had looked intently at me. 'Is that what you are?'

'What do you mean?'

'A baby-making machine?'

'Well —'

'Isn't that what they want you to think?'

They, I had wondered, but Laura had been in full flow.

'Even when it's a monster incapable of a decent life, they fix it up with tubes coming out of it and then they hand it over to you wrapped up and ready to wear you down for the rest of your life. Like with my sister's child. They said it was a gift from God and she had to put up with it. I'd like to see them minding a helpless, handicapped child twenty-four hours, those doctors in their white coats who go home each evening to the golf course and go to Mass on Sunday.'

The conversation had rolled around in my head since we had whispered like conspirators at her sitting-room window. It was not how I saw myself, I said. I wasn't able to make a decision like that. Anyway, Kevin would never agree.

'So don't tell him,' Laura had said impatiently. 'You and me, we can go to London for a shopping spree, can't we?'

Shopping! But wouldn't he have to agree, wouldn't he have to sign something? And where would the money come from? She didn't know or care.

For Laura it was a point of principle.

Lazily a bee circled in the air above my head. I lay down on the sweet-smelling grass and closed my eyes. The earth felt soft under me and I wanted to sink into it, deep down to where, I imagined, the bodies of ancient warriors were at rest with their belongings tucked around them: axe heads, leather pouches, coins. Such tidy housekeeping! Here was tranquillity and me dreaming that life could be anything I made of it. The droning of bees was untroubled, like a lullaby. As the sounds around me faded, I found myself sinking into oblivion. I was seeking illumination. What a foolish idea, I thought, for I'm a practical person. Light emerging out of darkness: isn't that what mankind has puzzled over ever since – I smiled sleepily – the dawn of time?

Suddenly a vision sprang to life. A woman standing imperiously proud, her head resting against white clouds, her flesh creamy and voluptuous. Her wild hair cascaded onto her shoulders and down around her body. The expression in her black-ringed eyes was steadfast. A bulwark against Nature itself, she gazed out across a stormy sea. Wrapped in a white shawl, the top of its head peeping above the wool fringing, a baby slept in the cradle of her arms.

I heard myself say: '*Yes, this my strength.*'

Astonished, I opened my eyes. Everything around me was absolutely still and I held my breath. In the next instant the wind lifted, tossing the heather and buffeting my hair. I had no idea how long I had been asleep. I glanced at my wristwatch: it had only been for a matter of minutes. I yawned and stretched my arms.

I had a dream, I thought, that was all. It didn't mean anything.

When I walked out through the entrance of the ring fort, a panorama greeted me. The hazy blue mountains of County Derry to the east and, to the west, the mountain of Muckish. The pale cone of Errigal. Lough Swilly probing its way towards Letterkenny and, like a whale's back emerging out of the sea, the island of Inch.

Far below me, a house was hunkered down in the trees along the water's edge. Even at this distance, I could tell that it was calling me home.

The Morris Minor looked at me quizzically when I arrived back at the car park.

'I'll manage,' I said, 'so you can stop asking right now.'

I was putting the car into gear when a shadow fell across the window. Outside, a man was bent over and gesticulating at me. He was thin, sharp-nosed, with narrow eyes and lank greying hair. What could he want – directions, maybe? A lift back to Letterkenny? I rolled down the window and I was about to ask when he stood up, his back still arched like that of an old countryman. For a frozen moment I did nothing, felt nothing. There were the stained cavalry-twill trousers in my line of sight, the edge of a tweed jacket flapping above the open flies and his member swollen and moving in his agitated hand. I heard myself shriek a silly girl's shriek that drove a flock of crows out of the treetops, and I felt my body tighten as I forced the car to turn, brakes screeching, on the gravel. I was panting with fear and yet, beneath my panic, there was something slithering in my brain like a water snake. *What drove a man to that?* I wondered, unable to resist a backward look in the rear-view mirror. I caught a glimpse of his ecstatic smile as he buttoned his jacket across his chest and wiped his hand on its lapel. If I had needed a better view I would have stopped the car. I'd have even turned it around so I could face him. Filled with disgust, I wondered which was stronger: his compulsion or my curiosity?

Later, on the phone, Laura said, 'Tell you what I'd have said to him.'

'What?'

'That I'd seen bigger on a budgerigar.'

3

A small head rose up at the side of the bed. Under a fringe of mousey-brown hair, fierce blue eyes, his face in shadow. Behind his skinny shoulders, sunlight poured through the bedroom curtains, bringing a raw, unweathered promise of the day ahead.

'What's up?' I asked.

'I don't want to go to school.'

'Why not?'

'*Because!*' A sudden squall of rage filled the air.

Conor climbed up onto the bed. His body was so light he could have been floating on the mattress as he wriggled towards me. I put my arm around him. He sighed deeply and rubbed his nose.

'Why do I have to go?'

Why indeed . . . I wanted to wrap him up in the blankets, hide him away from the world. He didn't deserve to be facing whatever terror lurked in the thickets, waiting for him at the school door.

'Will I tell you a secret?' I said.

'Mmmmm.'

'When I was your age, I didn't want to go to school either, but Granny told me that my guardian angel would always protect me.'

He was unconvinced. 'But why do *I* have to go?'

'Well, you go to learn things and to meet your friends. They'd miss you if you weren't at school, wouldn't they?'

'They could come here and play,' he said stoutly.

I smiled and touched his cheek.

'*Why* do I have to go?'

'Because.'

He growled and buried his head in my neck.

'Conor!' Kevin shouted up the stairs. 'Breakfast's ready!'

The little boy bounced out of the bed and disappeared downstairs.

Abruptly, I sat up, conscious of an unexpected stickiness between my legs.

Oh, thank you, I thought, thank you, God or Holy Mary or whoever is out there. *Thank you.*

I got out of bed and went to the bathroom to get a pad to stem the flow.

I sank back under the sheets and turned on my back to gaze at the ceiling. So my dream had been wrong: there was no baby. I'd had a lucky escape. As I lay there, eyes closed to the bright morning light, Laura's challenge still nibbled at my consciousness. *A baby-making machine, is that all you are?*

'Oh, shut up,' I said aloud.

Even Kevin, who never noticed anything, noticed.

'You slept it out.'

'Sorry.'

'That's okay,' he said. I was clearing the table and he was halfway out the door. 'But are you all right?'

'Why do you ask?'

'You look,' he paused and gently cuffed his daughter on the head, 'you look like Aoife does when she can't do her sums.'

Aoife squawked. I said nothing. After he had gone, I washed the breakfast dishes, feeling the suds squeeze between my fingers. The sun was heating up and yet, in the west, clouds were already banked high in the sky. Later it would rain, I told myself, and everything would be back to normal again.

In the garden I knelt at a flowerbed and pulled at the dead heads of flowers with a new kind of savagery. Purring, the cat wound itself around me. Cursing, I pushed her away. She padded to a sunny spot on the grass, stretched out and closed her eyes.

I looked at the cat with envy. Now that I was safely not pregnant, I could indulge my sense of grumbling discontent. Even though I knew I didn't want another baby, I still couldn't say what I *did* want. I couldn't complain about my life. It was the one I had chosen, but I was afraid of the silences, of long, empty afternoons. I thought of my mother: how her life had been one long struggle. If I had asked her what she had wanted out of life, she would have known what to say. She had one ambition: to see her two daughters settled and secure. My older sister, Mona, had got out as soon as she could and gone to London to train as a nurse. Mona had capability written all over her. She had sailed through the hospital exams and then she met a man from the North of England who proposed to her when she was twenty-one. A Protestant son-in-law was not what our mother wanted but Terence Bishop was a solid, load-bearing man with good prospects in the British police force. Mammy had to be satisfied with the promise that the children would be raised in the Catholic Church. Eight years and three children later, Terence converted and my mother was gratified that all her prayers to Our Lady hadn't been in vain.

When it came to my turn, Mammy had taken advice from the head nun in school and I had been sent to university to study architecture. I did what I was told and my mother continued to make ends meet and pay the bills. It seemed such a waste to me now, all that effort being squandered by me, but she didn't complain. As far as Mammy was concerned, with Kevin I was secure and settled, and that was enough.

The transistor radio, perched in the flowerbed, kept me company while I worked. There were the usual stories about trouble across the Border which I barely took in, and then a reporter came on and talked about student unrest in Dublin. I sat back on my heels.

'Nineteen sixty-nine has turned out to be a tumultuous year for UCD,' he said. 'It is the first time that disruption on such a scale has been witnessed in an Irish university, although now that students are getting down to their examinations, it does seem that the mass meetings and occupations have fizzled out. The administration has conceded some changes, so far unspecified, to the college structures and it is worth noting that, at one of the student rallies, a motion that proposed a Student/Worker Alliance was voted down.' He paused. 'Whatever *that* might be . . .'

'So nothing has really changed?' the interviewer asked.

'Well, you know, I suppose it's best summed up by the two posters I saw last week in the Main Hall of the university. One said: *Smash the pedagogic gerontocracy.* The other one said: *We like paternalism but we want*

Daddy to talk to us. I suspect that the second poster is a more accurate reflection of the view of students at UCD these days.'

The interviewer chortled. 'Oh, that's very good. Thank you. Now we have to move on to the situation in eastern Cambodia.'

I lifted my trowel and faced into my task. Although the herbaceous border was choked with weeds, I was encouraged by the way that some flowers and shrubs still battled for space. The garden was my delight. It tumbled down towards the water's edge, and along its boundaries was a hedgerow of whitethorn and bramble. For better and for worse, I had told myself when we bought the house. All the same, this was backbreaking work.

I bent over and dug my hands into the depths of foliage, searching for weeds. The greenery reminded me of Dublin and St Stephen's Green on an early October day. There were leaves on the ground and ducks splashing in an alginate pond. Barlo, Richard and I sauntering towards Earlsfort Terrace. Not a cloud of dissent on the horizon. A time of innocence and docile students. Bridget, I remembered, had been with us that day. Whatever happened to Bridget, I wondered as I stood up and stretched my cramped legs. All that upheaval and unspecified changes had come too late for her.

Suddenly the thought of my lucky escape hit me again and I skipped around on the grass. '*Oh thank you,*' I sang out loud as I twirled, '*thank you, thank you, thank you!*' Startled at my movement, the cat jumped up and stalked off towards the house.

But I couldn't get Bridget out of my mind. All I could do was hope that she'd had a lucky escape too.

4

I met Bridget for the first time in the autumn of 1962. In the crowd of university students she stood out as being different: her stockings were laddered, her skirt sagged, her coat was holed, her face was covered with spots and her nails were never clean. But there was a repressed passion about her, as if her life was full of mysterious triumphs. Despite her appearance, she had a shabby grandeur that made me think of the poem I'd learnt at school, 'The Old Woman of the Roads'.

The first time we met was in the UCD library. Bridget was leaning across the counter berating a librarian. Along the reading tables, heads were raised at the racket she was making.

'Gimme them books!' Bridget was shouting. A drop of spittle hung on her lower lip. When she lifted her hand to wipe it away, it looked for a moment as if she was going to strike the woman.

The librarian pursed her lips. 'I cannot release five books to you. Only four at a time. *That* is the rule.'

Such desire for learning was a novelty to me. It seemed wrong to thwart it.

'*I'll* take the book out,' I offered.

Bridget swung around in surprise.

The librarian hesitated. 'I'm not sure if that is allowed.'

I showed her my student card. She examined it with exaggerated attention. Then she wrote down my details and handed me the book. 'You have a fortnight,' she said to me. 'After that you will be fined.'

'That was real nice of you.' Bridget grasped the pile of books to her breast as if she was afraid someone might wrest them away. 'I'd buy you coffee only I haven't the price of it.'

So I bought her a coffee instead and we talked. She was from Offaly, on a scholarship, and wanted to become a teacher. I was intrigued by her hunger: for food, for learning, for experience.

In my life she became a combination of companion and corporal work of mercy. Whenever I had money, we went to the canteen where she wolfed down a plate of chips and sausages. Under the fluorescent lights, her face was smudgy, like soft cement. There were barred windows overlooking a yard and, in the corner, a baby-faced seminarian crouched over his beans on toast. The air was dank with grease. Behind a pillar a table was reserved for staff who, unlike the students, never had to queue.

Summer and winter Bridget wore her old school gabardine coat. Once, when we were queuing in the canteen, I saw her slip a fried egg, a slice of toast and a chocolate biscuit into her pocket while the woman serving food from the stainless-steel vats was momentarily distracted. I was too embarrassed to say anything. Stealing was a sin, I'd been taught, but Bridget lived by rules of her own making. All the same, did she actually *eat* that fried egg, I wondered, trying to imagine the inside of Bridget's coat pocket.

One day curiosity got the better of me.

'Do you steal just for devilment?' I asked.

She burst out laughing. 'To keep the devil away, more like!'

'I've no idea what you mean,' I said coldly. I was unhappy about the whole business. Bridget looked like a tramp and I wondered what I was doing in her company.

'I'm squatting in a room over a store in Burgh Quay,' she said by way of explanation. 'There's no light and it's as cold as a witch's tit.'

She had captured my interest now.

'So what do you do after lectures?'

'Stay in bed mostly and read. It's warm. I've a torch.'

But it's warm outside, I wanted to say.

Later, when I went into St Stephen's Green, the air smelt sweet, like newly made jam. In the distance, I could see Manus coming towards me. His shock of blond hair was unmistakable. Manus was not handsome. There was something distorted about his face – his face was too long and angular, his mouth too wide – but he had an animal quality that I found irresistible. When he saw me, I thought there was tenderness in his eyes, just for an instant. Then his face closed up. Manus O'Rourke, for whom I felt a deep, undying devotion. What was I to make of him? I was ignorant about the male psyche. To me, he was as exotic as a unicorn and as unfathomable. His hands were rammed deep in the pockets of the rumpled trench coat that gave him an air of a private detective.

He stopped in front of me. 'Fancy a flick?'

This was happiness. I knew no other way to express it but I wanted to kneel down and give thanks. Dumbly I nodded. He smiled and then his face settled back into its mask. As we walked, I was conscious of people's glances – him striding out and me trying to keep up, swinging my long mane of black hair that was tied back with a ribbon. I almost whinnied with delight.

The film was in French. It too was unfathomable, although there were subtitles. The audience of twelve people appeared to be asleep until the word *erection* appeared on the screen and there was a collective intake of breath. What exactly was an erection? I wanted Manus to tell me and, as we walked back across the Green, he gave me an explanation in a strangled voice. Oh, I said, mortified, and we walked back to the Main Hall in silence.

Although he hadn't even held my hand in the cinema, I was giddy with excitement at the thought of him and I wanted to tell the world – or at least my friends. There was one big difference between university and school: for the first time in my life the friends I had were male and, instinctively, I knew that neither Barlo nor Richard had any interest in what interested me most.

I was conscious of that gulf between them and me as we sat in Barlo's bedsit overlooking the canal on one of those nothing kind of student days generated by having too much time and no money. The walls of the room were painted white, the floorboards black. A desk was pushed up against a board of cork tiles which was covered with sketches, maps, photos and, disconcertingly, a full-size drawing of a man's penis. Barlo was a flamboyant dresser, with flowing hair and a penchant for cravats. In UCD he stood out. Male students, in the main, had short hair, wore white shirts and woolly jumpers or sad-looking serge suits.

Richard Horan was sitting on the floor rolling a

cigarette. Unlike the rest of us, when he qualified he would have a job waiting for him in his father's architectural practice, Horan, Birch and Nash. Richard Horan Senior was a cousin of the Bishop of Killaloe. While other architects struggled to get work, their practice flourished on contracts from Archbishop McQuaid to build churches in the new suburbs around the city.

'Since they have the market cornered,' Barlo grumbled, 'the least they could do is make decent architecture, instead of that ghastly Italianate pastiche.'

To Richard's annoyance, Barlo had taken to referring to the architectural practice as Whoring, Church and Cash.

The cigarette Richard had rolled looked as if it was made from newspaper and old tobacco. He lit it and took a deep breath into his lungs.

'What is it?' I asked.

'It's lovely.'

Wide-eyed, I looked at him.

'Here,' he handed it to me. 'You try it.'

The acrid smoke in my lungs made me cough and my eyes water. He laughed and offered the cigarette to Barlo.

'It's shit, you know.' Barlo waved it away.

'Yeah,' Richard agreed.

'You don't need that crap,' Barlo said. 'It rots your brain. Ideas are what keep us alive, not that rubbish. A work of art halts time for one glorious half-hour. In our short time in this world we can come to terms with only a mere fraction of existence. The rest we leave to fantasy and creative thought. Jesus, Richard, we have to rely on our aesthetic sense.' The tone in his voice had become urgent. 'Use your eyes, man. Read books. Travel. Experience life. You'll be building churches and yet you haven't seen the chapel at Ronchamp. *That* will make you high in a way that nothing else can. Then go to America and see Frank

Lloyd Wright's work. I was in Fallingwater last summer. They let me in with open arms. Me, a bogtrotter from Navan! I got to go through every inch of a world masterpiece. I'll never forget the sight of those cantilevers over the waterfall, the penetration of light and, inside, the interior like a bear's vagina.'

I giggled. I knew it wasn't very funny but I couldn't help myself.

'So you keep telling me,' Richard said.

'Get my point!' Barlo's voice rose in irritation.

Richard cackled. 'I get it. My body is inviolate. It is a sacred temple.'

'Oh for Christ's sake!'

Richard blessed himself, his hand crossing his chest. 'In the name of the Aalto, the Corb and the Holy Wright.'

A silence and the two young men staring at each other.

Then, 'Get out of this hole, Richie,' Barlo implored as he moved closer. 'Get out before they bury you.'

There was love in Barlo's eyes when he said it. I didn't see it then: that hidden thread of desire silvering their conversation. If Richard knew about it, he never let on. Where was I in all this? I was the button-lip, the child behind a door eavesdropping. Afraid of saying the wrong thing, I said nothing at all. The two of them talked while I listened. It was an arrangement that suited the three of us.

The truth was I wasn't bothered about aesthetics. All I wanted was Manus. I scoured the Main Hall, trying to catch a glimpse of him. Any free time I had, I wandered through the crowds of students, my breath fluttering in my throat in anticipation.

But there was no sign of him.

Often, in the distance, I could see Bridget's pale face as she waved to attract my attention. I pretended not to see her. There was a desperation in her that mirrored my own.

I didn't know if she could read my expression or even if she realized that I was deliberately avoiding her. I didn't care. Her dependence irritated me and I wanted to shake her off as, relentlessly, I pursued my quarry.

Then one day Bridget dropped out of sight.

It took me a while to realize that she was no longer there in the crowd, gazing at me while I looked past her. Life folded in over her memory. I hardly thought about her or wondered what had happened to her.

Months later, on a Saturday night coming up to Christmas, I was with a group of classmates, huddled around a table in the corner of Dwyer's pub when I heard my name being called. When I turned, a girl from Third Arts, whom I'd known in school, made a beeline for me. Had I heard about Bridget, she wanted to know. Her face was too close to mine, her need to talk too pressing. I wanted to freeze her out and return to the intimacy of the group, but she had her hand on my arm and wouldn't let go.

'Bridget's had a nervous breakdown. She's in a looney bin, somewhere down the country.' Her voice dropped. 'I hear she tried to do herself in.'

I closed my eyes. In the darkness Bridget's face pressed up against the barred window of a gaunt building. I saw the flailing movement of her hand behind the glass. It was my fault: I had pushed Bridget away and she had fallen off the edge. That night I went home and cried hot tears into my pillow. I didn't know if I was weeping for Bridget or for Manus. Both had become entangled in a great lump of guilt that I carried with me for days afterwards.

I was so miserable that when Barlo asked me to go to the Architects' Dinner Dance with him, I said yes. I went because he'd asked me and because I would have died rather than stay home on a Saturday night. Dressed in our evening clothes, we met at the Nelson Pillar where a bus took us out of the city and through the black, flat fields of County Kildare.

An avenue of lime trees led up to a large Georgian house. Its shuttered windows overlooked a parkland, spectral in the November moonlight. We went in through a side door that brought us into a long, basement corridor under the west wing of the house. In the gloom a vaulted ceiling crouched above our heads. As we moved down the corridor, light spilled out from the Servants' Hall to welcome us.

Inside, the room was heaving and couples were already sitting down along the trestle tables set for dinner.

Barlo wore a skin-tight, mulberry-coloured velvet jacket, white sailor trousers and a pair of spiv's two-tone shoes. He had cut his hair short and it gave him a military look. I was wearing a long, strapless, blue dress that made me look fat.

I looked at him crossly. 'You're prettier than me.'

'Ah, but you have the brains,' he said and then suddenly contorted his body to see across the crowd. 'Oh, my Heaven!' He pointed across the floor to a tall, sandy-haired boy who was tipsily wiggling his fingers in someone else's direction, and then he whispered into my ear, 'I'd love to suck his cock.'

Scandalised, I squealed with laughter. Barlo's face collapsed into gloom.

'Come on,' I urged him over to one of the tables. 'Drink. Eat.'

After dinner Barlo disappeared into the crowd. In a way, that suited me; I liked being left alone and free to explore the great house. To my disappointment, the door to the main floor upstairs was bolted. The corridor curved away from the Servants' Hall and, as the noise of the band faded behind me, I became aware of faint strains of a different kind of music. I opened a door and found myself in a high-ceilinged kitchen with a stone-flagged floor and a few students lolling on wooden benches. Around the hearth, which was big enough for a man to stand in, sat a group of musicians. They were playing music unlike anything I had ever heard before. Irish music, as I knew it, was played by céilí bands on Radio Éireann with a dull, repetitive beat that could drive you mad with its predictability. In that stone room with its shelves of cooking pots and pans, I was transfixed. Each musical instrument was a wild thing barely controlled by the musician playing it. The fiddler was bouncing off his stool and the uilleann pipes were shrieking like a maddened spirit let loose in the air.

Abruptly the music stopped. The musicians leant back in their chairs and talked among themselves. I sat down and waited. Then the whistle-player moved into action. His lips touched the mouthpiece. His fingers splayed out and he blew from his whistle the falsetto bark of a fox. Other musicians joined in and the yelping sounds of a pack of hounds followed the sound of the horn, sweet and shrill. Then the drumming of horses' hooves carrying in the riders, coat-tails flying, their whips cracking in a gathering rhythm. Thunder growled in the skin of a bodhrán. By now, no one in the room was sitting still. The hunt was up. We were all in a race through hedges, over stone walls and across the fields and away.

I thought of a day in Donegal: Mammy and I cycling back to Burnfoot, dreamily tracing our way along the narrow road. On each side, hedges dipped over our heads and the winter air was cold and still. Suddenly, our bodies shook with terror and our bicycles slid away from us as if the Devil himself had raged up from Hell. I screamed at the crazed eye, the flying mane, the heaving sides as a riderless horse, its reins flying, soared over us. The horse dived through the hedge and disappeared. My mother dragged me with her into the ditch and we clung together, waiting for other horses and riders to follow. The air quivered with fear. With our heads down, we shrank into the icy brambles and the ferns stiff with hoar frost, unaware that the huntsmen had already ribboned off in a different direction, following the hounds.

'Mother of God!' she murmured. I knew she was thinking of the fox, scrambling through the undergrowth. As I knelt, whimpering, in the sanctuary of her shoulder, I could hear the tiny sound of my mother's heart beating.

'Would you like to dance?'

Startled, I swung around as the music ended. His evening suit was crumpled and his bowtie undone. He looked like an unmade bed. Damn, I thought, not another big, thick engineer. My silence would have unnerved a lesser man but he didn't waver. Later, he told me that, at that moment, he couldn't have looked away even if he'd wanted to, that he had been mesmerized by the dark flecks in my grey eyes, the curve of my forehead, the widow's peak of my hair.

'I can wait, wee girl,' he said.

The musicians were striking up again, the piper tucking the bellows under his arm. I said nothing. I knew it was rude not to answer but, at that moment, all that mattered was the exquisite sadness of the first notes of a lament. I was in the hands of the musicians while they, in turn, submitted themselves to the music.

'When you're finished here, I mean.'

'Oh, all right,' I said quickly to be rid of him, my voice barely audible as the great wash of music pulled me beyond reach.

I had no idea how long I stayed in the kitchen but, when I got up from the wooden bench, I was stiff and my back was aching. Instantly, he reappeared in the doorway and extended his arm so that I found myself leading the way into the corridor. It was an odd feeling for me to be in charge.

On the dance floor in the Servants' Hall, we were sucked into an unwelcome clinch. I give you full marks for trying, I felt like saying, but if I were you I wouldn't bother.

'Aye, you liked the music back there,' he said. It was not a question. Then it sank in. The way he had said it: *I can wait, wee girl*.

'Where are you from?' I asked.

He named the parish on the Inishowen peninsula that was next to my mother's homeplace.

'It came to my mind, when I heard that tune,' he said. 'The Strabara and Donegal Hounds.'

So he saw it too: the freeze of a winter morning, the restless horses, their hooves sparking on the tarmac road, the excitement of the hounds milling about, the riders starting out. One man, trotting ahead, reins in one hand, while he made a clenched fist of the other behind his back to warn the rest, *Mine's a kicker* . . .

Without thinking, I leant closer into his shoulder.

'Me too,' I said.

When the music stopped and the couples began to move off the floor, we hung back awkwardly.

'I'm Kevin McAvady,' he said.

5

I stood up and surveyed my work. The pile of weeds on the grass was evidence of the progress I'd made, but the flowerbed didn't look any different to how it had looked when I had started weeding it that morning.

'I'll tame you yet, old house,' I muttered, setting off to get the wheelbarrow that, I remembered, was propped up in the yard at the back of the house.

As soon as I opened the yard gate, I knew that something was wrong.

'What is it?' I asked the grey cat who had followed me. Usually she whiled away her days by sleeping on the kitchen windowsill until she got hungry and came scratching at the back door. Now she was standing rigid, her fur raised along her back and a wild look in her eyes.

Then I saw it: a rounded shadow in the yard, a piece of heraldry come to life. With its long white neck and heavy wings folded over its back, the swan could have been a mediaeval intruder that had tumbled out of the sky. It drew itself up and hissed a grey tongue at the cat. The cat withdrew to the safety of the wall while I stood and stared at the orange beak, the calligraphic swoop of black skin, and its small, bright eyes. The swan ignored both of us, its head bobbing gently on its neck. Then it settled down, like a feathered cushion, on the cobbled floor of the yard.

For some reason the swan reminded me of my maternal grandmother, Mamo. That knowing look in its beady eye was familiar. Mamo, who was always in a hurry, giving a sharp glance over her shoulder before she went away up the fields or into the yard where the butter was churned. When she was only fifteen, Mamo had gone to America, where she had married a man from Ardara who was later killed in a railway accident outside Boston. With four children in tow, she had come home to the family farm beyond Burnfoot, to a mean cottage and thirty acres of poor ground.

Years later, when we came on our visits from Dublin, I was aware of a transformation in my mother. In that cottage, she became young again, almost a child herself, and happy. Acquiescent to the daily routine, she worked with Mamo until it was dark, her bare legs pale and vulnerable in wellington boots. After nightfall, while the two women stretched out in armchairs by the fire, smoking their cigarettes and talking, I fell asleep to the smell of turf on the sheets, to the shifting sounds of their conversation and the wag of the clock on the wall.

What do I do now? I wondered as I stared at the swan.

For a moment I felt like a spectator: here was me, looking at the swan and there was the swan looking away. The bird burrowed its beak into its wing and then, unspooling its neck, gazed up at the sky.

It was embarrassing, at times like this, to discover just how useless I was at living in the country. I remembered a time when the neighbour's cattle got out and trampled over our lawn and I had cowered with the children inside the house until Kevin came home. Simple things still unnerved me: the racket in the trees that crows made at evening-time and, in summer, the sight of a tick clamped onto a child's skin. For me, this house was home in a way that nowhere else could ever be, but that did not mean it was always a comfortable place to be in.

'A swan can break a man's arm with its wings,' I told the cat.

Then I thought of the children. I couldn't leave a dangerous bird in the yard to meet them when they came home from school. Feebly, I shooed at the swan but I realized that both of us were at a disadvantage. It had landed in an area of the yard that was too narrow to take off from and I was too scared to tackle it head-on. The bird stood up on its wide webbed feet and waddled away into the corner. Its flatfooted progress was comical. It walked like a pregnant woman. How I look, I thought, when I'm pregnant.

I withdrew to sit on the wall beside the cat. The swan swung around at us and hissed. I had the power to release it if I only knew how.

'Come on, Rosaleen,' I muttered, 'think of something.'

Then I remembered Mr Mundy.

Earlier, I had seen him walking with the dog across the fields but the fields were empty now, blanked by a slight, ghostly mist that had crept in from the lough. He would help me, I knew.

It took only a few minutes for me to walk out along the road. Mundy's was the next house to ours. It was a substantial, double-fronted house with acres of good land attached. A lilac tree, heavy with blossoms, scented the air as I came near. At the back door, the sheepdog woke from her sleep and wagged her tail.

'Hullo, Liadh,' I said rubbing her behind her ears. 'Good dog.'

The dog wriggled in a paroxysm of delight.

The back door was ajar but I stood outside, unsure what to do. We were neighbours, but I was shy about entering into the man's house uninvited.

'Come in.'

His voice came from somewhere inside the house. At the door there was a holy-water font made of white marble and inscribed with the words *A Present from Lourdes*. Automatically I dipped my finger in the chilly water, blessed myself and went in.

The dark, narrow kitchen was neat. Much tidier than mine. A formica-topped table, pushed up against the wall, was set for one person and the fridge hummed a cracked tune.

Mr Mundy was sitting in an office off the kitchen that was full of files and ledgers packed into bookcases. There were more files on his desk and documents scattered on the floor.

'Bloody paperwork,' he grumbled, putting down his fountain pen and peering at me over his glasses.

I had forgotten that Mr Mundy was the Master of the Hunt. In fact he was Master, secretary and treasurer rolled into one. He managed everything: the meets, the notices, the accounts. Tall and rangy, he was an old man and yet he still rode to hounds, his back straight, his face impassive, his eyes looking oriental under the peak of his riding hat. He had lived alone since his wife had died, years before, and his four sons had gone away. When Mr Mundy died, it struck me, the edifice to which he had dedicated his life would die with him.

'You're in some trouble?' he asked, seeing the look of my face.

Feeling foolish, I told him.

'A swan, is it?' He looked grave.

I nodded.

'Now what would Betty the Yank have done with a swan?' he teased.

Betty the Yank was Mamo, my grandmother. He had known her and a lovely girl she had been apparently. I wondered sometimes about Mr Mundy and Betty the Yank, but this was not the time to ask.

Before I could speak, the old man rose from his chair and took down a long black coat from a hook behind the door.

'Stay, Liadh,' he ordered. The dog whined and burrowed her head between her paws.

As Mr Mundy pulled on a pair of gloves, his wrists protruded as if the tweed jacket he was wearing belonged to another, smaller man. He had a gaunt look that made him seem half-starved.

Living alone, did he eat properly, I wondered as I padded alongside him, trying to keep up. I felt guilty – we were neighbours and yet I had never asked him into our house before. At his back door he slipped off his shoes and pulled on his boots that had been left to dry outside on a rusting boot-scraper.

'Your lilac tree is beautiful,' I said, looking at the pale racemes trembling among apple-green leaves.

'Aye, once I buried a dead kid under it.'

'*Pardon?*'

'The nanny goat sickened and died soon after.' If he was aware of my shock, he wasn't letting on but I sensed that there was a twinkle somewhere in the depths of his deadpan expression. 'I buried her under the apple tree and you won't get a finer crop in all Donegal.'

Mr Mundy strode ahead, up our driveway and around the side of the house. For a moment the yard seemed empty but the swan was still there, hunkered down by the wall, grooming itself. Indignantly, it pulled back and hissed as the old man landed the black coat deftly across its back.

'Shoo, shoo!' Mr Mundy said as he circled around the bird.

The swan roped its neck low to the ground. With one hand holding its body and the other gripping its neck, Mr Mundy scooped it up. Immediately the bird surrendered in his arms. I was charmed by the beauty of the tableau before me: of the man and bird united. Holding the bird across his body, Mr Mundy walked down the yard while I ran ahead to open the gate. Then I had a sudden thought.

'Please, oh please, just wait one minute. Don't move.'

I ran into the kitchen and picked up the camera from the dresser. I was thinking of the children, how they would enjoy seeing a picture of Mr Mundy with the swan. When I returned and held up the camera, Mr Mundy's face broke open unexpectedly in a smile. It was a shock to see those impenetrable eyes fill with laughter. He straightened his shoulders while keeping a firm hold on the swan as I took the photo. Then – why, I don't know – I put the camera on the wall, set the timer and I positioned myself alongside him. I had to stand on my tiptoes before I could snap the two of us.

'I'll give you a copy when I get them developed,' I promised.

Gently, Mr Mundy released the swan onto the grass. It faltered and then, luxuriantly, it spread its wings. I held my breath but, instead of flying off, the swan closed its wings down over its back.

'She has space,' he said. 'All she needs now is time.'

The swan nuzzled into its feathers.

'Will you have a cup of tea?' I asked, partly in gratitude but also to detain him long enough to see the swan fly off.

Mr Mundy bowed his head and I led him into the house. I was glad that the kitchen looked cheery, despite its shabbiness. There was a smell of fresh baking and the plates on the dresser shone in the sunlight, but the old man didn't show any curiosity about his surroundings. Instead, he stood, looking out the window.

'The wind will help her,' he said. Then, with a murmur of satisfaction, 'There she goes.'

Wordlessly we gazed as the swan, its wings outstretched, motored towards the lough.

'Freedom,' Mr Mundy said, 'is a fine thing.'

I put the kettle on the range.

Freedom, I thought: yes, for me too.

'I'm sorry about the mess,' I said.

Earlier I had washed the kitchen floor and it was still strewn with sheets of newspaper. Indicating to him to sit down, I pulled out a chair from the table. Gingerly he gave a little pull of his trousers at the knees and took a seat. When the kettle squealed, I lifted it up to scald the teapot.

'We'll let the tea draw,' I said as I cut some of the soda bread I had made that morning. It was still warm and floury and I was satisfied with the look of it.

Mr Mundy stretched out his hand, took a slice of bread and lashed on the butter and jam that I had set out on the table.

'Thank you for looking after the swan,' I said as I poured out the tea.

'No bother, wee girl,' he said, his cheek bulging.

I struggled to think of something to say.

'Kevin will be sorry to have missed you.'

'Oh aye.' The old man raised his head and looked at me, 'Sure, I never see that man any more. He was great with the horses once. Is it marriage that has him distracted?'

I laughed and sat down across the table from him. 'I doubt it. His great love now is shooting. He has three guns and he's away at weekends with the Club and often I won't see him for a whole day at a time. As soon as the season starts, he's gone out shooting.'

It was a bone of contention. Me looking for a break from the children, him arguing that he deserved a break from work. Me wanting to go out as a family, him out the door before I'd finished speaking.

The narrow black gaze was suddenly full of interest. 'Isn't it better that he's shooting when he goes out than shooting when he comes home?'

For a moment I was flummoxed. Until I saw the mischief in Mr Mundy's face and I began to laugh.

'Don't ask me. I don't understand any of it. Men only, and killing defenceless birds like that. I wouldn't do it if you paid me.'

'It's the country way,' Mr Mundy said peaceably and stretched for another slice of bread.

I moved the plate closer to his elbow. The country way: hunting, shooting, killing animals. I sighed. He smiled a ghost of a smile as if he could read my mind.

'This is a good place to live,' he said, 'with good people.'

'Oh, yes,' I said hurriedly, thinking of Laura. 'I have super friends here now. And, as for the children, this is their home. It's just, I suppose, that I grew up in Dublin and well, it is *different*.'

'Tell me,' he said, 'do the people in Dublin have two heads?'

I laughed again. Mr Mundy was like many Donegal men I had met who were direct to the point of hardness in their speech and yet, in their bones, there was a gentleness. It felt right somehow: the two of us sitting there in the warm kitchen, with mouthfuls of tea slipping down our throats. Under our saucers, the oilcloth on the table was patterned with little sailing boats.

'You have the place looking well,' he said.

'Oh, I don't know – there's so much to do. It was in bad shape when we got it. She had got too old . . . the previous owner, I mean.' I paused.

Mr Mundy bent his head over his teacup and drank. Then he looked up at me and said quietly, 'Around here they say that the land can change hands many times but that it never changes religion.'

I had not met Mrs Bascombe, the previous owner, but her name didn't sound Catholic to me. Jesus, I thought, I was becoming like the people around here, cataloguing everyone into two camps: Catholic, Protestant. Know your tribe. Why, I often wondered, did any of it matter?

As if he knew what I was thinking, Mr Mundy laughed and said, 'Molly Durkan married a pauper Presbyterian from Manorcunningham and brought him back here and within a year she had him turned. He was down in the chapel more times in his life than the rest of us.'

His laughter died as suddenly as it had risen. I turned to look out the window. The sight of the wheelbarrow on the gravel reminded me of work not done.

'Would you like me to tell you,' Mr Mundy broke the silence, 'what is the difference between city people and country people?'

'Mmmm, yes. Please do.'

'Well, there's not much difference, but there is one thing I can think of and it's not always obvious.' He paused then as if waiting for me to comment.

I said nothing but smiled encouragingly.

'Country people,' he said, 'like to hear the same story told over again, whereas, when it comes to city people, they want to hear a new story every single time.'

I mulled over this while he stirred his tea and, holding up the cup with his gnarled hands, took another gulp. Aoife and Conor would enjoy getting to know him, I thought. I imagined them invading his silent house with their chatter. Since they had no grandfather of their own, he could be a replacement. And Liadh, the sheepdog, would be a great draw. How often Aoife had pleaded for us to get a dog and I had palmed her off with vague promises! But a dog next door would be perfect.

'Will you look at thon Antichrist!'

I jumped. Mr Mundy was bent over, looking at a page of the *Irish Press* on the floor at his feet. I peered down at the fleshy jowls, the horse's teeth behind curling lips, the black hair and pale slab of a face above the deep, clerical collar: the Reverend Ian Paisley.

'See him?' Mr Mundy snarled. 'I know what would stop his slabber.' He raised his fist in the form of a gun. Then he pointed his index finger and pretended to shoot at the photograph. 'Good enough for him.'

An involuntary shiver ran down my spine. A goose walking over my grave, I thought, or maybe even a swan. Acting as if nothing had happened, Mr Mundy picked up the last slice of bread from the plate, spread it with butter and jam and opened his mouth wide.

The dreaminess of the day was broken. Deflated, I looked out towards the lough, to the scraps of white rocking on the water. The only sound in the room was the thrumming of Aoife's hamster on the wheel of its cage.

Without speaking, Mr Mundy stood and gathered his coat and gloves. He drained his cup and then bowed politely.

'I'll bring you in the photos when I have them,' I said again, wanting to detain him a little longer, but it was clear that he had already withdrawn into himself and wanted to be off.

Silence held no terror for him, I thought with a twinge of envy, as I watched him sauntering down the driveway, looking for all the world like a man who had just been set free.

Rain swept in from the west, darkening the day. At the school gates a gaggle of mothers in thin raincoats were huddled under umbrellas. Laura wasn't among them. She was on her own, smoking a cigarette as she sheltered beside a tree. She wore a white plastic jacket, a mini-skirt and a headscarf tied fashionably under the point of her chin. Even at a distance, I could see that her legs were purple with the cold. She waved at me cheerfully, just as the children erupted from the school.

'How're you doing?' she cried.

I grinned at her excitedly and gave her a thumbs-up. She looked puzzled.

'My monthlies,' I mouthed at her. 'I got them.'

'Well, Mother of God be praised, aren't you the lucky one!'

The children clustered around each of us so that, inexorably, we were pulled farther apart.

'Tomorrow,' she called as I moved off. 'I'll see you tomorrow.'

In the evening, after the children had gone to bed, I lit the fire in the living room and pulled the curtains closed. I was pleased to see how cosy the room looked. The wooden floor was spread with a frayed Persian rug. There was a second-hand couch and armchair and, on either side of the chimney breast, we had constructed makeshift shelves. Kevin was dozing in front of the television while I darned the children's socks. His body was too big for the armchair, with legs sprawled out awkwardly and head bent into his chest.

'Why don't you go to bed?' I nudged him. 'Or you'll be stiff as a board.'

As he struggled up out of depths of unconsciousness, for a moment he was a stranger. There was a look of panic in his eyes and his fists grasped at air as if something, or someone, was about to attack. It was only when he was fully awake that he softened, yawning and stretching his arms over his head.

'Make us a cup of tea, love,' he said, smiling at me.

And so we sat in front of the turned-down television set and I told him about my day, about the swan and Mr Mundy and how I thought that the children might like to visit the house next door but, before I was even finished, he interrupted me.

'You are not to go near that house!' His voice was harsh. His skin was blotched and red and he ran his hand through his hair so that it sprang up in a rage.

'*What?*'

He shook his head.

'But why, Kevin?'

He refused to elaborate. Instead, he buried his chin into his collar and glowered at the television screen.

Neither of us said anything for a moment.

Then: 'You have to give me a reason!'

'You don't need to know,' he muttered at the screen. 'Just do what I say.'

'But I– '

'Jesus Christ, Rosaleen!' he shouted. 'I know what I'm talking about and I don't have to explain it to you. Or to anybody else.'

The air in the room trembled. Upstairs the children slept on or, at least, I hoped they did, oblivious of the jagged sound of our voices. We hardly ever argued and never like this before. I knew, because she had told me, that Laura and Cathal had stand-up rows that were so noisy that, sometimes, their neighbours complained. Kevin and I were different. Or so I thought. Tears lurked at the back of my eyes at the shattering of the picture I had in my head. I didn't want to fight; I wanted to find a way back to the quiet evening and the sleeping giant in the armchair.

'Kevin,' I lowered my voice, 'what is eating you?'

'This is about trust, Rosaleen.' Kevin spat out the words as if he hated me. 'Do you even know what that means? You have to trust me and support me. Can't put it any plainer: *keep out of that man's way*. And the children too. It's really that simple, believe me.'

He turned up the television and hunched down to watch the *News*. There were the usual riots in Belfast. Then a comedy show came on and we sat watching it without laughing. The pall of his anger set him apart, as if he no longer belonged in this house, to these children and this wife.

Even when I closed the sewing box and stood up to go to bed, he didn't speak.

'Goodnight, love,' I said.

My words fell like flakes of ash in the grate.

It was late when Kevin came into the bedroom and, without a word, undressed in the dark. Then he burrowed under the blankets, his back curled away from me. Tearfully, I gazed up at the ceiling. I wanted to speak but the words died in my throat. His breathing was even, like waves on a beach. In his sleep, he shifted nearer to me and the sudden warmth of his body disarmed me. Instinctively I reached out. His back was unyielding, but I ran my hand down his spine and, after moistening my fingers in my mouth, circled around his body to seek him out. Slowly, rhythmically, I caressed until he stiffened in my hand.

'Well, at least, *he's* glad to see me,' I murmured in Kevin's ear.

He grunted and turned over onto his back. I clambered between his legs and stretched up to kiss his mouth. Tenderly, he touched the dried tears on my cheek and, at once, he became a familiar spirit again, one who had momentarily lost his way but now had come back to me.

'I have my period,' I whispered.

'So what?' Kevin said, gripping me tightly.

In the darkness our bodies moved together so easily that words weren't necessary. We made love and, afterwards, we lay, loosely entangled, under the blankets.

'Sorry for being cranky,' he muttered.

'Mmm,' I said. 'What was all that about?'

He rolled over to face me. 'You know, Rosaleen, you live here in a world of your own, with the children and the house. I mean, that's the way it should be. I'm not complaining. All the same, there are times when I envy you.'

Kevin wanting to be a housewife was such a funny idea that I giggled. Then I realized he was serious.

'What do you mean? You like your job – everyone says you're great at it.'

'I am an excellent engineer,' he said proudly, 'but things are getting bad. Every day that I go to work in Derry I wonder is this the day when the city is going to explode? Nobody knows where all this trouble is going to end, how it's going to end. With Terence O'Neill out of the picture, we have gone from bad to worse, and the jokers in charge are sitting on a powder keg. It's like waiting for Armageddon.'

I listened in silence and wondered what this had to do with us.

'I have to look after you, and Aoife and Conor . . . and I'm afraid, afraid . . .' His voice trailed away for a moment.

Then he continued as if he were talking to himself: 'Anything could happen. The work could dry up and I'd be out of a job.'

'Surely not, Kevin. Schools will always need to be built, and factories.'

I stroked his hair as we lay together, listening to the small, quiet sounds of the night. He has a point, I thought: I am living in a kind of cocoon.

An owl hooted in the trees.

'Kevin,' I whispered, 'are you asleep?'

'Uh-huh.' His voice was drifting away.

'What about Mr Mundy?'

He was wide awake again. 'Tom Mundy is in the IRA.'

The old man who led out the Hunt and drank tea in our kitchen? No, I could not believe it. That sounded crazy to me. Then I remembered the pointed finger, the venom in his voice. His words. *Good enough for him.*

'Really! How do you know?'

'Everyone knows except you, you idiot. He was interned in the Fifties. They reckon he nearly blew himself up in a raid on a barracks in Tyrone, but the case was thrown out because nobody was willing to testify.' He yawned and turned away in the bed, pulling the blankets with him.

I lay on my back and stared at the ceiling, waiting for sleep. So this is the archaeology of marriage, I thought: we scrape along the surface without thinking and then, when we least expect it, we stumble upon a discovery. Kevin was not, as I had presumed, invincible. At times like this, he was more like a small boy looking for reassurance. Kevin and Conor, father and son, more alike than I knew, both of them haunted by an anxiety about the world, a world over which neither had any control.

'Night, love,' I said softly.

'Night, sweetheart.'

6

Wednesday was a half-day in Letterkenny. The empty doorways and darkened windows gave the main street the sucked-in look of an old man who has taken out his false teeth. Only the chemist shop was wide awake. There's always money to be made from maladies, I thought as I opened the door to the sound of a bell tinkling somewhere in the back of the shop.

'Can I help you?'

The woman had bulging eyes and black hair in a bouffant hairstyle with flicked-out ends. I gave her my docket. She pulled out a drawer and riffled through a row of Kodak envelopes. With her head bent over the drawer, I could see that the roots of her hair were white, like a slick of icing sugar along her parting. Never, I swore, when I'm her age. Never, ever. Without so much as a by-your-leave, she opened the envelope and examined the photographs inside.

'These yours?' She fanned them out for me to see. There we were: Mr Mundy. The swan. Me.

'Well, yes,' I said, unable to bring myself to protest.

She gathered them up like a deck of cards and rammed them back into the envelope.

'There you are then.' She took the money and, as if she were doing me a favour, handed me over the photographs.

After picking up Aoife and Conor from school I drove out along the road towards Rathmullen. When we reached a large entrance defined by eagle-topped gateposts, I turned the Morris Minor off the road and slowly drove up the long avenue. On either side stood giant, tangled trees. In the undergrowth, mossy branches mouldered under ferns and brambles. A Georgian house rose up ahead, its pale pink walls glowing out across the boggy fields. At an open gate a *Tradesman's Entrance* sign pointed drunkenly to the ground. Above it, a new sign had been erected: *The Hall Riding School.* Here was old money plummeting in the world and having to work for a living, pressing rundown stables into use and leading out lines of besotted little girls astride ponies that had names like Peaches and Queenie.

One besotted little girl was mine.

I had promised Aoife that, for her sixth birthday, she could have riding lessons. *It's far from riding lessons . . .* I wanted to say, but the truth was, even as I laughed, I was gratified, deep down, that I had sparked such excitement in her. Kevin's anxiety about the future had made me conscious of the world outside, its price as well as its possibilities.

As I waited for Aoife to have her riding lesson, I thought: this is what money can buy – the different lives we can lead and the changes that tumble out, unannounced. I could earn my keep somehow, I had realized, and now I was impatient to get started. Otherwise, one day, when the children were all grown up, I'd be left alone to silent afternoons pressing in on me. I could imagine Aoife as a young woman in jodhpurs, sloshing around some muddy stable yard, breathing in the horsey smells, the tang of leather, the garbled vowels. She was only a child and already she was brave enough to teach me a thing or two. I remembered the gloomy house in Terenure, three storeys high and chopped into flats where Mammy, Mona and I had lived like nocturnal creatures in the basement flat. After Daddy died, I was always afraid when Mammy went off to the hospital in Meath Street to do the night shift that she would never come back. It was worse when I got older and Mona had gone to England. In the dark, every creak was mouse-like or burglar-like to my fourteen-year-old self, lying in bed with the bread knife beside me, trying to sleep as the house shifted around and under me, like a ship.

Carried on a slow tide of horseflesh, the children circled around the stable yard while a clutch of mothers waited. Aoife's face loomed up under her riding hat, her wide cheeks spattered with mud. Her expression, closed in concentration, reminded me of the first time I had seen her in the fluorescent glow of the labour ward: the crown of her head, her squashed purple face when she escaped out of my spent body. My first-born. To me it was a miracle, knowing her then at the moment of birth and, now, seeing the fearless child she had become.

Aoife grinned at me and, swaying in the saddle, led her pony through the crowd. She stopped and, leaning down, gave the pony an expert slap on its caramel-coloured flank.

'Isn't she beautiful, Mammy? Her name's Toffee.'

'Good enough to eat.'

The animal turned a frantic eye towards me. I flinched.

It knows, I thought, even the bloody horse can sense my fear. I patted the animal's neck nervously. From a height, Aoife looked down at me. She had Kevin's black eyes, warm and liquid. Like him, she looked as if she was in charge.

'If you had a carrot or an apple, she would eat it out of your hand,' she said.

Thankfully I had neither.

'Time to go, Aoife,' I said. 'Conor's sitting in the car and we have to call in to Laura.'

I watched as she manoeuvred the pony across the yard. She dismounted beside an open stable-door and carefully knotted the reins on a post. Unwilling to say goodbye, she turned and buried her face into the pony's shoulder.

That was the moment when I saw him, my mouth shrivelling at the sight of him. The man moved like a shadow out of the stable, past Aoife and down the steps. Without looking around, a bucket of feed in his hand, he sidled between the waiting mothers, trying to make himself invisible. But I knew him. Every single thing about him was nailed in my brain: those sharp features under the lank greying mat of hair, the skinny stoop, the soiled cavalry twill trousers. It was the man from the church car park.

Ignoring Aoife's protests, I went forward and grabbed her hand. I wanted to leave and never come back, but Aoife, her face puce, dug in her heels and held on for dear life to the pony's halter. For a moment I had a mad picture in my head: of mother, child and pony forming an undulating chain as we flew off, like cartoon characters, scattering pandemonium in our wake.

I gritted my teeth and, using all my strength, managed to prise Aoife's fingers off the animal's halter. I was vaguely surprised when she didn't scream and, instead, in silence, let me drag her along behind me.

Clara Hall-Davidson, who ran the stables, was on horseback at the far corner of the yard. From the sound of her loud, whinnying *YaYaYa* answers on the phone, I had envisaged a large, horsey woman in tweeds with a riding crop and a shadow of a moustache, but Clara Hall-Davidson had turned out to be a wiry girl in her twenties, with muscular arms and mousey hair tied back in a ponytail. She was dismounting from an enormous bay stallion when I approached. At the sight of the horse pawing the ground, Aoife whooped with delight. *Calm down*, I thought, and, breathing slowly, I came as near to the girl and the horse as I dared.

'Who is that man?' I asked, pointing to the distant figure in the stable yard.

'Who is he?' Clara Hall-Davidson's attention was on the horse while she abstractedly repeated my question.

I nodded, unsure suddenly where this conversation might lead, but determined that it was going to lead somewhere.

'Yes.'

'He's my father,' she said. 'Gosh, why on earth d'you want to know?'

Without warning my foot slid in the mud. As if in slow motion, I felt myself slipping, inexorably, under the shadow of the stallion. My sudden movement panicked the horse and it reared up, rattling its powerful head and drumming its hooves in the air. Its heart-hammering bulk towered over me and I screamed. Arms flailing, I tottered backwards, unsteady on the shifting ground. I managed, somehow, to regain my balance.

As soon as I was upright, I fled towards the car, while Aoife, in fits of giggles, bobbed alongside me.

'You should have *seen* the horse,' she said to Conor as she climbed into the back seat. 'His hooves were as high as the sky.'

Even after I had reached the safety of the car, I was shuddering with terror. What kind of a mother was I, I wondered, my mind in turmoil, what kind of protector of the innocent?

Consumed with shame, I buried my head in my hands. If I had been alone, I would have surrendered to the balm of hot, soothing tears until there were no more to be shed. But I wasn't alone. I was never alone, I realized. I was always on duty, watchful and waiting for some new danger to rear up and with animal malevolence to envelop me. In the back seat the children chattered, oblivious of any disturbance in their lives, and outside, under the trees, other mothers began to drift off in their cars. Although I was not alone, a wave of loneliness oozed into the marrow of my bones. Was this to be a part of my life for ever, I wondered: this endless vigilance, this sense of helplessness, this ache of defeat?

At Laura's house the children tumbled out of the car and rushed into the back garden, to where a knotted rope and a tyre hung from the apple tree. Shouting, they jostled each other to have a go at the slow pendulum-swing through the shady air.

'The energy they have,' Laura mused. 'Maybe if we stopped feeding them – what do you think?'

Niamh, her daughter, an anxious bespectacled child, who was older than the others, idled beside her.

'Off with yourself, Niamh,' Laura said sharply and gave her daughter a pat on the behind. 'Rosy and I want to talk.'

Sullenly the little girl moved away.

'Come inside, we can leave the back door open.'

Even the sight of Laura, somehow, lessened the unhappiness that had returned to gnaw at me, but I didn't feel like unburdening myself to her.

In the kitchen, the sink was full of breakfast dishes and, on the table, a bunch of marigolds wilted in a vase. We sat down at the table and she opened up her handbag and took out a packet of Carrolls No. 1.

'Want one?'

I shook my head. She lit a cigarette, inhaled deeply and looked hard at me.

'*So?*'

How well she knew me!

'It's nothing. How about you?'

A giddy, secretive look crossed her face like a cloud passing over the sun. Then it was gone.

'Laura?'

'Did you hear Mother Columba talking about the holidays?' she said as if there was nothing untoward to talk about. 'School closes this Friday and they get an extra two days in September. What a bloody nuisance!'

'We're not having a holiday this year,' I said, 'but next year, if we can afford it, we're going to Brittany to a campsite. Kevin' – I had to be discreet. Kevin would have been cross if he knew that I was discussing him with anyone, particularly Laura, whom he considered to be flighty – 'Kevin's been working so hard he could do with a break now but, still, France! Can you imagine how fantastic that'll be?'

Laura took a drag of her cigarette. 'Lucky you – all that wine and *oooh la la*!' She winked at me. 'Although camping sounds like hell.' Restlessly she ran her hand through her hair and then she slapped the table with a loud bang.

I jumped. 'What is it, Laura? What is up with you?'

Again the covert grin appeared. She pulled on her cigarette.

'I think I'm in love.'

'You can't be!'

Quizzically she looked at me. 'Oh, why can't I?'

'I mean, who is he? How long do you know him? Do I know him?'

I was beginning to enjoy the frisson of scandal. Laura had such a nerve.

'He's my type – sandy-haired, Irish-looking,' she said airily.

I looked at her suspiciously. Laura was able to conjure up excitement out of nothing. Our humdrum lives were a seedbed for her snarled-up emotions, for arguments with the neighbours over a child's burst football or an out-of-control dog, schoolyard tussles with the parents of children who were terrorized by Laura's twin boys. High drama was her speciality and it was fun to listen to her tales of battles won, lost and ongoing. But Laura had never said anything like this before, nothing subversive enough to destabilize her life. Our lives. My life.

'But how did you meet him?'

'Oh, it wasn't exactly romantic.' Laura burst out laughing. 'He delivers the bread to Montgomery's shop, but he is *so* gorgeous. I was passing the shop today and he gave me a wolf whistle. I was going to ignore him but then he did it again, so I turned around and glared at him. It didn't bother him in the least. He just grinned and told me that a mini-skirt is like barbed wire. Of course, I had to ask. "It protects the property," he said, "without spoiling the view." Cheeky git. So I told him his bread wasn't half as fresh as he was.'

In the cheerful chaos of Laura's kitchen, the two of us rested our arms on the table among the dirty dishes and drying clothes, and looked out at the children charging around on the muddy grass after a squashed football that was getting ready to give up its last gasp under the onslaught.

Gusty laughter died in my throat when I became aware

of a shadow in the doorway: a slight figure, unease in her eyes, who gripped the door handle and stared at her mother.

'Oh, God, Niamh, will you go away and stop earwigging.' Her mother raised her voice and pointed dramatically towards the door, '*Scram!*'

The girl fled.

What had the child done to deserve it, I wondered. To be born was a risky business at the best of times, but her daughter brought out the worst in Laura. Still, I reminded myself, Laura was my best friend. For good or ill. While she seemed unconcerned about Niamh's intrusion, I worried that the little girl had overheard our conversation.

'His name's Johnny,' Laura continued blithely.

I sighed.

'So how about you?' Laura stretched across the table and pulled the ashtray nearer to her. 'Aren't you ever tempted?'

I shook my head. 'Now that you've got the breadman, there's no one left for me. The only news I have is that I'm not pregnant and you know that already. Other than that, I'm just a misery guts.'

I, who should be thanking my lucky stars for getting my period, for house and home, husband and children, for good health and all the rest of it, had said it at last. It sounded so ungrateful but my sense of guilt didn't make it any less true. Laura tapped the cigarette delicately on the ashtray and then shook her hair back onto her shoulders.

'I know, I know,' she said. 'There's two of us in it. I often wonder what life would have been like if I hadn't been up the pole by my nineteenth birthday. When it happened, I felt sorry for Cathal as well as for myself. It was a hardship either way but, in the end, it's wild harder for girls. Men get away with it,' her voice hardened into grit, 'although I'm sure Cathal doesn't think he did.'

Skinny, owlish Cathal Gillespie who worked as a teacher in the Vocational school and had a passion for Gaelic football and left-wing politics. Prematurely bald Cathal who was known to his pupils as the Moon behind the Hill.

'Do you know how much I envy you?' Laura asked.

'Me!'

'Yes, you. You're the one with a qualification. I've nothing except a year's secretarial course and most of the time I was supposed to be learning I was puking up in the toilet.'

'Well,' I said doubtfully, 'I wasn't much good as an architect.'

'That piece of paper, though,' she waved an imaginary certificate in her hand, 'that makes all the difference. It's your passport. You could work to suit yourself. Some people work part-time, you know. I've a cousin in an architect's office in Derry. Even if *he* couldn't, someone would take you on, no bother. You'd cost them less than a man, so why wouldn't they?'

'No, they wouldn't.'

'Betcha they would. I bet you half my next children's allowance they would.'

Laura loved to bet. She had lost a week's housekeeping money at a card game once. Between the two of us, we had managed to buy enough groceries so that Cathal never knew. Was it my turn now to deceive? No, I thought, if I wanted to get a job I would have to tell Kevin but not straight away. I wasn't sure how he'd take the news. Maybe he'd be relieved. After all, he had his worries about the future and I was in a position to help. Laura could have been reading my mind. I had been thinking about looking for work, ever since that night a week previously when Kevin had told me about his fears.

I looked in wonder at Laura and asked, 'But who would mind the children?'

'I could, you eejit. Well, for a while anyway. You'd have to pay me something and it'd only be part-time. You'd be fantastic, Rosaleen McAvady – you'd be the cat's pyjamas.'

Something flickered inside me, some instinct took me over. There was always a possibility that she was right. I might feel better about myself then. I might finally grow up. It seemed to me that I was still living a childlike existence – *cocooned* as Kevin had pointed out.

And so Laura sat down at Cathal's typewriter and together we constructed a letter. She wasn't satisfied with carbon copies and insisted on typing it out four times. I signed each one, trying to make my signature look as architectural as possible. She was so pleased with herself that when Niamh came in, crying from a fall, she wrapped her arms around her and gave her a hug.

'Now,' she said to me over the child's head, 'we'll go into Derry tomorrow morning and try our luck. No jeans, either. Wear something businesslike: your green trouser-suit – that will do nicely.'

It's a game, it's not for real, I thought as I drove home. I can always turn down any offers. I could say my husband wouldn't let me. How could I have let Laura talk me into this? But, deep down inside, another voice refused to be ignored. As we climbed the bend in the road, Lough Swilly spread out in front of me. In the distance, the mountains were a delicate eggshell blue in the evening light – but the view was no longer enough to hold me. Go on, Rosaleen, the voice urged, *be brave.*

In the back seat the children were bickering, so I got them to sing with me, *Heigh-ho, heigh-ho, it's off to work we go* and, after a while, as the motion of the car rocked them, first Aoife and then Conor fell asleep. The throbbing of the engine was my sole companion and I let my mind drift. As I drove past Mr Mundy's house, I noticed that his car was gone and there was no sign of the sheepdog. Beside me, on the passenger seat, the envelope of photographs was a reproach. I had made a promise. Here was my chance to keep it and Kevin need never know. I stopped the car, extracted the photograph from the envelope and then opened the car door quietly so as not to wake the children.

Mr Mundy's house had a disconsolate air. Streaks of moss discoloured the grey plastered walls, and the paintwork was peeling off the window-frames. Inside the porch, a lone, faded deckchair was propped up against the window. Nervously, I opened the flap of the letterbox and pushed in the photograph.

In the back seat Aoife and Conor were still sprawled out, fast asleep. I turned on the ignition. *Heigh-ho,* I thought as the engine started up and I drove the car into the evening light.

7

Laura and I walked up Shipquay Street towards the Diamond and then farther along streets of brick and red-brown stone buildings that huddled together beside the massive city walls. Derry was a city made up of compartments: the Bogside (Catholic), Creggan (Catholic), the Fountain (Protestant), Pennyburn (Mixed).

We were now heading up Bishop Street towards the Fountain and Laura was bucking mad.

'What are you thinking of?' she said.

I shrugged and said nothing.

Just before we reached our destination, Laura stopped and leant against a wall. Around us the street was empty of people and the air smelt of warm dust and distant cooking fumes. With her wavy, red hair and big, hooped earrings, it struck me that Laura looked indisputably Catholic.

Her face was a picture. Her head was down and her

75

lower lip jutted out. She looked like a petulant child in her rose-patterned dress with its full, short skirt.

'Oh, come on, Laura,' I pleaded. 'It's just another architect's office.'

'I'm not going in there,' she said sulkily.

We had nothing to lose, I thought, since we weren't getting anywhere, anyway. The office where her cousin worked had turned out to be closed. On the door someone had put up a memorial card to announce the death of the beloved mother of an esteemed colleague. We wondered about the etiquette of dropping in a letter on the day of a funeral. 'Blast it, anyway,' Laura had said and shoved the letter into the letterbox.

I walked on and, gritting my teeth, rang the doorbell of a tall terraced house. There was no reply. From her stand against the wall, Laura threw me a vitriolic look and pulled her cardigan over her shoulders. I rang again.

A girl opened the door. She was young, with brown curls that tossed about her head when she spoke. Her high sweet voice made me think of a bird chirping among leafy, windblown branches. When I followed her inside the building, I was reassured by the familiar signs of the architect's trade: framed sketch plans on the walls, a T-square leaning against a desk.

I gave her my letter and asked if I could see Mr Welland RIBA, as was written on the brass plaque on the wall outside.

'Who shall I say?'

'Rosaleen McAvady.'

Her face widened with surprise. Then she took the letter and disappeared. A few minutes later she returned. Her face was expressionless.

'Mr Welland is too busy to see you,' she said, and moved quickly towards the door to usher me out.

Outside, Laura was sitting on the step of a neighbouring house, twirling a strand of hair between her fingers. She looked up at me, a smile playing on her lips.

'Ha!'

I said nothing.

She persisted. 'Didn't I tell you?'

This stupid demarcation, I thought. Catholic, Protestant, Hottentot, Jew, what did any of it matter? I wanted to say so but I said nothing.

'I told you so,' Laura gloated. 'I don't know why you bothered.' She stood up and flounced out her skirt. 'They won't have a Catholic around the place.'

I would never understand the nature of the fault-line that ran under the surface of our lives, but this incident was the kind of constant reminder that ensured that I did not forget the bitterness. I was getting as bad as them. The previous day I had told Kevin that I knew our postman was a Protestant because he had a long chin and big feet.

Laura began to walk away. I sighed and followed her. The search for work was proving to be much harder than I had expected. Laura stormed on, as if she was afraid to stay in the Fountain area a minute longer than she needed. By the time we made it back to the Diamond, she had calmed down and she turned to rest her hand on my arm.

'Rosy?'

'What?'

'Bet you half a crown that the next office will be the one.'

Her sudden cheerfulness was not infectious. Doubts crowded in on me and, despondently, I shook my head and said, 'Maybe we should just go home.'

'Come on, Rosy, I can feel it in my wee-wees.'

On Strand Road we found the next office. It was three storeys high and up a winding stair, so when we got to the little reception room we had a bird's-eye view down into the street below. Laura sat down to wait while I went into an inner office.

Daylight blazed down from two large skylights. The white, airy room was sparsely furnished: a desk and chair, a drawing board, stool and a shelving unit for drawings. Cormac Grealish of Eoghan McPartland and Associates sat on the edge of his stool and raised an elegant eyebrow when he saw me. He was a handsome, middle-aged man with a long sculpted face, a wide mouth and a mane of rich brown hair speckled with grey. A casual check shirt with rolled-up sleeves and grey corduroy trousers gave him an air of calculated ease. On the back of his chair hung a jacket of brown herringbone tweed that exactly matched his colouring. He waved me towards the chair.

'Any relation to Kevin McAvady?' he wanted to know.

Of course, it hadn't struck me until then; Kevin and he had worked together, building factories mainly. As we talked, I took out my college thesis to show him. Without comment, he opened it up and slowly turned over the pages of the folder. I chewed on my lip. There was a pause. Then he closed up the folder and stared down at his graceful hand that lay whitely on the dark green cover.

'Nice cover,' he said as if he was saying something profound.

His sharp glance trapped me into replying.

'I'd have thought that *inside* the cover is what matters.'

Silence ballooned in the drawing office. I've done it now, I thought, but he ignored me and gazed intently at the sheet of drawing paper pinned onto the board. Between his fingers he spun a pencil. Suddenly, a slim whistle escaped from between his lips.

'Aha! Now I see . . .'

He bent over and carefully drew lines and angles on the

paper. Engrossed in his work, he appeared to have forgotten that I was in the room. I thought of Laura sitting in reception waiting for me and I stirred in my chair. Deep in thought, he concentrated on his work. Then he spoke, his head down, as if talking to the drawing board.

'We could do with a bit of help. No one in this office seems to do colour schemes, interiors, that kind of thing. Sort of things that a girl knows about.' He turned to look at me. 'Do you?'

I wasn't just a *girl* fresh out of college any more. I was a woman with children and a home but that was beside the point. This was work that I knew I could do. Instead of being put out by his abrupt manner, I was amused by it.

'Yes.'

'I'm only the associate. I'll have to speak to the guv'nor.' He rubbed the pencil between his palms and then placed it on the ledge of the drawing board. He stood up and stretched out his hand to shake mine. 'I'll be in touch,' he said vaguely. 'When. If.'

Uncertainly, I waited for him to finish but he sat, twirled on his stool and bent down again over the drawing board. A languid hand waved me off.

'I think, but I can't be sure,' I said to Laura when we got out into the street. 'I think he's going to take me on.'

'I *knew* it!' Laura said triumphantly and clapped her hands.

A weight lifted off my shoulders. I realized that her belief in me had made all the difference.

'Have we time to celebrate?' I asked. 'I mean coffee, or something?'

'Don't think so. We've the kids to collect, don't forget.'

Usually Laura would drag me into a pub at any opportunity but I thought no more about it until we were driving back to Letterkenny. Suddenly, at the sight of a van coming towards us on the other side of the road, Laura gave a little shriek of excitement. She leant out of the window and waved. As the van neared, I got a glimpse of a raised hand, a cloud of sand-coloured hair. Then the van swerved across the road and came to a screeching halt a short distance ahead of us.

'*Stop*!' Laura shouted.

Surprised, I stopped the car on the verge and turned off the engine.

'Laura . . .' I turned to face her but she was gone out of the car like a bullet.

Through the windscreen I watched her run towards the figure stepping down from the bread van. I was reluctant to admit, even to myself, that, somehow, standing on the verge, the lush summer greenery providing a backdrop, the two of them made a striking couple. They could have belonged together: her auburn hair falling onto her shoulders, the pink roses of her dress glowing, and his sandy hair standing up in a cloud around his head. Like brother and sister.

Or like lovers, I thought with dread.

He said something that made her laugh, her hand fluttering up to her neck. And I understood why she was wearing her best summer dress and had the cardigan slipped off her shoulders and the wide neckline to show off the swell of her breasts, and why she'd been so keen to get going on the drive back to Letterkenny.

Jesus! I thought. With a breadman of all people.

The door opened and she was in beside me again, her exhilaration filling the Morris Minor.

'Jesus, Laura, have you no sense?'

Laura ignored my question. 'That's him, that's Johnny,' she said, sitting back into the car seat contentedly. 'Isn't he the bee's knees?'

Startled, I jerked my head up as a shadow loomed up outside. Laura rolled down the passenger window and, resting his arm a hair's breadth from her bare shoulder, the breadman bent down to peer in. His face filled the window. His eyes were the colour of green marbles, like the marbles that Conor kept in neat rows on the mantelpiece: yellow and green spirals, frozen in glass. His eyes had the same quality: a cool, translucent deadness. There was a cigarette stuck behind his ear and his brown coat was dusty with flour. How *common* he is, I thought.

'Who's this?' he asked.

'*This* is my friend,' Laura said pertly.

'How you doing, friend?'

I couldn't bear to look at him. I stared down at the rim of the open window where his pale stubby fingers rested. His hand was covered in freckles and nicotine stains, his thumbnail was black, and on his third finger he wore a wedding ring. I felt slightly sick.

'We have to go,' I hissed at Laura. 'The children will be out from school.'

'Better not keep the wains waiting,' he said. While he was speaking, he lightly stroked her bare shoulder with back of his hand.

'Stop that,' she giggled and began to wind up the window. He jumped back in mock alarm.

Without looking at him, I revved up the car. As I waited to drive out into the traffic, the bread van shot out in front of us, crossed the road and disappeared in the direction of Derry. Laura waved after it.

'Laura, what are you playing at?'

'Ah Rosy, only a bit of fun. There's no harm in it.'

She was so brazen, I was afraid to ask her what *it* was. A mean glint of anger sparked inside me.

'Oh really,' I said, 'and would Cathal think so?'

'What Cathal doesn't know won't hurt him,' Laura said. She stretched back in the seat and pointedly closed her eyes.

My throat constricted as if I had swallowed something toxic, something I wanted to regurgitate before it disappeared inside me and contaminated us both. I couldn't, wouldn't, let it go.

'Laura, do you realize he's married?'

'Oh, honey child, and so am I.' The car filled with the ugly hoot of her laughter as she raised her arms and pulled her hair up into a knot. 'Don't worry, it's only a bit of fun. You know, it's like ice cream – it's nice to eat but you wouldn't want too much of it.'

Unconvinced, I drove in silence to Letterkenny. When we arrived, the school was beginning to disgorge its children. I slowed the car carefully and parked. My brain was still buzzing with resentment. I knew it was none of my business what Laura did, but she had implicated me all the same. I got out of the car and slammed the door behind me. She stayed put.

I was going to walk away from her when my heart suddenly pounded with fear. Across the road a rusting old Cortina was parked. Inside the car a familiar figure was crouched, his hands on the driving wheel. I recognized the sharp nose, the grey straggling hair and hunched-up shoulders. I jumped back into the Morris Minor and yelled into Laura's startled face, my words tumbling out incoherently. Immediately she grasped my hands in hers.

'Now, calm down,' she said, 'and tell me again.'

And so I told her again. Slowly this time while her eyes became hard. She opened the car door and hitched up her cardigan around her shoulders. With her head down, she careered between the parked cars until she stopped and rapped sharply on the window of the Cortina. Afraid to move and cursing my fear at the same time, I watched from a distance. What drives a man like that, I wondered again. Then I thought of Aoife and Conor and Laura's children and all the other mothers' children. I couldn't hear what Laura was saying but I could see her mouth move and her raised arm pointing at him.

For a moment nothing happened. Then the man started up the engine, wheeled the car around and disappeared in a cloud of dust.

Laura zigzagged between the cars and sat back in the seat beside me.

'What a creep,' she said.

'What did you *say* to him?'

'Waiting outside a school for little children! He won't be back,' she said with satisfaction.

'Oh Laura.'

With a theatrical flourish she lit a cigarette, inhaled deeply and then blew smoke down her nostrils. 'It was easy, girl.'

She was revelling in her moment of triumph. Her skin was golden, the hairs on her forearms glinting in the sunshine. In my eyes, she was transformed into a fabulous creature, beautiful and strong. At that moment I wanted to *be* Laura. She was so brave and so smart and sure of herself. Everything I wasn't.

When she turned to look at me, her eyes were dancing. 'I told him I knew people in the IRA and what they do to perverts when they catch them. Only I was stupid and said *prevert*s by mistake,' she giggled, 'but he got the message, right enough.'

'God, Laura, do you?'

'Do I what?'

'Know people in the IRA?'

'Now you're being stupid,' she said.

In the crowd of children I saw Aoife and Conor, satchels

on their backs, walking slowly across the school yard towards us. Without saying a word I looked hard at Laura.

'Course I don't,' she said, 'but that old queer will never know.'

Did she hesitate before answering or did I just imagine it?

8

A week after my interview in Derry, just when I had given up hope, the 'guv'nor' phoned and offered me work. Two days a week – was I interested?

'Yes,' I said without hesitation.

Then as soon as I had put down the telephone, doubts crowded in. What if . . . ? How would . . . ? Could I . . . ? *Kevin* . . . how would I handle telling him? I fretted as I circled around the garden and in and out of the kitchen. On the windowsill the grey cat gazed curiously at me. 'I'm being ridiculous,' I told her. In reply she curved a little pink tongue around her outstretched paw and writhed in ecstasy.

When dinner was over and Kevin and I were sitting quietly together on the sofa in the living room, it seemed like it was as good a time as any, but I didn't know how to begin.

'What are you thinking of?' Kevin's voice was gentle as he slipped his arm around my shoulders.

So I told him.

'*Jesus*!' Abruptly he stood up, his face drained of colour. I watched as he angrily paced the room.

'I just can't understand you. I thought you were happy. *You* wanted to give up work. *You* wanted to buy this house.' He stopped in the middle of the room and looked at me. 'And now this.'

I thought of the sinkful of crockery still to be washed, the chores that never went away. I hadn't been sure about the idea until Kevin's reaction made me feel that actually, yes, maybe I *did* want the job. Anything was better than staying at home for the rest of my life. I frowned. It was a choice I had to make now.

'Don't you think you should have asked me first?' Kevin said.

I looked into the empty grate. I was about to say that I didn't need his permission, but I shrank from confronting him. Then I remembered a phrase that Mammy was fond of saying to Mona and me when we were growing up . . . *softly, softly, catchee monkee.*

'Yes, Kevin,' I lied. 'You're right, of course. I should have. I'm sorry.'

Uncertainly Kevin looked down at me. I seized the advantage.

'Listen,' I said, reaching out for his hand, 'you know the office. I mean, you've done work for them. I've heard you say yourself that they're good architects.'

It was true. Kevin did a lot of his work in Derry with Eoghan McPartland and Associates. As soon as I said the name, I realized that this fact was my trump card.

'And it's only for two days a week,' I added sweetly.

Shoulders slumped, he dropped down onto the sofa and clasped his hands tightly together under his chin. I waited. Even when I had got the phone call and I had stammered out my thanks, I still hadn't been sure that I'd go through with it but now my doubts had dissipated. I had won the argument.

Kevin sighed again. 'On one condition.'

We had moved from war into negotiating peace terms.

'What is it?'

'If things get rough – if there's any trouble in Derry, I mean – you have to promise me you'll leave the job.'

His tone was so grave that I could feel my mouth twitching into a smile.

I nodded.

'Stop smirking at me,' he grumbled. 'Anyway, in a few months' time you'll probably be fed up and itching to come home again.'

'Well,' I said peaceably, 'you could be right.'

I rumpled his hair. Irritated, he twisted his head away and rested it against a cushion. Too tired to get up and switch on the lights, we sank further into the sofa as a dusky languor filled the living room. In the garden a ball thudded on the ground and the voices of our children came to us, clear and full of life.

Kevin stirred out of his torpor. 'And who's going to make my –'

'*I* will make your dinner,' I said, 'just like I always do.'

'Well, at least I look the part,' I said to my reflection in the bathroom mirror. I checked my green trouser suit, white blouse, and white summer sandals.

At my side Aoife's face reared up, her expression wary.

'You look nice,' she said.

I bent down to give her a hug.

She pulled her head back and gazed at me.

'Mum?'

'What is it, my dotey?'

Although she was still a little girl, her face had a womanly, flat-cheeked, dark-eyed air about it. She looked at me hard. 'Will you still bring me to horse-riding?'

Knowing what I knew, I wondered what was the right thing to do. Her gaze was steady, daring me to refuse, ominous as a dark cloud on the horizon when a storm is forecast. It wasn't fair, I thought, on my first day going to work that I had to contend with this. I was nervous enough without forcing a confrontation. A little, warm hand slipped into mine.

'Ummm,' I said.

Aoife's eyes filled and her lip quivered.

Oh God, I thought, *not now*. Maybe someone else keeps horses, I thought, and gives lessons. Anyway, I had a week to find out.

'Yes, of course,' I said. 'I'll still be taking you.'

I slipped an Alice band on my head to keep my hair back and gave one last anxious look at myself in the mirror.

'Wish me luck, dotey,' I said but Aoife was already rattling down the stairs ahead of me.

Eoghan McPartland hitched up his trousers, straightened his tweed tie and gently patted his balding head. Known to those who worked for him as 'the guv'nor', it was a nickname that suited his cheery, Pickwickian splendour and rolling double chins.

'Warehouses, banks and factories were the making of Derry.' He spoke in a staccato rush. 'They kept its heart beating. Aye, commerce and trade first. After that, dereliction and decay. Oh aye, it is now such a great city that our university goes to those dunces in Coleraine.' He paused and gazed sorrowfully at his thumbs. 'There's no shortage of halls and churches of every kind. Always been good, old-fashioned competition here, in trade and religion and in war.' He waved expansively to the view from the window of rooftops and church spires. Then he pointed to a framed drawing on the wall. 'St Columb's Temperance Hall. Look at it. You'll not see such swagger in a building anywhere.'

Earlier that morning, standing outside the office of Eoghan McPartland and Associates, I had to quell an urge to cut and run. Once inside the building, I relaxed. I had not, as it turned out, been given colour schemes to design. The guv'nor had taken me into his office – fading lithographs of classical buildings on the walls – where he had handed me a folder and then launched into a lecture on Victorian Derry. Mystified, I had listened while he talked about the brick and timber warehouses and mills decaying along the waterfront, the coastal trade, the emigration to America and Canada.

'Two of my grand-uncles walked from Donegal town to Derry quay and sailed out to New York and out of history,' he said. 'The third brother who came with them was my grandfather. He liked the look of what he saw here and he stayed. He sold his ticket and spent the rest of his life complaining.'

Again the hand's fond sweep over his bald head and for a moment his burbling laughter filled the room.

'I want you to do an inventory of buildings that you see: buildings of particular significance in the city. I offered to do the job myself for the Ulster Heritage Society but I'm up to my tonsils in work.' He looked at me shrewdly. 'So now you're the one to do it for me.'

His enthusiasm unnerved and excited me at the same time. I didn't know anything about historical buildings but, somehow, that didn't matter. It was as if my brain was stretching to match his exuberance and the task he was giving me shimmered magically ahead.

'I do have a camera.'

'Good girl,' but already his attention had shifted away. He stood up.

'Should I start now?'

'First I'll introduce you around. Get you set up right.'

He opened the door for me. Head high, I walked out of the room. Then I stopped to let him pass in front of me.

'You've already met Cormac,' he said, opening a door.

The room was disappointingly empty. The skylights glared down into a silent space. He opened the next door and we entered a studio where four drawing boards were set up.

The two young men in the room fell silent at the sound of the door opening. I was still tingling with a nervous confidence when I shook hands with each one in turn: Malachy, a lanky, shaggy-haired young draughtsman from Strabane with acne-destroyed skin, and an older man, Andrew from Cardiff, who had a tic and black eyebrows that wriggled like worms.

Andrew was extravagantly polite, ooohing and aahing like a Welsh comedian. Jumping up from his stool, he led me towards an empty drawing board near the window. After the guv'nor had left, I sat down, put the folder on the drawing board and stared at it.

Now what, I wondered, my confidence draining away in a flood of embarrassment.

In the hushed room the two male heads bent over their work. The only sounds were of their breathing and the rumble of traffic outside. Cigarette smoke curling up from Malachy's drawing board dissipated in the air.

I opened up the folder to a jumble of maps, references, sketches. When the guv'nor had handed it to me, his relief had been palpable. This was a job that would keep me busy for ages, I realized, but it was also a job that I was capable of doing. A thin thread of certainty uncoiled inside me as I took a deep breath and began to separate the pages to examine them more closely. A sociable silence settled in the room as we worked.

Suddenly, the door smacked open.

'Yo fuckin' boys, yo have –'

On seeing me, the stranger stopped in mid-sentence. Thickset and strong, he was in his thirties, I guessed. He had a monumental slab of a face, like a headstone, and wore a navy fisherman's sweater and jeans. Has to be a foreigner, I thought, with that tan and that haircut.

'Who is this person I have not met before?' He turned to Malachy and Andrew, who had both straightened up expectantly.

Before they had a chance to speak, I introduced myself.

'And I am Frederick from Antwerp – architect,' he said.

Formally we shook hands. He lumbered over to the unoccupied drawing board and emptied out his pockets.

'This country is crazy.'

I realized that Frederick was talking to me in his rubbery, indistinct voice. I sat back on my stool and looked at him.

'I want to know where I can get French letters, you know?' he said. 'When I go to a pharmacy here in this town, the man get angry and will not serve me, so, please, I ask these fuckin' boys here where can I get them and they send me over to the Waterside. But they also beg me to get some for them, so I go into the shop – this girl working there, when she sees me it is the same girl I have met in the dance last night and she is not happy when I ask her for a hundred French letters. She thinks I am making a joke but it is not true. It's just these stupid fuckin' boys are afraid to buy themselves.'

His face expressionless, he waved the packages in the air and dropped them on the desk. Malachy and Andrew swooped. Frederick shrugged, sat down and picked up a pipe from among the items he had taken out of his pockets. Striking a match on the edge of his drawing board, he noisily lit the pipe. Then, clenching it between his teeth, he bent over his drawing. The sweet, heady smell of tobacco wafted across the room. In the silence that followed I could sense that the other two were watching me.

'Never you mind Frederick, there's no harm in him,' Andrew said to me softly, the tic under his eye working overtime. 'He just takes everything literally. He's a foreigner.'

So are you, I thought and then, *so am I*.

'Aye,' Malachy echoed.

For a moment I thought I would tell them that Kevin and I could do with a few French letters ourselves but I didn't. I just smiled sweetly and said nothing. This was my world now. I was back in the labyrinth of office life as if I'd never left.

My other world, I found, was managing very well without me. When I went to collect the children from Laura's, they begged me to let them stay there for their tea but I put my foot down.

And when we arrived home, Kevin was back early and sitting at the kitchen table. He didn't baulk when I asked him to peel the potatoes.

'Oooh,' I teased, 'maybe I should go to work for more than two days a week!'

'*No!*' said Kevin, spearing a potato in mock rage.

Outside, the evening sun expanded the green, dappled garden in a burst of light. Then the sky darkened and the light fled. Like a moment of happiness, I thought, that fires up everything and then dies. And so we worked together in the kitchen, the children running in when I called them and the smells of thyme and freshly chopped onions scenting the air.

9

I was conscious that my life was taking on a different shape. My week formed a pattern: days of domesticity interspersed with days that I spent moving through the streets of Derry. I felt I was being altered by the change in my circumstances. Even when I was at home, working in the garden or when Laura and I and the children piled into the Morris Minor and barrelled out to the seaside at Buncrana, I knew, in my heart, that I had taken a step forward: a small, significant step of my own.

Laura told me she was green with envy.

I had no experience of recording buildings but, somehow, I knew I could do the job. I just had to become more observant, I decided, and take note of everything: gargoyles on a portico, the dressed stonework of a gable. When an oriel window came into view, I photographed it. Camera in one hand, sketchpad in the other, I made my way through the city, learning about its layout and concentrating on its physical form. The guv'nor was right about the rich repository of buildings, but many of them were falling apart. Often the brickwork was soft and crumbling and yet, it was still, unmistakably, part of a wall of a church or a warehouse. It was built with a purpose in mind: solid, unyielding, inevitable. Such stability was a pleasure to me. Buildings didn't have tantrums or answer back, they didn't fall down and beat their fists on the floor until they got riding lessons, or demand biscuits in the middle of the night – all of which, for me, made a satisfying change. Not only were the structures quiescent, they also had a story to tell. Slowly and hesitantly, I began to set down on paper what I saw, taking photographs and making sketches. Once I had satisfied myself that I had captured the essential nature of a building, I went to the public library and examined the parish records or went up to McGee College for information. By acquiring the language of the city's architecture, I found that I was also learning about the history of Derry from its beginning, from 'Doire', the acorn of a settlement.

Then the little world that I had constructed so diligently collapsed.

In my dim, unthinking way, I'd known about the situation across the Border. There had been civil rights marches before, and skirmishes and raids, sudden bursts of conflict followed by periods of calm. Kevin had talked to me about the political causes of the unrest: the discrimination against Catholics, the gerrymandering of constituencies, the repressive policing, the sectarianism, but, to me, the turbulence had always seemed at one remove. For all I cared, he could have been talking about another country.

Then, on 12 August 1969, the city of Derry exploded.

This was trouble of a different order, and impossible for me to ignore. The Apprentice Boys' March had been the trigger and, initially, there was a weary familiarity to the riots that filled our television screen. Not for the first time, stones were thrown and were met by a police onslaught. This confrontation was different: a wave of rage and hurt and a sheer physical appetite for battle swept through the streets of the Bogside and crashed over the Royal Ulster Constabulary. Armed with stones, bricks, petrol-fuelled rags in milk bottles, a mobilized community fought back.

Each night we watched, on the television screen, the movement of rioters advancing, falling back in clouds of tear gas, and then pushing forward again. Armed with batons, helmets and shields, the RUC looked terrifying, an alien army. Along the parapet of the block of flats overlooking Rossville Street, a line of youths, like cowboys with handkerchiefs over their mouths, rained down stones and petrol bombs. Below them, talking into a television camera, stood a girl, tiny and ferocious. Bernadette Devlin was her name, I learnt from the commentator. A factory I recognized was set alight and gutted in a heavy pall of black smoke. Into our living room came Kevin's worst fear, thundering out of the streets of the Bogside, spewing stones and flaring flames in its wake.

'I told you this would happen,' he said. 'They'll have the whole place destroyed. And nobody to stand up to them and take control. The Unionists and the Irish government both. Jesus! You couldn't trust any of them. I heard a man on the radio saying the only answer is to send in the United Nations.'

Kevin forbade me to return to the office in Derry. The riots filled me with fear, so I didn't argue. I wrote a letter to the guv'nor and explained that my husband was concerned about my safety and that, as a result, I could not return to work but I added a postscript – without telling Kevin – to say that if things settled down I would love to come back.

Despite my compliance, the city invaded my life. Full of anxious excitement, I pored over newspaper photographs and television news programmes. Standing in the garden, I watched the seabirds shimmy over the placid waters of the lough and wondered how near the battle would have to get before the sounds of it could be heard. In my imagination, the streets that I had come to know attained a new, mysterious grandeur. My fingers seemed to touch the stones that were skimming through the air. Flames scorched my face and I breathed an atmosphere contaminated with CS gas. The city was taking a step towards anarchy and I could only watch from afar, my sense of longing mixed with horror.

'What is happening?' I asked Laura when she phoned. '*Why* is it happening?'

I wanted to know everything but all she said was, 'What's happening is bloody murder and I have Mammy and our Pauline and Jamie here and they'll put me in the madhouse the way they're acting, calling themselves refugees. They came out here in a taxi with bagloads of clothes. I'll never be rid of them.'

I had hoped to take Laura and her children to the beach at Buncrana, I said. We could sit on the sand and talk about what it all meant.

'Och, Rosaleen, Jamie's away up to the hospital with Cathal.' In her excitement I noticed that her Derry accent became more pronounced. 'He got hurted last night in the fighting. Come on down, Rosy, will you, just for a wee while? Jesus, I can't do this on my own.'

This turned out to be a pile of bags in Laura's hallway and a haze of cigarette smoke in the kitchen, and Laura arguing with her mother, who had her sleeves rolled up and was scrubbing pots and pans at the sink.

'Mam, will you stop that?' Laura caught her by the arm. 'You'll have my pots wore out.'

'I'm that worried, Laura. Our Jamie wounded, and us having to come over the Border. The RUC could've killed him.'

'I know, Mammy, I know, but you can't take it out on the saucepans. They're not used to it. Here, sit down and have a smoke and tell Rosy all about it.'

Laura directed her over to an upholstered chair with wooden arms in the corner of the kitchen. Panting heavily, her mother sat down and rummaged in her handbag. Mrs Bradley was a woman with sharp, intelligent eyes, steely permed hair and tree trunks for legs. Silently, her other daughter Pauline, who had been sitting at the kitchen table, came over to her and gave her a cigarette.

Laura turned her back on them both and began taking cups and saucers down from the cupboard.

'I'll just settle the children,' I said hastily and led Conor and Laura's twins down the corridor to their bedroom. Within minutes, under Conor's direction, the twins had taken the blankets off the bunk beds and draped them across the room to make a tent. As the three children crawled inside the tent they had made, I shut the door quietly and came back into the kitchen.

Mrs Bradley burst into conversation as soon as she saw me. 'You'll not believe it, girl!' Smoke streaming out of her nostrils, she said excitedly, 'If I live, I'll never see the like. Grown women fighting the polis, and wains no bigger than Niamh there setting fire to the houses.'

At the mention of her name, Laura's daughter melted out of the room. Aoife followed her.

'Not the houses, Mammy,' Pauline said. Older than

97

Laura and unmarried, she was an indistinct carbon copy of Laura, a faint, colourless version of her younger sister. 'Although, right enough,' she continued in her quiet, neutral voice, 'last night with the fires we were all afraid for the cathedral.'

Her mother chimed in, 'And my own son choked with the gas and the arm hanging off him.'

Just then a car drove up and parked outside the bungalow. Car doors slammed. Laura and I ran to the window to see Cathal and a skinny, long-haired young man wearing a donkey jacket getting out of the car.

'Speak of the devil!' Laura threw open the front door. 'Well, what did the doctor say?'

Her husband gave her a withering look and walked past her into the kitchen. 'Town is full of clapped-out Irish army trucks up from Ballykinler, and soldiers.' He took off his glasses and polished them energetically as he spoke. 'That's what kept us.'

Reluctantly the younger man followed him in and sat down on a kitchen chair.

'Well, our Jamie,' Laura said, 'what did the doctor say?'

Her brother twisted away from her and looked at the wall. His mother bent towards him.

'You can tell me, son,' she said solicitously. 'Is it broke like you said?'

Cathal snorted, 'Go on, show your mam how broke your arm is.'

'Doctors don't know nothing,' Jamie said.

'A bit of sticking plaster was all and he's fighting fit.'

'You're joking!' said Laura.

Cathal turned to her, 'Is there any tea in that pot?'

'You wee shite, the fright you gave us.' Laura cuffed her brother on the head.

Jamie ducked, then straightened up and ambled across

the room to stand beside his mother.

'Thanks be to God,' she said, blessing herself quickly as she settled back in her chair.

Laura poured a cup of tea and carried it over to her. With a trembling hand her mother spooned sugar into her cup from the bowl Laura proffered. For a moment their heads were close together, auburn and grey, almost touching. Without speaking, the young woman and her mother exchanged surreptitious smiles.

Laura straightened up and turned to Cathal. 'Turn on the radio there for the news.'

Her husband opened up the glass-panelled doors into the living room and went over to the corner where the radio was on its stand. Tinnily, the Beatles' 'Love Me Do' sang out in the room. As she set the table, Laura joined in the chorus.

'Good on you, girl,' her mother said, tapping her hand on the chair.

Then suddenly, the room froze when the music stopped for a newsflash and that was how we heard that the British government had taken the decision to deploy their soldiers into Derry and other troubled areas of Northern Ireland to reinstate public order and protect lives and property.

The announcement was met with a stunned silence.

Then. 'Protect *us*!' Jamie said. 'Fuck me.'

'What does it mean?' Laura's mother wondered.

'It means, Mammy,' her son shouted, 'that the British Army is sent in to keep us taigs quiet. Oh, Croppy, fucking lie down!'

No one said anything for a moment.

Jamie pounded the table with his fist. 'It's a fucking disgrace. Now we have the Unionists beat, we should keep on fighting and get rid of the Brits.'

Pauline opened her mouth to speak but Cathal interrupted her.

'Actually, Jamie is correct.' He spoke as if he were giving a lecture at school. 'It happened before in Suez and in Aden. British imperialism flexing its muscles. The ruling class sends in the Army to keep the natives in their place and now they are on Irish soil for the very same reason. Of course those soldiers are only pawns, working-class lads from Scotland and the North of England, following orders.'

'Well,' said Pauline, 'at least it means an end to the rioting.'

Jamie ignored her. 'I wouldn't trust the Free State and that Jack Lynch neither. We could've all been dead and he'd be still making speeches. And the pipe stuck in his gob. Fuck me.'

Suddenly Pauline, her face pink, stood up. 'Mind your language, you wee bugger!' Her voice quivered as she spoke but there was steel in her words. 'Know something, boys? I'm glad the Army has come in. *Glad* – do you hear me?' Her hands on her hips, she looked at the men defiantly. 'All I care about is that we can go home and we'll be safe in our house and thank God for them soldiers.'

Her mother looked at her thoughtfully. 'Aye, right enough. We might get a bit of peace now.'

Laura was leaning against the kitchen table. She looked down at her hands.

'What do you think, Laura?' her mother asked.

Laura smiled at her mischievously. 'You'll have those soldiers carrying home your shopping from Wellworths and everything now, Mam. You won't know yourself.'

'Don't you be cheeky, Miss. At least the B Specials won't be battering down the doors of decent people now.'

'That's right, Mammy,' said Pauline. She added spitefully, 'Oh, it's easy for them that are living down here in the Free State in comfort and well out of it all. Aye, safe and secure in their bungalows.'

'*Jesus, Pauline*!' Laura took a step towards her. For a split second they looked like cats ready to spring.

Arms outstretched, Cathal moved quickly between the two women. Imperceptibly he shook his head at Laura. She turned away to the sink and began peeling potatoes furiously.

No one spoke. On the radio Bridie Gallagher sang about the hills of Donegal.

With difficulty, Mrs Bradley stood up and tucked her handbag under her arm. 'Come on, our Jamie, and get our bags,' she said. 'Time we went on home.'

'Ah Mam!' In dismay, Laura looked over her shoulder at her mother. 'You'll surely have your tea before you go? I'm making egg and chips.'

'No, child, I'm away long enough. If we go now, we'll be home in time to see it all on the TV.'

Cathal helped Mrs Bradley on with her coat and scarf. She hugged Laura and me and then the four of them went out to the car. Laura followed them while I waited behind in the kitchen.

As the sound of the car faded, Laura walked back into the living room and turned off the radio. Her face had lost its animated look, the lines on her neck were more pronounced and her skin was mottled. In her eyes, tears glistened.

'What's up?' I asked.

She shook her head and gazed down at the table without speaking.

'Come on, Laura, this isn't like you.'

She busied herself, gathering up the cups and saucers scattered around the kitchen. I stood at the sink and watched the soapsuds churn under the running tap. In a companionable silence we worked. I washed and she dried and, when we had finished, I wiped my hands on a tea towel.

'Come on, Laura, tell me.'

She grimaced at the shrieking sound the chairs made on the floor as she pushed them under the kitchen table. I waited.

'I worry about them, that's all,' she said at last and then, wryly, 'I even worry about our Pauline – can you believe that?'

'But, Laura, things will surely settle down now that the British Army's in charge.'

Laura hooted with laughter. 'Wise up, Rosy.'

'What do you mean?'

'This isn't the Home Counties for God's sake,' she said with a heavy emphasis. 'It's *Londonderry* we're talking about, Rosy.' She sat down at the table, gnawing on her knuckle. '*Nothing* ever gets settled in Derry.'

At the mention of the city, a vision rose before my eyes: the canyon view of Strand Road from the office window, the hilly tangle of spires and roofs, smoke curling around chimneypots, warehouses yawning along the waterfront above the curved smile of the river, the great fortress walls, their colour reminiscent of old brown donkeys. It's over, I told myself bitterly, that freedom that I had, that small and contained life in which I was able to ramble about, lost in thought, and be myself.

'I'd better go home.'

Time to go, yes, but home was not where I wanted to be. I picked up my handbag from the floor and was about to leave when I realized that Laura wasn't listening to me. Shoulders hunched, her bony, freckled hands gripping her face, she was crouched over the table. Suddenly she was sobbing like a child.

'Oh Laura!' I felt helpless. Laura was the strong one, she knew how to take on the world and here she was weeping.

Her daughter Niamh appeared in the doorway, looking

drawn and frightened at the sight of her mother's distress.

'Mammy . . .' she began but Laura stood up in a fury, her eyes blazing, her hair flying out around her wet cheeks.

'*Get away from me!*' she screamed and Niamh ran out of the kitchen. Somewhere inside the house, boys were shouting. A door slammed. Outside a dog barked.

I patted Laura's hair while she hiccupped and talked through her tears. She wanted to go home, she said. It broke her heart, she said, to be away with all the trouble going on, and . . . and . . .

'Take a deep breath,' I said.

Laura wiped her nose on the tea towel and said, 'Pauline's right. I am safe, living in the Free State away from it all, but the truth is, if she only knew it, I'd change places with her right now. She could have all this and welcome to it.'

She gazed around the kitchen and then jerked her head angrily towards the door that Niamh had left open. 'If I hadn't got pregnant on that wain, I'd be my own woman now instead of being stuck here. How did it happen? What did God have against me? All it took was one lousy time behind the dog track and I didn't even enjoy it.'

'But Laura, you have a family now —'

'Don't you get it? That's the whole point, Rosy.' There was spittle at the corner of her mouth. A tear dripped off her chin as her face collapsed again in her hands. 'I hate it all. I hate Niamh and I hate everything else about my life.'

'Laura!' I recoiled. No one could say that about their child. *No one.*

In the doorway a figure stood, a small, composed figure. Conor. Head cocked, he was listening, a look of curiosity on his face. The look of a wise old man which I knew only too well. I waved him away and he disappeared out of the kitchen, his little sandals slapping along the corridor.

'Oh Laura.'

She shook her head impatiently. 'And stop saying "*Oh Laura*" – just because I'm a coward doesn't mean I'm stupid.'

'You're not a coward!' I said, surprised. 'You are anything but. Believe me.'

'I must be a coward to be still here in this house when the world is being changed all around me. Something has happened, Rosy, these last few days. Our house at home in the Bogside. Do you know where it is?'

I shook my head.

'When I look out of our bedroom window in Westland Terrace I can see the city walls and the Walker monument and all those Protestant buildings that you're so keen on these days. All my life they've looked down on us like *we* were the outsiders, not them. Do you want to know something, Rosy? I used to have nightmares, always about the same thing. I dreamt thon buildings were chasing down the hill towards me and landing on top of our house and burying all of us under the rubble. Used to scare the shite out of me. I'd wake up screaming and gasping for air every time. Isn't that some dream for a wain to have?'

She paused. The kitchen was quiet, reflective: at peace again after the invasion of people. Now it seemed to be waiting. Were we all waiting, I wondered, for something to happen?

When Laura spoke again, the tone of her voice was light, 'Well, not any more. The Bogside will never be the same again. We've driven the RUC out for ever. With our bare hands. Imagine, Rosy,' her eyes were shining, 'I come from Free Derry now.'

'Yes,' I smiled at her. 'History in the making.'

Suddenly, she slapped the tea towel hard against the counter and wailed, 'And I wasn't there for any of it!'

She twisted the tea towel as if she were strangling it and then, abruptly, threw it on the floor where it uncoiled wetly like a dead fish.

'Well, it's over now and the British Army is in charge,' I said in an effort to comfort her, but she wasn't listening.

'Just because I come from Free Derry,' she said, 'that doesn't make *me* free.'

Her hand fluttered to her neck before travelling up to her forehead as she turned towards the window and presented a face of tragedy to the evening light. It was a moment of pure theatre.

I couldn't help myself: I burst out laughing.

'Oh, *Laura*!' I said.

10

I felt silly, like a mother hen fussing over her chicks as, holding their hands tightly, I led Aoife and Conor across the stable yard. There were a few mothers standing around as usual but there was no sign of Clara Hall-Davidson's father. All the same I wasn't taking any chances. At the sight of Toffee waiting at the timber railing, Aoife pulled on her riding hat and then clambered up into the saddle. The pony shook its head contentedly as the two of them waited to be led off.

I was glad I hadn't told Kevin about the incidents in the car park and outside the school. I hadn't the stomach for a showdown. He would have insisted on stopping Aoife's riding lessons. He might have even gone to the gardaí and made a complaint. I just wanted to keep the peace and to enjoy the look of bliss on my daughter's face which sitting astride a horse generated. Anyway, I rationalised, with all this talk of civil rights, Aoife had a right to learn horse-riding if that's what made her happy. I could give her that much. I had decided to be vigilant while continuing to bring her every Wednesday afternoon to the Hall riding school. I had checked around but there weren't any other riding schools in the area and I shrank at the prospect of a direct confrontation with my daughter.

'We are staying here until Aoife's finished her class,' I said to Conor.

He shrugged, sat down on the ground and began picking at a scab on his arm. His face gave nothing away.

'Want to play?'

He looked at me suspiciously. 'Play what?'

'Chasing, maybe?'

He shook his head.

We watched in silence as Aoife and the other riders disappeared down a track through the trees.

'We could follow them,' I said hopefully but he shook his head again.

I watched as he wandered off in the opposite direction, towards a tree trunk lying in the undergrowth. Then he disappeared. I stood up from where I'd been sitting on a step.

'Conor?' I called uncertainly. Then louder, '*Conor*?'

His head reappeared out of the greenery and he scrambled up on the tree trunk. He paused, wobbling slightly, his wide-open gaze seeking a response from me. I clapped my hands as, with his arms outstretched, he walked with the exaggerated steps of an acrobat along the length of the tree trunk and then jumped into the brambles.

'Did you see me?' he hollered and ran towards me, arms flapping like wings. 'Did you *see* me?'

Who did he remind me of? Who had performed for applause like that, his face turned full-on to make sure that

I was watching, watching, and ready to respond? Then I remembered. Daddy. Of course. Daddy who sang loudly and long, his eyes watchful for attention as he did so. *'I met her in the garden where the praties grow . . .'* His Cork accent coming through each line and his fleshy gaze spanning the room. Look at me. Look at me. And how we looked, Mammy and Mona and I, sitting spellbound at the swoop and leap of his voice, the self-assurance in his straight back and his short, stout legs planted on the sitting-room carpet. Daddy sang like a performer on stage even when the audience was only us girls and his two brothers when they were up from Cork and joining in with him on 'The Boys of Wexford' and, with tears in their eyes, 'The Banks of My Own Lovely Lee'. To me it felt as if the house itself was playing out its own rhythm in the crescendo of their voices.

The house in Terenure was the only home I remembered. When Daddy inherited money from a bachelor uncle, Mammy, with two little girls to raise, had set about buying the house. As far as she was concerned, it was perfect: set in flats and already bringing in an income. The peeling wallpaper, the sagging roof, the drench of dampness, she ignored. One night she had brought home a crate of porter along with Seán Cross the auctioneer, who had a sheaf of papers in his briefcase, and the three of them had sat down together in the sitting-room and, when he was nicely mellow, Daddy had signed for the house while taking a breather between finishing 'Three Lovely Lassies from Bannion' and starting the ten verses of 'Paddy McGinty's Goat'.

Mammy said to me years later, 'Surely it was best to put the money in rooms than it going down his throat?' She had a way of straining her head forward, nose twitching, when she wanted an answer. She was small, lean as a whippet, and muscular from all the lifting and pushing at work. Her nursing job kept our family going while Daddy's profligacy kept her on a financial knife-edge. All the same, he was no match for her. He was a roly-poly, curly-haired man who cried easily, and had that seductive lilting voice. While she was sinewy and strong, he was plump and yielding. There was a haven for a little girl in the cushioning of his woolly black suit and waistcoat smelling of beer and tobacco. I loved to huddle, like a kitten, into the folds of the rough cloth that covered his comforting bulk, and stay there until I fell asleep. As he talked over my head, his words rumbled out from the depths of his chest.

'Mammy, look at me!' Conor called. '*Look at me*!'

He was lugging a branch through the undergrowth. Dutifully I watched as he propped it up against a fallen tree trunk. He hunkered down, concentrating on the task of building a shelter with branches and sticks.

'I'm looking.'

'See what I made.'

'What is it?'

'You have to guess,' he shouted.

'Is it a fort?'

'No.'

'Is it a train?'

'That's silly, Mammy.' He was offended. 'You have to guess again.'

'I give up.'

'It's a house, of course.'

'That's lovely, Conor,' I said but he wasn't listening. All his attention was bound up in his work.

A house. A home. The place where, when you get there, they have to take you in. Poor Daddy! That baleful eye staring up at me. His body splayed out on the floor beside the camp bed and the old brown blanket bunched up around his legs. Left out in the cold while the rest of us slept in our beds.

Whenever my father went on a drinking binge, Mammy refused to let him inside the house. She locked the doors and he was forced to sleep in the garden shed for the night. The shed door was swollen and warped. It was impossible to open it. We would hear him cursing in the darkness as he pulled himself up through the window and into the shed.

It was so long ago, I told myself. And yet . . .

'You've made your bed, now you can . . .' her voice sharp as grit in the night air.

'Aggie, Aggie,' he'd croon as he swayed in the moonlight.

The sound of their voices would wake Mona and me where we were sleeping in the lumpy double bed. The bedsprings screeched whenever we moved. We'd lie still and hold our breath and wait for the silence to be shattered by his '*You're a bitch – a cruel, cruel bitch!*' When he was drunk, he found the courage to berate her, but even so, she never gave an inch.

'Away on!' She'd close her bedroom window. *Bang*.

'Oh poor Daddy.' Unable to stop my tears, I'd cover my head with the blankets.

Beside me in the bed, Mona, who was thirteen years old and wordly-wise, would stretch out a hand and pat my arm. 'He'll sleep it off. So Mammy says.'

But whatever *it* was, neither of us quite knew.

Next morning, Daddy, a hangdog expression on his face, invariably arrived in for his breakfast, his tie askew and his suit covered in dust. A chilly silence met him at the kitchen table. Not a word was said on those occasions. Mona and I crept out to school but, by teatime, Mammy and Daddy would be back talking. If anything, the tone of their conversation would be tinged with a new, edgy warmth. As

111

she moved around the kitchen, he was there at her side, reaching over to take the weight of the ancient kettle with its blackened sides and lifting it onto the hob; or else, she sat down wearily while he fussed around her, setting out the cups and saucers, the milk jug and sugar bowl, cutting slices of bread. Sometimes as the day began to fade, he sang across the kitchen table – 'The Last Rose of Summer' or 'The Darling Girl from Clare' – gazing so mournfully at my mother that Mona and I would burst out laughing.

'Away on and get your homework done' was all Mammy ever said when she stood up to get ready to go on night duty. Even she couldn't stay cross for ever.

'Go out and tell your daddy his breakfast's ready.'

I got down from the kitchen chair and padded out into the garden: grey cement walls on each side of a patch of muddy grass, a line of dustbins, the shed made from concrete blocks and a corrugated iron roof, rotting timbers, a broken windowpane. A derelict pram sprouted dock leaves. I made my way through the nettles and climbed onto an upturned crate so that I could see through the window into the shed. In the dim light an eye baleful, unblinking, stared into mine. His head lying back on the floor, the old blanket bundled around his legs.

'Daddy!' I called. *'Daddy!'*

His silence sent a shiver through me.

'Are you sick?' I was frightened of this strange, motionless being whose marble eye implored me to save him.

Mammy came running when I screamed. She took one look and lifted me down from the crate.

'Go into the kitchen, alanna,' she said. *'Now.'*

I ran into the house. My heart was beating like a church bell. The oilcloth on the table was torn at one corner and I rubbed at it with my fingernail. The tear grew bigger and bigger as I fretted.

Breathlessly my mother followed me back into the house. 'Go up and tell Mr Adjouti that I want him here *now*.'

'Ah Mammy!' I was aghast but it was pointless to protest. She had already disappeared out into the garden again.

Mr Adjouti rented a room up at the top of the house. Shakily I clutched at the balustrade that snaked up the twilight canyon of the stairwell. I began to climb the stairs up to the third floor. Mr Adjouti had been the first black person I had ever seen. When I saw his glistening ebony skin, his full lips and brilliant teeth, I couldn't have been any more surprised than if he had sprouted a pair of wings from the shoulders of his well-cut suit. Mr Adjouti always bowed to my mother whenever they met on the stairs. He was studying medicine in the Royal College of Surgeons and was never a bit of trouble, my mother said – in fact, a nicer man you wouldn't meet. I was only seven; all I knew was that Mr Adjouti was going to be a doctor and that he was black   a cause of anxiety to me on both counts – but this was an emergency. I stopped outside his door, took a deep breath and knocked.

After a long pause the door opened and Mr Adjouti, in shirt sleeves, looked out cautiously. He smiled at me. He was always smiling. Day or night, he had a disconcertingly large smile, displaying a pink tongue in his cavernous mouth.

'Mammy wants you and Daddy's in the shed!' I shouted as if he was deaf.

Amazed, he looked at me for a moment. Then he closed the door and disappeared from view.

'Mr Adjouti,' I sobbed as I hammered on the door. *'Mr Adjouti!'*

Immediately Mr Adjouti reappeared with his jacket on, stepped out on the landing and locked the door behind him. Then, without warning, he leapt down the stairs, like a giant daddy-long-legs. Helter-skelter, the two of us descended flight after flight of stairs until we reached the basement and went out into the light-filled garden where my mother was standing. Her face was so white she was like a marble statue. I had never seen her afraid before and the sight terrified me. I ran to her side, but she didn't even notice me. For a moment she just stood there, staring at Mr Adjouti. Then she grabbed him by the arm and muttered rapidly to him. Deliberately they turned away from me so that I couldn't hear what they were saying.

My mother and Mr Adjouti walked to the shed and leant over the windowsill. I followed them and stood beside them without saying a word. I listened to them as they looked down into the shed and conversed. The tone in their voices was relaxed now, almost desultory. 'Now we can . . .' 'If he will . . .' 'Be careful,' she kept saying. 'Be careful. Be careful.'

Then Mr Adjouti walked around to the door of the shed and rattled the door handle. A flake of paint fluttered down and landed on the ground. Mammy and I watched without breathing as Mr Adjouti carefully removed his jacket and was about to lay it down on the wheelbarrow when Mammy stepped towards him and took it in her arms. Without a word he took a running leap at the door and kicked it hard with his foot. The door splintered under the force of his kick.

'*Wheeeee*,' I breathed as Mr Adjouti pushed the door open and disappeared inside.

'Rosaleen!' At the sound of my voice, my mother suddenly caught sight of me and shooed me away.

Reluctantly I walked back to the kitchen and sat on the doorstep as I had been told to do and watched Mammy's back. There was something reassuring about the tight dress material accentuating the roundness of her behind upended over the window-ledge of the shed and the ties of her apron ribboning in the breeze. Mona was away at our cousin's house for the night, so I was on my own, trying to unravel the mystery that had Mammy and Mr Adjouti talking in such serious tones. I squeezed my knees together with excitement. The story I had to tell Mona! And not even a mention of school for me. 'Mr Adjouti will get Daddy out of the shed and everything will be all right,' I said aloud, trying to convince myself, but everything seemed wrong: the daylight isolating out the strands of ivy from the walls, the overturned wheelbarrow rusting in the grass. The distant noise of traffic and birdsong jarred and the silence between Mammy's urgings and Mr Adjouti's grunts made me feel sick in my stomach. Slowly Mr Adjouti's black face emerged in the doorway of the shed, Daddy's head resting on his shoulder. The two men intertwined seemed to fall out of the shed but Mr Adjouti regained his balance and began a slow progress down the garden, Daddy's head lolling back on his arm. In Mr Adjouti's embrace, Daddy looked small enough to be a child.

'*Mammy*!' I wailed, but Mammy ignored me as she ushered Mr Adjouti, bearing Daddy's limp body, into the sitting room. She slammed the door behind them while I huddled at the kitchen table, my fingers tearing again at the oilcloth until it ripped with an ugly sound. Mammy'll kill me, I thought, crossing my arms guiltily. I bent my head and closed my eyes.

When I open my eyes, I tried to convince myself, everything will be all right.

In the distance the single line of horses and riders emerged from the woods and circled around the edge of the field.

'Where are you, Conor?' I called.

'Come and find me.' His voice was muffled.

I found him lying down in the little nest of branches and twigs he had constructed, looking happily up at the sky. A haven – that was all he needed to keep his worries at bay until he outgrew them. One day he would be a father and have children of his own and what he'd learnt he would have learnt from me. And from Kevin, of course, I thought quickly, but the great provider Kevin had never pushed a pram or changed a nappy in his life. Then I would be old. Sometimes I played a game with myself, trying to imagine what kind of a grandmother I'd make. Not one like Mamo, I hoped. She had ended up in the county home in Lifford, an angry little woman in a bed with high sides like a crib, in a ward with barred windows.

As for Mammy, I had hoped that she would move back to Donegal to be close to me and the children but she would have none of it.

'I've reared my own already, thank you very much.' By this time she had sold the house in Terenure and bought a little house in Rathgar. 'At my age, I'm near to the shops . . . and the cemetery,' she added as an afterthought.

Where Daddy was buried and where, she said, one day she would join him.

Occasionally she talked about him, but she never referred to the circumstances of his death or to the fact that, when he was alive, he could never hold down a job for long. She talked about how he could have been a professional singer if only he had put his mind to it; how he loved to eat jam with his black pudding and rashers; how they had met for the first time in the North Star Hotel and he had knelt down on one knee and sang to her there in the foyer and how her girlfriends from Donegal had fallen around in stitches of laughter. Once he was dead, Daddy was easily tamed: the arguments were disregarded, the bouts of drinking obliterated. She rarely mentioned him but when she did he was painted as a loveable, vaguely foolish figure. Even early on, when I was still a child, the image she concocted didn't ring true to me. There were many times, in the dark of night, when his cold one-eyed stare pierced my dreams and I woke up trembling in terror. Eventually, I outgrew my nightmares, and both the real and the invented stories about my father began to merge and then to fade.

In the meantime Mr Adjouti became Dr Adjouti and went away to America. We never saw him again. He must have thought that keeping your husband in the garden shed was some kind of tribal custom. Certainly he had been unfazed when Mammy had got him to lift Daddy out of the shed before the ambulance men came. By the time they arrived, Daddy's body was lying tidily on the living-room sofa, the way Mammy wanted it.

'I'd have been mortified,' I heard her say to Mr Adjouti. *Mortified*. I didn't know what the word meant but it rolled around in my head through the days that followed, and afterwards the word was for ever associated in my mind with death. Mort. Mortician. Mortified.

I sat on at the kitchen table, my arms covering up the tear in the oilcloth while Mammy cleaned our flat from top to bottom. By the time Mona came home, Daddy's body had already been removed to the hospital morgue and I got to tell her all about it.

Later Mammy brought the two of us into the sitting room and made us promise on the bible never to talk about Mr Adjouti lifting Daddy out of the shed. Solemnly Mona and I swore to Almighty God. In our rickety double bed we talked between ourselves but all anyone else ever knew was that Teddy O'Sullivan had had a heart attack and it had killed him.

I bent down to lift back the curtain of branches. Conor rolled away from me. I leant in and tickled him and he squealed with delight.

'Come on, little fox,' I said, carefully picking twigs and leaves out of his hair.

The air turned into a thin mist as rain pattered onto the undergrowth. In the shade, Conor's blue eyes were huge, fringed with long lashes. Love of my life, I wanted to sing out loud. Tower of Ivory. Temple of the Holy Ghost. Ark of the Covenant. I hugged him. He wriggled out of my arms and ran across the open ground to the stable yard where his sister was dismounting.

I followed him slowly past the old house and waved at Aoife, but she didn't see me. In the leaden light of day the house had an unloved air. There were mossy patches on the roof and slates missing. Rusty gutters sprouted tufts of grass. Out of the corner of my eye I caught sight of movement. Did a curtain twitch in a high window or did a shadow move across? I couldn't be sure if the impression of a human presence inside the house was real or not. I was drifting: weed in a stream, carried on a current and powerless, not knowing what might happen in my life, next week, the week after, and fearful that nothing at all would happen.

There was nobody there, I decided. I had imagined it. For an instant I was disappointed. As I stared up at the window, the moment was filled with an unnameable sadness. Then I heard voices behind me – female voices murmuring to each other. I presumed it was casual talk between mothers hanging around like me, waiting for their daughters to come back with the horses. The sound of raindrops tapping on the leaves overhead. I became conscious of a cloud of menace in the air. The words were indistinct and yet the conversation had an unexpected edge.

'*What?*' I said but by the time I turned around, the mothers had already moved off, gliding away through the trees, like woodland creatures vanishing into the forest.

11

A spring tide: the water in the lough sucked out into the middle of the estuary, exposing mudflats and rocks covered with shaggy seaweed. Long-legged birds scuttled back and forth, pocking the slime. In the sky a plane needled into a cloud and disappeared. Around the house, branches swayed in a crying wind that matched my mood.

The tone in my voice was querulous. 'It's not fair.'

Grizzling, my mother used to call it when I was a child. I had liked the sound of it then and I liked the sound of it now.

'Life isn't fair,' Kevin said.

'But everything's settled down now the British Army has arrived.'

Nothing ever gets settled in Derry. Laura's voice echoed in my head but I was determined to ignore it.

Kevin was a fortress: hunched shoulders, corrugated

121

forehead, mouth thinned into a line. How he'll look when he's old, I thought. Jowly. Impenetrable. Stuck.

'God almighty, you have a grand life. How many girls do you know have their own car? I work to keep you all.'

'But –'

'You're a mother now. You can't be taking risks.'

'Oh, tell me something I don't know!'

And on it went. Our argument was more a game of ping-pong than a battle of wills, each of us beating backwards and forwards until finally he moved away.

'We can't have what we want all the time.'

I glared at him as he got ready to go to work. He was escaping over the horizon and where did that leave me?

'Oh,' I said, 'you mean *I* can't have what I want.'

His back turned against me. His shoes crunching on the gravel.

'So tell me,' I shouted after him to make him feel bad, 'what do *you* want for your dinner?'

The car door slammed. He hadn't even heard me.

'It's not fair,' I told the cat curled up on the windowsill. Her mouth opened delicately in a pink yawn.

In the evening, Kevin came in from work and sat down at the kitchen table to read the newspaper. His face hidden behind the rustling pages, he said nothing for a while. Then suddenly: 'I met Eoghan McPartland in the street today.'

Carefully, I poured tea into a cup and stirred in milk and sugar. 'Did you?'

'He asked me when you were going to come back to work.'

I dropped the spoon and turned around to stare at him. The expression on his face gave nothing away as he turned to the Sports pages.

'And what did you say?'

'Hmmm?'

I strode across the room and grabbed the newspaper.

'And what did *you* say?'

'Keep your hair on, Rosy.'

His amused manner served only to irritate me further. I slapped down the cup of tea I'd made him. It slopped dangerously onto its saucer.

'*Tell me, Kevin.*'

'Oh,' he said, taking a sip. 'Whenever he wanted you back, I said, you were ready to go.'

He had the grace to look abashed. Anger rumbled in my gut. He could say it to the guv'nor but he couldn't say it to me. Kevin the strong, the resolute. Icily I examined him as, head down, he drank his tea. Not resolute enough, I decided. Even though I felt a leap of joy at the thought of going back to work, I had a compulsion to grumble. Out of principle.

'*Now* it's okay for me to go, now that the *guv'nor* wants it.'

'Jesus, Rosy,' Kevin sat back and scratched his head, 'are you never satisfied?'

I bit my lip and said nothing.

'I'm only trying to look after you and this is the thanks I get.'

The smell of burning custard brought me back to the stove. Kevin folded the newspaper, flattening the pages with the palm of his hand.

'Anyway,' he said, 'I always said things would improve once the British Army was in.'

No, I thought, stirring madly, you didn't *ever* say that.

I forgave him when he produced the bottle of wine he had brought home to celebrate. We could afford wine only on special occasions and I was touched by his gesture.

'Oh Kevin.' I stroked his cheek.

An ink-edged night stole in across the sky. After the children had gone to bed, we pulled out our chairs from the kitchen and sat in the garden, drinking the last of the wine. The cat gazed at us with half-closed eyes from her perch on the wall. Then she jumped down and stalked off into the undergrowth. Above us, a miasma of birds calling in the treetops.

Kevin leant over to me.

'Are you happy now you've got your own way?'

'I'm happy.' I smiled woozily at him and put my arms around his neck.

He stood up and went into the house. After a few minutes he reappeared, carrying a blanket.

'Oh my God! What about the children?'

'The children are fast asleep. I've checked.'

'Someone else might see us, though,' I said in alarm as he pulled off his shirt and unzipped his trousers.

'Oh yeah, Mundy's old dog might, or our cat maybe.'

Kevin wrapped his arms around my head and back and laid me down gently on the blanket. I stiffened.

'What now?' he said.

'Will you come out before . . . ?' The fear was always there. Working out dates. Today we can. Tomorrow we can't. My unruly body.

'I will. I promise.'

Under the warmth of his fingers my breasts ached for more. I opened my legs to take him in and there, on the blanket, in the lee of the house, we made love in the darkening shadows. Just before he climaxed, he pulled away and the cold slap and spray on my thigh made me shudder involuntarily. Carefully he wiped the white streak of semen from my skin with the edge of his shirt. Then, with closed eyes, we lay still, listening to the cries of the birds and the waves snuffling on the stones, his chest rising and falling, his breathing deep in my ears and his arms making a cradle for my body. *There is a lake in the heart of every man*: a phrase from a library book, or an English class at school. George Moore, that was it. There is a lake . . . yes, and I thought, I will remember this moment when I'm old. When we are both old.

And then a treacherous wraith of memory slunk up from the water's edge, a memory of other fingers tracking along my spine and spreading apart my thighs, of another's lips sliding down my pubic arch in search of pleasure – in a pool of lamplight I saw the blond hairs on his arm.

Manus, I thought, *go away.*

'Good boy,' I murmured and pulled Kevin closer to me.

We lay together until the cold night air drove us indoors. Clutching our clothes, we sprinted towards the back door, laughing giddily. Inside the kitchen we dressed and then sat down by the open door of the range to warm our hands at the burning coals while we waited for the kettle to boil.

'Happy?'

'Happy,' he said and smiled at me.

On the day I started back to work, I met Cormac Grealish on the stairs leading up to the office. He was coming down, his languid frame stooped under the low ceiling, his fingers resting on the newel post at the turn of the stair. He was a sight for sore eyes. Was it a blessing to be so good-looking, I wondered, or a curse?

'Good morning,' I said. Did he even remember who I was or what I was doing in the office? At my eye level I was conscious of a slight bulge in his corduroy trousers. A packet behind a placket, I thought and blushed.

'Ha, you've come back. Delighted,' he said, fanning back a strand of his hair behind his ear. His eyes crinkled, I noticed, when he smiled.

'I'm delighted too,' I said. 'How have things been?'

'Ach, don't we all know how things have been? The question is, how are they going to end?'

'I suppose so.'

Then, with a chuckle, he said, 'Aye, the genie's well and truly out of the bottle now.'

The office had been closed for four days. When I returned, it felt as if we had all taken a brief holiday away from our desks and everything was back to normal but, of course, it wasn't. There were checkpoints around the city, with armed soldiers in uniform leaning out over barbed wire barricades to talk to the local girls. There were occasional bursts of rioting in the Bogside but nothing to impinge on our office life.

At coffee break, Malachy, the draughtsman, read his copy of the *Racing News* as usual and took to slipping out to the bookies for a quick bet. Andrew had gone home to Cardiff for the weekend and brought back a bag of faggots that he threatened to cook for us.

Perplexed, Frederick looked down at Andrew's offerings. The Belgian architect was easily mystified. One day, in a pub he frequented at lunchtime, a customer had complained that the beer tasted like cat's piss and had turned to Frederick who was sitting by himself at the counter. Did his beer taste like cat's piss too, the man had wanted to know. 'But how do I know?' Frederick had asked on his return after lunch to the office. 'I have never tasted cat's piss.'

Now his eyebrows met in a line on the bridge of his nose as he inspected the grey lumps of meat inside the greaseproof paper bag.

'Faggots are to *eat*?' he growled at Andrew. 'But you said a faggot is –'

'Not in front of a lady,' Andrew interrupted him and warningly put a finger to his lips.

'Oh for God's sake, Andrew,' I said, 'I'm a married woman. I know what a faggot is.'

'Well, now *I* am not certain.' Frederick turned to me for help. 'Please tell me.'

I lifted my satchel of drawing materials over my shoulder and stood up from my desk. 'Oh, Andrew will tell you. Won't you, Andrew?'

The task the guv'nor had set me had grown during my absence. It would take me a lifetime to finish the inventory at the rate I was working, I reckoned, but somehow it didn't seem to matter. From the beginning the guv'nor had displayed a benign lack of interest in what I was doing. Any progress I made was recorded and I left him regular reports on his desk. When I decided on a building, I set about photographing it from all angles and then made a rough sketch of its exterior. In the public library I found Ordnance Survey maps and parish records which provided me with information to add to the material I was collecting.

I simply picked up where I had left off.

There is no time like the present, I thought, shutting the office door behind me. Outside, the pavements were wet and the sky threatened more rain. I walked past the courthouse (distinguished Greek Revival) where a few disconsolate men were lingering on the steps. St Columb's Cathedral loomed above the roofs of the houses in the Fountain. I hadn't been back to that part of the city since my ill-judged job-hunting foray that had put Laura into a sulk. Recording the cathedral was my most ambitious project so far. My confidence had grown during my enforced absence. Any strangeness I felt about the city had gone and affection had rushed in to take its place. The camera felt good in my hands and the satchel holding my sketchpad banged importantly against my thigh as I walked.

Exploring the past and making a record of it suited me better, I decided, than trying to cope with the terrors of a building site – wading through mud to meet some builder, waiting for instructions while diggers moved across acres of churned-up soil, or contending with the mysteries of working drawings. On my second day in the office Malachy told us about an architect he had once worked for who had absentmindedly designed a house with a bedroom that had no way into it. The builders had dutifully built the doorless bedroom in accordance with the drawings. That day I was the only one who hadn't laughed at Malachy's story. It had sounded horribly like something I might do. I worried that, some day, I might be held responsible for a doorless room, a tilting floor, a sagging roof or even – and this was my worst nightmare – a building collapsing on my watch. I should have studied history instead, I decided. It would have been much simpler: I couldn't do any harm to the dead. All the same, if I hadn't studied architecture, I would have never met Kevin and there would have been no Aoife and no Conor.

The cathedral reared up in front of me. I pushed open one of the heavy wrought-iron gates and walked up the gravel path. In the porch the church doors were locked. A stone inscription in the porch caught my eye.

If stones could speak
Then London's prayse
Should sounde who
Built this church and
Cittie from the ground
Vaughan AED

The planter's creed: praise be to Sir John Vaughan, the all-powerful Governor of the City of Londonderry. Sir John who built church and city from the ground and had no other gods before him – no Gaelic life, no medieval city, no Irish peasantry. Embedded in the cathedral walls was a history of conquest, siege, endurance unto death and a starving city awaiting God's deliverance.

I wandered around the outside of the building, taking photographs as I went. There wasn't another soul in the place to disturb me. I half-expected a Quasimodo figure to appear out of a door and berate me for intruding on hallowed ground. No one interupted me as I sat down on a bench and took out my sketchpad but there was only enough time for a hurried sketch before rain swept across the grassy cathedral close. It was a brief deluge. Even as I packed away my things and ran for shelter, the rain was already thinning out to a drizzle.

Damp and cold, I walked back to the gates of the cathedral. The old brick houses, tight as corset stays, crowded around me and, for a moment, I was disoriented. Ahead of me, a street tumbled down towards the river. It formed a spine from which identical brick-terraced streets branched off. I thought how quiet it was! And how empty. The only sounds were the rumble of traffic, the patter of rain. I was walking through the gates, having figured out the direction I needed to go, when I became aware of a new sound.

It was the throb of an engine.

Then a hearse emerged out of a side street: a shiny black monster rising out of its lair. I caught a glimpse through the hearse's windows of a wooden casket, brass handles, a wreath of flowers. Uncertain what to do. I stood on the narrow footpath as the vehicle, glistening with raindrops, glided towards me. Following it, a procession of people moved in concert as if they were huddling together for warmth, a sea of overcoats and umbrellas billowing in the grey light.

Always show your respect for the dead. My father's instruction. He had been a stickler for convention. Without thinking, I raised my hand to my forehead to make the Sign of the Cross as the hearse passed. At that moment a face in the crowd turned towards me. A man with bloodshot eyes that scorched mine, his face distorted into a fierce grin. Hunched against the cold, he halted and took his hands out of his pockets. I shrank back, afraid that he might strike me. He clenched his hands into balled-up fists and for a moment I stood, paralyzed by the hatred in his eyes. Then, straightening up, he looked away and marched on past me. The cortège continued on its journey through the cathedral gates and up the gravel path: a caravan of closed, immutable grief.

I hurried along the terraced streets. Blanked by net curtains, the windows kept any sign of life out of sight. The only relief was a bedraggled Union Jack and kerbstones painted a cheery red, white and blue. I stopped to take a photograph, lining up through the lens the coloured edges of the street.

Just then a door opened and a woman came out, a sweeping brush in her hand. When she saw me she stopped and stared. I could see the question in her face as if she had asked it out loud. Grimacing nervously, I answered her anyway.

'I'm just taking a photograph.'

The woman's hair was tied back in a ponytail. Although I sensed that she wasn't much older than me, her small, puckered features gave her an ancient, androgynous look. She wore a nylon coat and a pair of men's tartan carpet slippers that were too big. I wanted to talk to her. I wanted to find out about the siege mentality that I had heard about. To listen to someone who lived in this enclave with its defiant kerbstones and faded Union flags. Then the thought struck me that, for all I knew, she mightn't even belong there. Maybe she was like me: an outsider. Living in Donegal made me think that my life was a bit of a fraud sometimes and that I was play-acting at belonging.

The woman's face was expressionless, *sealed*, like the faces of the mourners I had seen. Then she surprised me: the arch way she swung sideways into the stance of a film star, and batted her lashes, one hand up to her hair, the other on her hip. 'This is my best side.' Her lips incongruously pouting to blow me a kiss and then, laughing, she disappeared into the dark interior, the door swinging closed behind her.

I didn't stop walking until I got back to the Diamond. If I hurried, I would be in time to meet up with Frederick and Andrew. It was nearly lunchtime and they'd be on their way to the pub. I needed their company, to laugh at male jokes that I didn't always get, to hear the clink of pint glasses and the inevitable talk about football.

The sun emerged from behind a bank of cloud when I arrived at the junction where the street inclined past Butcher's Gate, newly blocked by an Army post and barbed-wire fencing. I started downhill towards the pub on Waterloo Street. My pace quickened. I'd be just in time.

Then I saw him.

Below me, at the bottom of the hill, there he was, standing out from the shadows, his hair golden in a slash of sunlight, his hands rummaging in an old khaki trench coat until he pulled out a crumpled packet, took out a cigarette and stuck it in his mouth. Cupping his hand. The flare of his lighter. People walking up the street blocked my view. When they had passed, a gap opened up and I saw him again. I could describe that lighter with my eyes closed: its silver casing, his initials monogrammed on its side. An expensive object for a student to own but it came in handy.

He pawned it regularly – when needs must, as he used to say. On each occasion when he had money, he always went back to get it out of hock. It belonged to his father, who had the same name, I remembered, and who had given it to him when he had gone off to college for the first time. All this extraneous detail I knew about his life; everything I squirrelled up in my memory was as clear as a film ribboning out in front of me.

I watched as he turned and looked up but I was in shadow and he didn't see me. I held my breath as if I could make myself invisible, fold myself into nothing and secrete myself into the years that had passed since we had last met.

When he started to walk up the street towards me, a feeling of dread made me want to turn and run but I stayed where I was and waited for him to recognise me. I waited to see his expression when, wiping the blond fringe away from his forehead, he would shake his head with amazement, all the time smiling his broad, cracked smile. It seemed a long time before he looked up and saw me. I had the luxury of seeing his familiar gait, the cigarette dangling from his fist, his shabby coat with its torn lapel, the mixture of cockiness and clumsiness that drew me to him.

He thrust out his hand to shake mine and then took it back, laughing excitedly as he came close into an awkward hug.

'Hullo, Manus.'

'Well, hi there.'

We looked at each other and then both looked away.

'A drink,' he said, 'and I mean now.'

He had filled out; even his shoulders looked broader. The swagger was more pronounced as he walked, the belt of his coat swung and flapped behind him.

Suddenly I felt embarrassed. There was too much to remember. His easy-going manner, for all its waywardness, had a calculated edge to it. Be careful, I warned myself, but myself wasn't listening.

The nearest pub was empty apart from a young man slouched on a stool behind the counter, reading the *Derry Journal*. The air was soused in the smells of cigarettes and old beer and there was no food to be had apart from a jar of pickled eggs on the counter. The pale ovoids floating in brown liquid made me think of foetuses preserved in a jar.

'Do you have any sandwiches?' Manus asked.

'Café's down the road,' the barman shrugged, clearly waiting for us to leave.

Manus ordered a pint of beer for himself and a glass for me. He sat down and looked at me with interest.

'You've changed,' he said.

No, I thought, I'm the same. Then, yes, I supposed I had changed. A lifetime had passed since – was he thinking of it too? – that night when a madness had taken me up to his room and he had opened the door, the look of surprise on his face on seeing me, changing to a smile of covert intensity.

'Not really,' I said but the moment was over.

Manus's head was down over his pint and he was talking about the article he had to write. I'd heard that he had become a newspaper reporter. He had landed a job in a national daily paper. *The Irish Press*, wasn't it?

'I have to understand what is going on here and get my copy filed by six o'clock. Deadlines! This place is world news and I'm struggling to make sense of it. Free Derry, a town in revolt without laws or a police force.' He looked at me hopefully. 'I suppose you know all about it but I'm at sea here.'

'It's not a town. It's called the Bogside.'

'I know *that*. Go on, you live here, so tell me.'

I had to admit to him then that I had never been in the Bogside.

'Never!' He looked at me in surprise. 'Well, I've an interview to do now with one of the leaders. Stick with me,' he grinned. 'I'll show you places you've never been.'

'I can't.'

'Of course you can.'

That innocent smile. Those knowing eyes.

He rubbed his fringe back off his forehead. 'Come on, Rosaleen,' he said. 'I need minding.' He gazed forlornly at the torn lapel of his coat as if he hadn't noticed it before. 'And mending. You haven't a needle and thread by any chance?'

Laughing, I shook my head.

'I might get lost or attacked by the natives.' He leant towards me. The scent of his aftershave tickled my nose. I recognized it: Old Spice shaving lotion but under it, or behind it, was his own particular smell that had stayed on my skin afterwards when I'd walked out into the night. All the way home it had trailed alongside me, and when I had climbed into bed it had haunted me like a penance. Suddenly I realized just how easy it could be: Kevin at work, the children being minded, even in the office nobody ever noticed if I was in or out. I envisaged a room in the City Hotel, a torn raincoat draped across a chair, trousers in a mound on the floor, a net curtain lifting in a breeze, sunlight shivering on our naked bodies, a double bed. I thought: *if he could read my mind . . .*

A gust of beer hit the back of my throat, making me gag. Manus laughed and thumped me between my shoulder blades but the beer had done its work. I felt weightless, euphoric even. Our glasses drained, we stood up at the same time and then, as if we were on a mission, we walked into the street.

In the arched shadow of Butcher's Gate three British soldiers idled. The sight of their uniforms was a reminder of the new order. I expected an interrogation but the soldiers waved us on. We walked through a gap in the barricade and under the arch. Once out of the shadow of the walls, we stopped and gazed down into the Bogside.

Below us the wide, dusty road was littered with stones, bricks and broken glass. In the distance, the tablelands of terraced houses climbed up the hillside to the modern housing of Creggan. Manus began to walk down the road as it dipped past the ugly concrete block of Rossville Flats. I hesitated before following him, but the turbulent scenes that I had seen on television bore no relation to the vista ahead.

An awestruck stillness hung in the air. Nothing moved. Pompeii, I thought, must have known the same eerie silence. Broken kerbstones and rubble strewn on the road: the only evidence of the struggle that had died as quickly as it had erupted. Rising up, like war wreckage in a desert, were ramshackle barricades built to stake out the boundaries of a hard-won territory.

'This is where it all took place,' Manus breathed. 'The Battle of the Bogside. I wonder what's it like to live in a part of the UK where the Queen's writ doesn't run. This is what I'm here to write about – this no-go area.'

'It's not part of the UK.'

'Oh really?' He looked at me. 'If it's not part of the UK, then what is it?'

I couldn't answer his question. From studying the architecture, I knew some of the history but that knowledge gave me no insight into the lives lived in the cramped terraced streets that were identical, as far as I could see, to the streets of the Fountain which I had left earlier.

To our right, along Rossville Street, another point of entry into the Bogside had been blocked off and a barricade erected. It was made of builders' materials, iron bars, timber sheeting, old sofas. As we watched, two women in headscarves, gripping their handbags tightly, negotiated a breach in the barricade. Once safely on the other side, they straightened up, dusted themselves down and disappeared into the city. Getting on with their lives, I thought, and wondered what those lives were like. Not that much different from mine. Housework and cooking dinners always had to be done, in some fashion or another. Even in a war zone.

As Manus strode on ahead, he expounded his views about how the community had marshalled its forces to keep out the police. He pointed out the gable wall of a house on which the words **You Are Now Entering Free Derry** were painted in glossy black, assertive paint.

'Hard to believe that this was the heart of the action.' Thoughtfully he surveyed the scene: the maze of streets and beyond, to the grassy slope rising up to the city walls that towered above us.

It didn't look like much of a prize to me: a gaggle of bare, uncompromising houses hunkered down together and, between them, wastelands of rutted grass and mud.

'We're now in Free Derry,' Manus said. '*No Pasarán.*'

I waited without comprehending.

Suddenly he spoke, as if he was making a speech, as if somehow on the empty road a crowd had gathered to listen to him.

'A spectre is haunting Europe,' he declared. The portentous tone of his voice made me want to giggle but he continued, raising a clenched fist above his head as he addressed the imaginary crowd. 'Comrades, the proletariat have nothing to lose but their chains and they have a world to win! *Working men of all countries, unite!*'

Pro-le-tar-iat. I didn't know what it meant but I liked the way it rolled around in his mouth.

'What does that mean?'

He frowned. 'You mean you don't know?'

I shook my head.

'It's from *The Communist Manifesto*.'

All I knew about communists was that they tortured priests and pulled off their fingernails and that they lived behind the Iron Curtain.

'Really? I didn't even know that the communists had a manifesto.'

Manus took out a notebook from his pocket and began to scribble. Mystified, I looked over his elbow at the squiggles and stray words that he had written. He stopped, looked around and saw the bafflement on my face.

'You don't recognise shorthand and you've never heard of *The Communist Manifesto*.' He snapped the notebook closed and then gripped my arm. 'Know something, Rosaleen? Your education is severely lacking.'

I froze at his touch, at his fingers pressing into my skin. Manus was oblivious to my reaction and, linked together, the two of us walked along the road. My mind seethed with anxiety. What if anyone saw us, strolling arm in arm? We might easily be taken for lovers. If Kevin ever got to hear . . . Manus kept talking rapidly as we walked. Did I know there was an actual radio transmitter set up in the Bogside, and walkie-talkies – and they even printed a newspaper on a Gestetner machine they had somehow acquired? Being a newspaperman himself, this last piece of information made the biggest impression on Manus. And all the while he was talking, his hold on my arm was firm and unrelenting as he steered me towards a large pub on the corner.

Was he trying to get me drunk, I wondered. At this rate, it wouldn't take much, I thought, my skin prickling with fear. What am I doing here? I wanted to pose the question aloud but Manus had already come to a halt, and, with a flourish, opened the pub door for me. I hesitated. A knot of men lingering outside on the step stood back to look at us.

I hurried inside to an opaque dullness lit only by a series of barred windows, thick with dust. Along the walls of the pub, battered banquettes were silhouetted in the gloom. In our nostrils, a whiff of cigarette smoke and urine. The room was so quiet that our footsteps echoed uncomfortably on the floorboards. At the bar an old man was hunched over a pint of Guinness and a whiskey chaser. Systematically his shaking hand reached from one glass to the other.

Manus ordered drinks, stretched back on the banquette beside me and closed his eyes. An old habit of his. He had always been able to nod off, even in the middle of a conversation, and then wake up a few minutes later, refreshed and raring to go. I was at liberty to examine his cheekbones, high and pronounced, his long jaw and blond hair fanning his forehead and tumbling over his ears, the signs of an incipient double chin. There was something corpse-like about him in sleep, I thought, now that his skin was a faded beige, his strength collapsed into anonymity, his lips sagging to reveal a row of nicotined teeth. When compared to the sight of the sleeping Manus, my memory of him seemed fantastical.

I was sitting in a strange pub in the Bogside with a stranger.

I nudged him and whispered, 'Manus.'

'Hah?'

'Who are we waiting for?'

He yawned and stretched his arms. His eyes were filled with a sudden, raw vitality. I smiled at him. *This* was the Manus I remembered.

'I'm meeting a man here. One of the leaders. He should be along any minute. D'you want another drink?'

I shook my head. I had barely touched the one I had. As

he emptied his glass, the door of the pub opened and a couple came in. The young man was short and fat with downy, peachy-pink cheeks and small, amused eyes. Thick black hair fell onto his shoulders and black curls of chest hair erupted from the open neck of his tight nylon shirt. Following him in was a skinny girl wearing a miniskirt, a yellow leatherette jacket and vivid blue eye shadow. Her lipstick glittered. I recognised the shade: Coty's Frosted Pearl. The young man jerked his head and immediately the girl came across the room and sat down beside me. A wad of chewing gum circulated in her cheek as she rammed her hands into the pockets of her jacket and glowered. Her companion stayed standing.

He looked at Manus. 'You're the newspaperman.'

Manus looked up eagerly. 'I am.'

'How're you doing?'

In reply, Manus extended his hand but the young man was busy rummaging in his pockets for a cigarette. Finding none, he looked at Manus. 'Got a smoke, pal?'

Manus flicked open his pack of Benson and Hedges. The golden packaging glinted expensively.

'Good on you, mucker.' The young man extracted two cigarettes, lit one and put the other one in his pocket.

'I'm expecting Eamonn McCann.'

'Aye. He can't come but,' the young man said flatly.

He couldn't have been more than eighteen with his mantle of hair, his girlish complexion and dimples. I peered at him. Did he even shave?

'I've been sent to tell you. There's another meeting with that Brigadier that's in charge of the troops. He says he wants to know more about our demands and McCann's gone to tell him.'

'Jesus H Christ!' Manus growled.

The young man pulled up a stool and sat down as if he

hadn't heard him. The girl slid along the banquette to sit closer to me. For a moment, the only sound was a fly buzzing around the table.

'I'm fucked so,' Manus said. 'I'm supposed to interview him for the paper.'

The young man shrugged, 'No harm to you.'

'What the hell do I do now?'

Manus's question went unanswered. Sweat oozed gently along the young man's hairline. The chewing gum made a soft slurping sound in the girl's mouth.

She turned to me. Where was I from, she wanted to know.

'Dublin,' I said, 'but I'm living in Donegal now.'

'That's wild. What are you doing in Derry?'

'Well . . .' I began.

'I mean, reporters are up here from everywhere. Why are they bothered?'

'Well . . .' I tried again.

'Nothing ever happens in Derry.'

It was my turn to be surprised.

'It's a dump.'

The young man's face flattened with disdain. 'Never you mind her,' he said. 'Going to dances, that's all she's ever about.'

He looked for support from Manus, who grinned back at him annoyingly.

'Oh aye.' The girl examined her fingernails. She frowned as if she was trying to remember something. 'That's the exact same thing my da says.' She shifted nearer to me and, lowering her voice as if she was imparting a secret, said, 'And I don't give a shite about what he says either.'

'You shut your gob,' the young man said without conviction.

'Will you have a drink?' Manus offered.

'Thought you'd never ask.'

'Mine's a Babycham,' the girl said, 'since you're asking.'

When the drinks arrived, the young man kept his head down, emptying his glass stealthily. The girl snuggled down on the banquette, twirling the stem of her glass and chortling when the bubbles made her sneeze. She smiled at Manus but he had eyes only for her companion.

'Were you out in it?' he asked the young man.

'For the entire week. I was on top of the High Flats mostly.'

Manus gazed at him. 'I suppose I could interview *you* instead.'

The young man straightened up and flicked back his black curly mane. He twinkled, 'Way on.'

Manus flipped open his notebook, drew a line down the centre of the page and started to write. The young man waited.

'So what's your name?'

'Willie Hasson.'

Gloomily Manus scribbled as the young man talked about days spent firing stones onto the flanks of RUC men, the sickening power of CS gas in the streets, how to make petrol bombs, the steady resistance inbuilt in the barricades, the burnings, the exhilaration, the exhaustion, the relief in the end at the RUC withdrawal.

'Were you ever afraid?'

'I was. I was afraid for my life that we'd get lifted, but the peelers never got near to us,' he said proudly.

Manus waited, like a bird of prey biding its time before it swooped. 'And the aftermath – when it was all over?'

'What?'

'After it was all over – what happened then?'

'Sure, it was over.'

'But what did you do?'

141

'I went home for my tea, so I did.'

A pause.

The old man climbed down from his stool and weaved his way across the floor to the jacks. Manus chewed on his lip.

The young man swallowed a mouthful of beer, wiped his mouth with his sleeve. 'Now we can walk down the streets with our heads held high because we own them. We beat the bastards. Free Derry belongs to us now.'

'Bastards?' Manus prompted.

'Aye, the B Specials and the RUC.'

'And what about the Unionists?'

'What about them?' the young man said belligerently. Then his tone changed, 'Don't get me wrong now. I've nothing against working-class Protestant people. They're no different to us when it comes down to it. Workers being exploited by the ruling class, for slave wages. You know thon poor bastards: they swallow the line about us Fenians are after their jobs and their women. The Brits and their tricks — divide and conquer, am I right? What we stand for is the unity of Catholic and Protestant working-class people in a Workers' Republic.'

I looked at him. I had never heard anyone talk in such terms before and never about the unity of Catholics and Protestants of any class, let alone the working class. I thought of Laura in her best dress, leaning against the wall outside the architect's office, her face suffused with rage, and Mr Mundy sitting at my kitchen table – *the land can change hands many times but it never changes religion* – and the man in the funeral cortège raising his clenched fists. As if he were explaining a different way of seeing the world, this improbable harbinger in the form of a fat boy with long hair and a sharp-tongued girlfriend was challenging me to think for myself. All those times at university when I had sat and listened while Barlo and Richard had expounded about everything under the sun, I had been a passive witness.

Now I wanted to ask questions.

'But I —'

The young man ignored me and continued. 'And as for the Mad Major, when I see that eejit on the TV I know by just looking at him that he's talking shite. Even when I turn the sound down, I can tell.'

'Who's the Mad Major?' Manus asked.

'You know, Chichester-Clark. He thinks he's in charge.' His head ducked down as he drained his glass.

'So what are you fighting for?' Manus asked.

The young man hesitated. 'We want one man one vote, decent housing, jobs – well, *I* don't want a job for I'm off to university in Belfast – and workers' control of the means of production and we want an end to Stormont and the Special Powers Act.'

'And a United Ireland?' Manus asked.

'You must be joking. With the Free State? Sure they're as bad.'

'Really?'

The young man was looking down at the squiggles in the notebook. 'Have you got my name written right?'

Manus nodded and continued, 'So the demands that Eamonn McCann is making to the Brigadier. Any idea what they are?'

'You'll have to ask him.'

'Don't you know?'

Willie Hasson shook his head.

'Listen, I need to meet some of the men off the Defence Committee. Can you help me with that?' Manus asked.

'Aye, surely – we can go up to the headquarters. There's a meeting on and you can see them there.' Willie jerked his head towards the girl and me. 'But girls won't be let in. Them two will have to stay outside.'

The girl reared up, blue-lidded eyes sparking, and poked him in the stomach.

'On your granny!' she cried. 'You promised we'd go up to our Auntie Chrissie's after. She's expecting us.'

The young man blew out his cheeks. 'This is important,' he muttered.

'Know what? '

He looked at her glumly.

'I wouldn't be seen dead at your oul' meeting anyway.'

Manus scrambled up, clutching his coat.

'I'm with you,' he said to the young man, who had stood up and moved nearer to him as if seeking protection.

'Willie Hasson,' the girl said loudly as she lifted her glass to drain it, 'you're nothing but a wee git.' She turned and gave me a cheerful blue wink. 'I'm away. Are you coming?'

For a moment I wasn't sure if I was being asked to go with her out of the pub or out of Derry. I shook my head. She wasn't the only one leaving. Manus had his coat on and was heading out the door of the pub, followed by the young man. Bewildered at the turn of events, I didn't move. *Manus is leaving me behind,* was my only thought, *without saying a word to me.*

At the door he stopped and let the young man go on out ahead of him. When I saw him turn and come back towards me, a wave of relief flooded through me. My face opened in a welcoming smile. I couldn't help myself and I moved along the banquette to make room for him, but Manus didn't sit down. He leant over me and picked up the notebook he had left on the table. Then he straightened up, took a biro from his inside pocket and slid it through the ringed binding of the notebook.

'See you around,' he said.

The pub door swung shut. Silence rushed in to fill the dusty air. The lounge suddenly felt alien and cold. The old man at the counter turned his head to stare at me. Shivering, I looked down at my hands and remembered that I still had to run the gauntlet of men hanging around outside the pub.

I was being punished, I decided, for what I'd done. What *we* had done, although I was only too aware that I was the one who was guilty: giving myself to Kevin, and then, before long, flying up the dark stairs to climb into the bed of another man. That night had wrapped around us so tightly that I'd been lost in the reaches of his legs and arms, his pale skin and blond hair. That was years ago, I told myself, and yet I couldn't move from where I sat alone in the gloom, confounded by the arrival of Manus into my life and by his peremptory departure.

I realized that he had not asked me one question about me or my life. What did I expect? I was a wife and mother now.

'Do you want anything?'

I looked up and shook my head at the barman who had come over to clear away the glasses from the table. I resolved to bury the memory that hovered in the stale air. Stop it, Rosaleen, I told myself. Some things belong in the past, not to be spoken about. Not even to be remembered.

12

Laura was standing at the front door of her bungalow. She smiled when she saw me.

I parked the car and got out slowly. My smile was guarded. I had decided not to tell Laura that I'd met Manus. It wasn't just meeting Manus that had me in a state of bewilderment, I tried to convince myself. It was the whole thing: the sight of the Bogside, the barricades and deserted streets, the *unity of Catholic and Protestant working class* . . . what was I to make of it all?

Fortunately, Laura didn't usually ask me a lot of questions. In a way I think she didn't like to hear about the job that she had helped me get. It created a distance between us – a reminder, as she saw it, that I was moving on while she was stuck. As I opened the low gate and walked towards her, I knew that I didn't want to let her into my secret life, even if, as I suspected, it mirrored hers. Men on the edges of our little world spelt danger and I shrank from exposing myself to her cross-examination. I decided instead that I would give her a laugh by describing how I had gone to St Columb's Cathedral and sat in the close and how I'd made a fool of myself, making the Sign of the Cross at a Protestant funeral.

But Laura didn't laugh when I told her. At first she looked discomfited. Then nervy.

'You took a risk going up there,' she said.

'Don't be silly.'

'Do you know who was being buried?'

I had no idea. A man, a woman, no one I knew, that was for sure. It was a big funeral, that was all I knew, 'How would I know whose funeral it was?'

Laura shook her head.

'What?' I asked.

'My guess is that was they were burying a man called William King. Our Pauline was on the telephone and she told me about him. He's from the Fountain and he died on Saturday night.'

Puzzled, I looked at her.

Laura folded her arms and looked past me towards the roadway. When she spoke, her voice sounded far away. 'He got beat up by some lads and then he died. And the British troops just stood by and did nothing.'

A gust of wind swept under our skirts as we stood there, two young women taking our ease in the afternoon air. I felt goose pimples rise on my bare arms. The memory of the funeral cortège moving through the cathedral gates was sharp and cold, like an ice flow beneath our conversation.

'Laura?' But I knew she wouldn't be able to help me out of my ignorance. I thought about the conversation in the pub. The flare in the young man's eyes when he spoke. Was he sincere or was it just something he'd learnt to recite, parrot-fashion, to entertain the newspaper reporters who were swarming into Derry, hungry for a quote? I would ask Kevin. He understood politics.

Then I thought, no. I can't do that. Not ever.

'Mmmm?' Laura was barely listening. She knelt down to lift up the bottles of milk that had been left on her doorstep since morning. She nodded at me to help her and I carried two of the bottles into the house.

The warmth of the glass through my cotton blouse was comforting, like the smell of newly baked bread, or the sight of cows in a field of long grass, or the sensation of a baby mouth sucking at my breast. I closed my eyes. I knew that I didn't want any more children and, yet, here was my body expressing its own yearning, separate from mine. There was safety in motherhood, I thought, and a completeness. Would I ever have the experience again of a tiny life being utterly dependent on me?

My eyes snapped open. That kind of thinking was escapism, I told myself, and then I thought wryly that Laura wouldn't approve of what I was thinking.

In the kitchen there was an opened box of chocolates on the table. I put the milk bottles in the fridge.

'Laura?'

'Sit down.' She waved at a chair. She sat beside me and pushed the chocolate box over to me. 'Help yourself. Cathal won them in the school raffle. First prize was a springing sow. Second prize a laying hen.'

'You're joking!'

She grinned. 'No, I'm not. Someone else's idea of a joke, not mine, but they raised enough money to pay for —'

There were sounds of a commotion outside and the door banged open. Laura's daughter came howling into the kitchen. Her hair was scraped back into two stiff plaits behind her ears. Tears dribbled down her face.

Laura's hand hovered over the box of chocolates. She did not waver, taking her time to select the one she wanted. Under her daughter's gaze, she unwrapped the chocolate and, carefully, opened her mouth to bite into it. The little girl stopped crying and stared intently as the chocolate disappeared between her mother's lips.

'Yum,' Laura said. She stared hard at Niamh, daring her to protest.

The little girl said nothing. She stood absolutely still, her lips pressed together, and looked at the floor.

'Well, what ails you now?' Laura said at last, dabbing her mouth with her finger. Impatiently she listened as Niamh stuttered her way through her tale of woe about a fight over a swing and a torn skirt.

'L-l-look, it's ruined.' The child lifted up the material with its L-shaped tear.

'Go on into the bedroom and change out of your clothes,' Laura said angrily. Then she saw the look on my face and relented. 'Go on, love, and I'll sew it.'

Niamh did as she was told and came back into the kitchen to give the skirt to her mother.

Laura nodded for her to go outdoors again but Niamh dawdled, hanging out of the handle of the back door as she looked up at her mother.

'Mammy, can I have a dog?'

'Hmmm?'

'Can I have a dog?'

Laura looked up from her examination of the torn skirt.

'Course you can,' she answered airily. Her expression gave nothing away.

Butter wouldn't melt in her mouth, I thought. If Laura could lie to a child, she could lie to anyone.

Triumph lit up the little girl's face.

'*So there*!' she said, dancing out of the room. 'Told you

so! I'm getting a dog!' she shouted to the children scattered around the garden. Through the window I could see them run up to gather around her.

Laura lifted down a sewing box from a cupboard and, screwing up her eyes against the light, tried to thread a needle.

'Give it to me,' I said. 'I'll do it.'

Laura had striking grey eyes but they were weak and she was too vain to admit that she needed glasses.

'Are you getting her a dog?' I asked when I had threaded the eye of the needle and handed it to her.

'Are you soft in the brain?'

'But you said . . . ?'

'By tomorrow it'll be all forgotten about.'

On the drive home, I couldn't keep Manus out of my mind: his face up close to mine, his breath smelling of tobacco and tickling my mouth, the lights from the street seeping through the thin curtains of his bedsit window as I clambered awkwardly into my clothes. He hadn't even got out of his bed, I remembered, when I slipped out the door and sped downstairs and out into a Dublin street, glittering with rain.

'Mammy?'

'Yes?'

Aoife leant forward in the back seat and broached the subject head-on. 'Niamh is getting a dog.'

'Really?'

'So why can't we?'

I sighed. Laura wasn't getting Niamh a dog, I wanted to say; she is just fibbing to save herself the bother of telling Niamh the truth. And then I asked myself: when it came down to it, what difference was there between Laura and me? When did a fib become a lie and a lie become treachery?

'Why not?' Aoife clutched the back of my seat. I could feel her fingers at my shoulders.

'A puppy,' she breathed into my ear.

'Let's see what kind of dog Laura gets Niamh first,' I said cravenly, 'and then we can talk about it.'

As I drove past his house on our way home, the tall figure of Mr Mundy suddenly came into view. His dog bounded around him, her big tail brushing the air like the old-fashioned feather-duster that had hung behind Mamo's door when I was a child. At the sound of the car, Mr Mundy grabbed the dog by her collar. He looked up and tipped his cap in a salute. I pretended not to see him and pressed my foot down on the accelerator. As we passed him I sensed – even though I had given no sign – that he knew I had seen him emerging out of the undergrowth. On each side of the entrance to his house the gate-posts leaned like headstones, lichened and grey and weary. The only acknowledgement of his presence was made by Aoife, her face pressed against the window.

'Liadh, oh Liadh!' she shouted, waving madly in an effort to attract the attention of Mr Mundy's dog.

Tom

13

Tom Mundy opened the fridge door and peered inside. He took out a piece of cooked bacon and put it in a blue-rimmed enamel dish on the table. Moving across the kitchen he crouched down in front of the open oven door and lit the gas. As he waited for the oven to heat up he scrubbed potatoes and put them into a saucepan on the hob. Carefully he placed the dish of bacon in the oven. After shutting the door, he washed his hands under the cold tap. The regularity of domestic tasks filled him with a quiet pleasure. His house would always be neat and, when his time came, he intended to make a clean corpse.

Drops of rain spattered the window. Evening was drawing in as the sun went behind a battalion of inky clouds. When he looked up, he saw the battered Ford van moving up the driveway. There was a gritty sound to the engine as if it had made too many journeys on rough roads.

He didn't know who was in the car but he had a fair idea what they wanted. It struck him that he didn't have to let them in. He could disappear farther into the house and they'd get tired of knocking on the front door. He was an old man now. They didn't need him and he certainly didn't need them. All those arguments were beyond him and they would want him to take sides.

'Time was when we were all on the same side,' he said aloud, 'the few of us that were left.'

Even in the worst of times, when they were on the run, moving at night or bivouacking in a bog, he never doubted the hard-forged loyalty they had for one another. Now there was a new generation; he didn't know half of them and he didn't want to. He had turned his back on it all. The bitterness of Curragh life had served as a bed from which he had failed to rise. Others went on to criss-cross the country, organizing in their secret, military fashion. They had grown strong. He had gone back to the farm and, each night, when he got into the empty bed where previously his wife had lain down beside him, he drowned.

My poor Marnie, he thought – she had understood none of it. In the silver-framed picture beside the bed, her eyes crinkled into a smile. A great worker. She could milk the cows twice a day and turn the hay, and was strong enough to deliver a calf.

When he tried to remember her as she really was, not just a frozen image in a picture-frame, he thought of the day in the high field. That day when they had set out together to clear the sheugh before the winter came in. Each carrying a slash hook, they had begun to work at the far ends of the sheugh. The sun had climbed up in the sky by the time they met in the middle, weary and triumphant.

'Not a bad effort for a farmer's wife,' he had teased her. She had straightened up, shielding her eyes against the sun to look down along the stretch of sheugh on which he had worked.

'And I'd say, no great effort from the farmer's husband,' she had retorted.

She was a stout woman, as tall as he was. Her cheeks were bright with sweat, her mouth stained with blackberries, and her broad hands were scratched and bloodied by brambles. She put down the slash hook and turned towards him.

'Close your eyes,' she whispered.

Into the darkness she came close and he tasted the juicy warmth of the berries in his mouth and then he felt her lips on his. Their tongues swimming together while, gently, she held him in her arms. In his nostrils, the faint smell of fetid water coursing down the channels they had made.

Marnie was afraid of no one and she would stand her ground in any dispute. He admired her for it but, that night, when they had come for him, her courage had deserted her. Had she known about her sickness then, he wondered, and said nothing? That night he had brushed her aside – his hand stinging even now, with sorrow – and had gone with them out the door.

By the time he had been released from the Curragh, she was already in Letterkenny hospital, wasting out the last of her days.

He yawned. His work for the day was done. *Sufficient unto the day* . . . and his mouth salivated at the idea of sweet bacon fat and floury potatoes. Simple pleasures, he thought.

The knocking on the front door was quick, urgent, but he took his time, turning on the light in the hallway before he went to pull open the door,

There were two of them. One was a skinny, white-faced boy he didn't know. The other was Johnny Doherty, *Fresh*

Bread the Day It's Baked emblazoned on his blue van parked outside the house.

'We thought you'd died, the time it took you,' said Johnny.

'Is that so? I'm sorry to disappoint ye.'

'Ah Tom, we're here in peace. Can we come in?'

He stepped back into the hall. The two visitors walked in with an air of self-importance that he found almost comical. He bit his lip so that he wouldn't smile and led them towards the parlour. When he opened the door, the room reeked of must and damp. There were dead flies on the window ledge. Wizened apples, forgotten from the previous winter, lay in rows on the sideboard, emitting a cidery smell. Since Marnie died, he hardly ever went into the parlour. It had been her room. She had spent her evenings there, listening to Radio Éireann. Her wicker sewing box with its broken handle was still on the little table, beside the pile of Agatha Christie paperbacks and the book of Robbie Burns poems her father had given her. He gestured to the two men to enter the room ahead of him. They sat down stiffly on the sofa while he took his seat on the winged armchair. He leant his head back against the yellowed antimacasser and closed his eyes.

'So, Tom, how are you doing?' Johnny, leaning forward, asked him earnestly. His pale eyes scrutinized the older man.

Tom sat up and returned his gaze. Johnny was going bald, he noticed; the hair was thinning on top and the man looked fleshier than the last time he'd seen him. Which was when? That time in the hotel in Stranorlar, at the meeting when the row broke out, even though the Chief of Staff himself had been there. Tom had said nothing at that meeting. He had felt ashamed at the behaviour of some of them, including Johnny Doherty, shouting and roaring about politics. What about the Struggle, he had wondered silently, that our comrades died for? That it should come to this.

'Not good. Aches and pains . . . old age. It comes to us all. I'd say now you have more on your mind than the state of my health.'

'You're on your own a long time now.'

Tom Mundy grunted.

'A fine woman was Marnie,' Johnny persisted.

'She is well-remembered,' Tom said. His face was a closed door.

Johnny Doherty smiled his lopsided smile and leant back on the sofa. He had a lazy charm that got him into trouble sometimes, Tom thought, with women particularly. He delivered more than bread, it was said. The widow's solace, wasn't that what they had christened him? Beside Johnny on the sofa, the boy wriggled impatiently and plunged his hands into his donkey jacket, but Johnny still took his time, gazing into the empty fire-grate.

When he spoke again, his voice had a sober tone. 'These are terrible times, Tom.'

'Aye.'

'Catholics burned out of their houses and no one to defend them. There are walls in Belfast have written on them: *IRA – I Ran Away.* That's what's said of us, and the leaders that sold us out.'

Out of the blue, the boy spoke. His voice was high, like a girl's.

'Communists and traitors,' he hissed.

Thoughtfully the old man examined him. The boy reddened and relapsed into silence.

Johnny Doherty continued, 'We need equipment, Tom. There was practically nothing there for us when we went looking. No wonder old Dinnie was made quartermaster for there's no weapons worth the peelers' notice anyway. We have to be ready for the next time, God knows, for there will be a next and one after. This is our time, Tom: we can bring the whole rotten institution down, but not with our bare hands.'

'War is it, then?'

'Please God it is. This generation to end it once and for all.' Johnny Doherty sat back on the sofa and blew out his cheeks. 'We're under orders to bring in whatever we can.'

'Orders from Dublin?' Tom asked, surprised.

'Fuck Dublin! They're running the show no more. This is *our* war now. Beware the risen people.' Johnny grinned. 'It's not just the Brits that will get the message. In Dublin they'll get that same message soon enough. When they do it'll be wild obvious to the world then. Things are going to be different from now on.'

'I see.'

There was something in Tom's voice that made Johnny Doherty look at him closely. 'So, Tom,' he said quietly, 'are you for us, or against us?'

'I am for the Army Council, Johnny.' Suddenly the old man felt weary. Was he really, he asked himself. Did he even care? 'What about yourself, Johnny?'

Tom had seen the burning houses on the TV, like sacrificial pyres, and had heard the women interviewed as they pulled away from the homes they had built up over a lifetime, rage in their voices and a hopelessness weighing down their shoulders.

Johnny Doherty's reply was low and urgent: about the need to bring in arms, for the defence of people of the Short Strand and the Markets and closer to home, of the Bogside – maybe even, one day, it would spill over the Border – and how they'd all need to be ready.

'Would you say so?' Tom wondered aloud. 'I mind the

people in the Bogside drove out the polis all by themselves.'

'Aye, and they let the British Army in. The women making them cups of tea, for Jesus' sake. Next they'll be opening their legs for them.'

The boy gave a wide grin. Tom closed his eyes.

'This is our time,' Johnny said. 'Tom, we're going over the top this time. A United Ireland and victory at last. In a year it will be all over; we'll have the Brits on the run. Make the place ungovernable. We've always said that Stormont was illegitimate. Now we can prove it.'

'Why come to me?'

'You know the people around here that have guns in their houses. Shotguns, rifles, whatever. Now that you're well got with the hunting set.'

'I see.'

For a moment the room was silent, while outside the wind whined through the trees.

'You'll not get my airgun,' Tom said. 'I'm that scundered by rabbits.'

Johnny Doherty laughed. 'You can keep your oul' airgun. It's not what we're after.'

The old man fell silent again before rousing himself to squint across the low table at the two men. 'Is that all you want?'

'Aye, Tom, that's all. We can take it from there. Names, addresses. You'll never be known. It's for the Struggle. The least you can give us.'

'Squeal on my neighbours – is that what you want me to do?'

Johnny Doherty's laughter exploded around the room. The boy giggled and then began to scratch his head energetically. The old man looked impassively at them. His silence hung suspended in the stale air and the other man's laughter died. Outside, the branch of a tree banged against the windowpane, like a frustrated child.

'The old man can't remember any names,' the boy suddenly snarled. 'Can't remember or maybe won't remember, would you say?'

Tom Mundy swivelled around in his chair to get a good look at him, 'Tell me, son, what's your name?'

'*Seán MacGabhann is ainm dom.*'

'MacGowan, aye. And how is your father?'

'Do you know my da?'

'Of course I do.' Tom bent towards him. The young man looked defiantly at him. Tom continued. 'And I mind who your grandfather is too.'

The boy grimaced.

'And his name. Fergal McGowan. Isn't that right?'

The boy grunted and wriggled down into his jacket.

'Aye, that's right,' the old man said. 'Fergal the informer.'

'Ah now,' Johnny said quickly.

With a faint smile, the old man lowered his head and said nothing.

'Wise up, Tom,' Johnny said. 'This is getting us nowhere.'

Tom Mundy could see in the other man's eyes a look of disgust: what he was thinking of him, an old man settled nicely into his chair and, if the smell of bacon was anything to go by, thinking more about his tea than about the Cause.

'If you're not going to help us, then we'll go. There are others that will, although I always believed you were a true republican. I'd be disappointed to think –'

'Just give me a minute.'

Stiffly Tom pulled himself out of the chair and left the room. When he opened the kitchen door, he was met by a blast of steam. He turned down the gas flame under the pot of potatoes. As he stood for a moment at the oven, he caught sight, on the dresser, of the photograph of himself holding the swan around his body and, beside him, his young neighbour smiling impishly up at the camera.

When he turned to go out of the kitchen, Johnny Doherty, to his surprise, was standing in the doorway, blocking his way.

'What?'

Johnny Doherty shrugged but did not reply.

The old man smiled wryly. 'Trust no one, is that the way?'

'Come on, Tom, what do you say?'

The old man raised his face and looked into Johnny Doherty's eyes. That strange green colour reminded him of gooseberries. He saw his younger self reflected in those eyes: living out a double life, straining every sense to be alert for a tell-tale shadow, or listening out for the whirr of a hidden tape recorder, or finding a safe way out of the dark, his nerves on a constant edge. Tom Mundy had nothing but compassion for the man he had once been, that young man who had believed in the Struggle, and for the others who had shared that belief with him. His comrades. The best of them were all dead now and lived on only in his memory. In his weariness, his heart softened towards the two young men stranded, so it seemed to him, in the dusty, ghost-filled parlour across the hall.

'I didn't say I wouldn't help you,' he said.

Rosaleen

14

Without a backward glance Aoife clambered up onto the pony. She gripped the reins, pressed the horse's sides with her heels and moved off to join the line of riders. Conor was at a friend's birthday party and I was free to spend the hour as I wished. It was only a taste of independence and yet enough to make me feel lightheaded. I sauntered down the avenue of trees. The sight of rushy fields stretching out on either side and the sound of branches clacking cheerfully above my head made me smile for no reason at all except that I was at peace with the world. It was one of those moments, it seemed to me, that make everything worthwhile.

This is my life, I thought, yes, and Manus doesn't belong in it.

When I returned to where the car was parked, there was still no sign of Aoife and the other riders, so I continued walking up the driveway. The banks of shrubbery opened onto a wide lawn and the house loomed up ahead. Uncertain, I paused, but curiosity got the better of me. Skirting around the front portico, I followed the path as it curved around the side of the house.

Then I saw the man.

He was slumped on a bench as if he were asleep.

Or dead, I thought, fear pirouetting along my spine.

I backed into the shade of the trees. I wanted to run but I was mesmerized by the sight of the solitary figure. Was he the man from the church car park: the man whom I now knew was Clara Hall-Davidson's father? He was dressed in an old plaid shirt and corduroy trousers. The bench he sat on was propped precariously against the wall of the house. He was like a ghost, carrying no weight. Around him were the traces of a phantom conservatory: a groove along the wall showed where, a long time ago, a glass roof had leant up against the house. Under the man's feet were the remains of a terracotta tiled floor.

A walking stick rested between his knees. Around his neck was a woman's scarf incongruously patterned with pink and purple flowers. It formed a cradle in which his arm lay, with his fingers protruding out of the folds of silk. His other hand lay idly on his lap as if it, too, had been rendered powerless. Then he lifted his face towards the sun and I could see it was a grotesque distortion: one eye was closed, the cheek puffed and swollen around it, and a dark red bruise encircled his forehead.

I tried to make out some distinguishing features: where was the lank hair, the narrow eyes, the stained cavalry twill trousers? Where was the agitation, the energy, the menace? Frantically I tried to convince myself otherwise, but there was no mistaking him. This was the man whom Laura had threatened outside the school, after I, like a modern-day

Judas, had pointed him out to her. Now a horribly disfigured version of the man, it was true, but still, undeniably, him.

Someone was to blame for what had happened to him. Was it me?

Laura wasn't at home when I arrived outside the bungalow in Church Road. However long it took, I decided I would wait for her. Aoife and I sat in the car while raindrops bounced off the roof and smeared the windscreen. From the back seat came a plaintive 'Can we go home now?'

'Oh dotey, we can't. Not just yet.'

My hands were sticky as I twined them together in an agony of suspense. *Come on, Laura!*

By the time she appeared, it felt as if I'd been waiting for hours. The rain had reduced to a fine drizzle. She walked up the road, bags of groceries slapping at her knees, looking back occasionally to shout at the twins, who were jumping into puddles. Stoically Niamh walked beside her. The young girl was weighed down by a bag of potatoes and her wet hair was flattened on her forehead like strands of seaweed.

Laura was unsurprised to see me.

'You must have read my mind because I want to talk to *you*,' she said as she turned the key in the back door and we went inside. The children ran on ahead into a bedroom to play.

As soon as Laura had put down the bags of groceries on the kitchen table, I confronted her.

'*What did you do? Laura, tell me!*'

'What are you on about, Rosy?'

Breathlessly I told her what I had seen. Then I stepped back and tried to interpret the expression on her face. It was smooth, serene and impenetrable, but Laura's denial did not satisfy me: her hesitation and then outraged innocence.

'Course I didn't do anything.'

I realized that, knowing what I knew about her, I couldn't even trust her to tell me the truth. How could I believe her, I wondered as I stood against the door jamb with my arms folded. I felt like a police interrogator. She looked up at me solemnly, the way children do after a fight.

'Sit down, Rosaleen,' she said, pulling out a chair. The freckles on her face were brighter than usual, like paint splattered across a canvas. Her expression was unswerving. There were times when Laura had the pale, unknowable eyes of a wolf. Elaborately she made a cross with her finger at her breast, 'Honest to God, I did not say a word to anyone.'

I sat down reluctantly. 'Are you sure, Laura? I mean, you said you didn't know anyone in the IRA.'

'Well,' she bit her lip, 'I do but . . .'

'Oh Laura!'

'No, no, keep your hair on. I do know some of them. In fact, one of them would have been only too glad if I'd asked him.'

When she giggled, I wanted to slap her.

'Laura, this is serious!'

'I swear to God I didn't ask him or anyone else to go after that man. Cross my heart and hope to die.'

Silently we stared at each other.

'Do you not believe me?'

I sighed. I didn't trust her but I had to believe her. If she was responsible, if she *had* gone to someone in the IRA – and I quaked at the thought – then that made me responsible. Yes, I would be to blame. I tried to make sense of what I'd seen. Despite her protestations of innocence, I still wasn't sure if Laura hadn't whispered in someone's ear. And yet, deep down, I knew I had to believe her.

'Whatever happened,' Laura said, her face close as she leant across to touch my arm, 'it has *nothing* to do with me.'

She was so eager now to be trusted that I weakened and told her that I believed her.

She grinned and clasped my hand. 'Not, mind you, that I wouldn't have done it.' Her eyes were dancing now. 'Someone else just got in there first. And good luck to them, say I. He deserved what was coming to him.'

'But who do you think would do something like that?'

'You know what, Rosy, anything could have happened – a car crash or maybe he got kicked by a horse.'

Startled, I looked at Laura without seeing her.

A recollection of the conversation I had heard that day when the mothers were gathered together, whispering among themselves, came to me. I had seen a curtain twitching in an upstairs window of the great house and a phrase had flitted into my consciousness then, like a bird or a bat emerging from the huddle of colours: blue jeans, pink shirts, a yellow dress, navy-and-white stripes. Miraculously the words carried weight now, dragging out a meaning that became clear to me as I sat in the safety of Laura's kitchen. It broke through the world of children, horses, mothers where nothing much ever happened. If somebody died or someone was sick it was a predictable event: a relative dying in old age, neighbours coming in with cakes. Nothing prepared me for what I had heard and I had suppressed the memory. Now the meaning of the words was obvious. It was a crazy message written across the sky outside the kitchen window: *She did it*.

Who was *she*? I could ask all I liked but there was no one around to answer. My imagination shrank from the place where the solitary figure had turned his face upwards to drink in the sun's heat. He had looked broken and defeated, like a patient in a nursing home waiting for his dinner to be served up at four o'clock and bored out of his brains. I thought of his ravaged face and there was only one answer. I had heard the conversation without understanding what it meant. Until now.

Can't believe it, his own daughter.

I had suspected Laura but now I knew that, despite her posturing, she had been innocent all along. I thought of Mr Mundy, an old man who lived in the past and was supposed to be in the IRA and who had been kind to me. In spite of Kevin's fears, I was beginning to doubt that the IRA even existed any more. As for Laura, she was such a show-off I couldn't take anything she said at face value.

'Clara Hall-Davidson,' I said and, as soon as I said her name, I knew that it had to be her.

Laura looked astonished. 'You think she did it?'

I nodded.

'She *horsewhipped* her own father?' Laura laughed a gurgling laugh, loud enough to chase away the shadows. Leaning back in her chair, she said admiringly, 'Well now, the wee bitch!'

'Can you believe it?'

'That is *wild.*'

We looked at each other in wonder.

'Who'd have thought?' said Laura. 'It wasn't Professor Plum in the library after all. It was Lady Clippity-Cloppity in the stable yard.'

I smiled grimly.

'It makes sense though,' Laura said. 'The gentry may be down but they're not out. In fact, all things considered, they've done very well for themselves, more's the pity. Only a few of them burnt out of their mansions and gone to England.'

'That was years ago. For goodness sake, Laura, it's 1969 now.'

Laura wasn't having any of it.

'Don't you kid yourself,' she folded her arms and declared. 'Violence is the hallmark of their class.'

Class. A strange word to come tumbling into our conversation. I was middle-class because I had a university degree. Laura was working-class because she came from the Bogside. Now that we had children and husbands and houses, was there any real difference between us?

'Still I never thought,' I said.

'Well, she has a business to run,' Laura said, ever the pragmatist. 'She must have found out about him.'

'Her own *father* . . .' but I wasn't thinking of Clara Hall-Davidson or about the man nursing his injuries in the sunlight. I was thinking of a body sprawled out on a shed floor: an outcast in a ramshackle garden, weeds dancing in the wind, the apron ties flapping around my mother's back, cold cement walls, an old brown blanket. Daddy.

Laura said cheerfully, 'All those nice mummies – if they'd ever got wind of what he was at, she'd have been finished.'

'They must know. I heard them talking.'

'Oh, they'll keep coming *now*,' Laura said crisply. 'After what she's done to him, they'll be queuing up for riding lessons.'

I didn't reply. I was thankful that Laura hadn't noticed my distress, my hands trembling on my lap. It was a shock to discover, after all the years, how the past still had its grip on me. A strangled breath caught in my throat.

'So am I off the hook?' Laura asked.

Yes, I could say with certainty that she was. And if she was, I thought, then so was I. *Off the hook.* I liked the sound of the words and their promise of a wriggling escape. I couldn't go on for ever feeling responsible for what had happened to my father. I had been seven years old when he died, in a world that was beyond my comprehension. My sigh of relief was audible.

Laura, her hand resting gently on mine, shifted on her chair in order to peer closer into my face: 'What is it?'

'It's nothing. Nothing whatsoever.'

'Are you sure?'

'Yes,' I replied firmly. 'Now tell me what you wanted to talk to me about.'

'Huh?'

'You said you wanted to ask me something.'

'Oh God, aye.'

To my surprise Laura looked nervous, unsure of herself. She hesitated and walked over to the sink to pour herself a glass of water. After taking a gulp, she turned around to face me again and said breathlessly, 'Will you and Kevin come out with us on Sunday night?'

'What for?'

'It's Cathal's birthday. He's going to be thirty.'

Thirty. The two of us fell silent. Our turn would come and then, one day, we would be old.

'You mean go to the pub?'

'Yes – he's watching a match in the afternoon, so he'll give us a blow by blow account.' Laura rolled her eyes. 'Lucky us!'

'Kevin will enjoy that. Of course we'll go.'

'Thanks, Rosy.'

Her gratitude was lightly expressed but it was heartfelt, I could tell. Were things really that bad between her and Cathal? Her hand fluttered up to her mouth and I realized that I didn't need to ask. I knew the answer already.

15

'I'm not going,' Kevin said flatly.

'Oh please. I promised Laura.'

'Jesus, I can't take Cathal Gillespie talking crap all night.'

In the end, I knew, we would go out to the pub and, as usual, Kevin and Cathal would spend the night arguing with each other.

'He's not that bad,' I said.

'Not that bad!' Kevin groaned. 'He's getting worse.'

If Laura and I hadn't been so close, I doubt if Kevin and Cathal would have spent any time together. They had nothing in common – except a propensity to disagree. When the two men met, it always led to an argument about something: sport, politics, money. Cathal was a fanatical GAA man. Kevin followed soccer. Increasingly, these days, their discussions turned to politics. As the situation deteriorated across the Border, Kevin and Cathal talked about the whys and wherefores, the might-have-beens. Apart from work colleagues and the members of his shooting club, Kevin didn't have any friends, so I think it suited him to go to the pub to lock horns with Cathal, even if he complained about him.

Cathal Gillespie had a spindly, bookish air. He chose to wear round, gold-rimmed spectacles that gave him the look of a Russian revolutionary from *Doctor Zhivago*, a look he cultivated, wearing a donkey jacket and a navy peaked cap to hide his baldness. He spoke with such a heavy emphasis that a comment about the weather sounded like a classroom lecture. And Cathal talked a lot, spreading out his hands as he warmed to some theme or other: the final kick of a match, the latest news from Belfast.

Kevin, on the other hand, was a cautious listener, pedantic in his own way, but cool and logical. His approach to an argument was to parse and analyse what the other person had said and then, bit by bit, to dismantle it.

In the afternoon Kevin went over to his older sister's house. Maureen had never married. She lived in the family house on the outskirts of Letterkenny. A gaunt house built on the Dublin road in the nineteen forties, with miserable grey walls and a square of mossy grass for a front garden. The hot-water cylinder was giving trouble. Margaret didn't believe in paying workmen to fix anything and the house was falling down around her. In winter it was so cold she always wore her overcoat and woolly hat indoors. Maureen was an unhappy woman by choice, I thought unkindly. She brought out the worst in me, even though I had reason to be grateful to her. In return for fixing the water cylinder, she had promised Kevin that she would baby-sit.

Once Kevin had left, the house was at ease with itself. I dawdled at the kitchen table. What an unexpected turn of events: to find Manus and then to lose him again! Not that he was mine to have in the first place. He never had been, I thought sadly. That night when I had climbed the stairs into the dark recesses of his room, I had no insight into what I was doing. Now, looking back, I felt I had been like a bitch in heat. It meant *nothing*, I told myself firmly. I wasn't going to emulate Laura, out roaming the roads in search of her lost liberty. I had seen the look on her face, her hand touching her cheek, and the incendiary nature of her unhappiness.

When Kevin came back, I realized that something was wrong. Imperceptibly, a shadow shifted across his face when he looked at me and then turned away.

'What?'

He shook his head and muttered, 'Nothing, it's nothing.'

At the dinner table I tried to find out what was bothering him but he kept blocking me, fending off any enquiries.

'Daddy?' Aoife said.

'What?'

'Can I have a dog?'

'Not until you're old enough to look after it.'

Silently, she absorbed this information. Aoife had inherited Kevin's habit of reflecting before she spoke.

'Daddy?'

'What?'

'Can I have piano lessons?'

'*Jesus*! You must think that I'm made of money.' His voice was unusually harsh.

Aoife blinked in dismay. Bemused, she gazed down at her plate.

'Eat your potato,' I told her.

'Yeah,' shouted Conor as he shovelled a spoonful of

mashed potato into his mouth. 'Eat your poppies, *Eefie*.'

She cuffed him with her fist. 'Shut up, you!'

'Christ!' Kevin's head reared up at the sound of Conor's wail. 'Keep quiet, both of you.'

Silence. Then:

'Can we ask Santa Claus for piano lessons?' Aoife looked earnest. Her hand crept across the table to touch Kevin's clenched fist. 'Please, Daddy?'

Kevin ignored her and kept eating. Aoife looked down at her pile of mashed potato, her face scrunched up in distaste. She put down her knife and fork and folded her arms.

'Aoife, eat some of it at least,' I said.

She stared ahead.

'Aoife!'

'Noooo.'

Kevin exploded. 'Either eat your dinner or go to your room *right now*.'

Immediately Aoife scrambled down from her chair and left the kitchen. The sound of her shrieks diminished as she went up the stairs. The bedroom door breathed open and then – *bang*.

'God, Kevin, was that really necessary?'

Two faces looked at me. Conor, ears pricking up at the possibility of conflict, and Kevin, sullen and heavy. I stood up and began to clear away the plates. I took Aoife's plate and scraped the mashed potato into a bowl. Kevin strode into the sitting room and turned on the television. More trouble in Belfast. Riots. Gunfire.

I sighed and began to collect up clothes the children had scattered around the kitchen.

'Come on, little fox,' I said to Conor. He slipped off his chair and we went upstairs, his cool little hand clutching mine.

Aoife was sitting on her bed, reading a book.

'Mum?'

'What?'

She lifted a tear-stained face and looked at me. '*Why* can't I have piano lessons?'

I took her hand in mine and examined her stubby fingers. 'Do you think your fingers are big enough to play the piano?'

Aoife stretched her hands as wide as she could. 'Course they are.' She had an innate sense of her own worth. It was a characteristic I liked. Soon she would be moving beyond me, I thought, flexing and testing herself in ways I could only imagine.

Piano lessons, why not indeed?

'We'll see,' I said.

Aoife sighed.

I changed into my shift dress. In the mirror I looked at my reflection and saw a young woman, small in height – was I getting dumpy? – with clear blue eyes and glossy black hair pulled back in a ponytail. Had Manus been impressed by what he saw? I tried to remember the expression on his face. Had he seen a new confidence in the way that I had come towards him down the street, carrying a sketchpad and camera, my voice even and strong? Don't be foolish, I told myself as I pulled off the rubber band and let my hair tumble freely onto my shoulders. Manus was my secret life, a harmless fantasy, and he was no contest when it came to the things that Kevin was good at – being a father and provider, protecting Aoife and Conor and me. I put on my high-heeled sandals and clattered downstairs.

In the living room Kevin was standing looking at the empty fireplace.

'Aren't you getting ready?' I asked.

For a moment he didn't move. Then he turned and stared

at me. His gaze was a mystery, impossible to read.

'What?'

'Why didn't you tell me?'

'What?'

'You know.'

All at once I felt hot and cold.

'I hear you met up with an old flame.'

Oh.

How did he know? His face was implacable. Was he hurt, angry or just truculent? I took a deep breath. It was inevitable, I supposed. No secret life allowed.

'Kevin, I –'

'So tell me, Rosaleen, how is Manus?'

His face was a mask.

'Jesus,' he said, 'I just don't understand you.'

'It's nothing.'

His voice was clipped and cold, 'Then why can't you tell me what's going on unless . . .' He stopped. 'Are you?'

'Am I what?'

'Seeing Manus?'

'Oh Kevin, don't be daft.' I went up to him and slipped my arms around his waist. 'It's nothing, I swear. I just bumped into him in the street, that's all. We had one drink.' Two drinks, I reminded myself, but decided to keep going. 'He works for a newspaper and he wanted information about the situation in Derry. And no, I have no intention of seeing him again.'

'What the hell is wrong with you that you couldn't tell me about it?'

I couldn't tell him because I wanted a secret world for myself, just like Laura did. The difference was she wanted it for real while I was content for mine to be an imaginary part of my life.

'Is that really too much to ask?'

Without speaking, I shook my head.

'Makes me look like a fool when I hear it from someone else.'

'I'm sorry,' I said and meant it.

'Just don't keep any more secrets from me, all right?' He was calmer now, lifting a lock of my hair and turning it between his fingers as he looked down at me. He smelt of diesel oil.

'You'd better get changed.' I said.

'Promise me?' he whispered into the crown of my head.

Promise. A door clanged shut somewhere inside me and the air in the room grew expectant. He wasn't happy to let me be. He had to burrow inside my head.

'Okay,' I muttered. 'Okay. Okay. Now go and get changed or we'll be late.'

Just then the doorbell rang. I looked out the window to see who it was. A familiar figure stood at the front door. *Maureen.* Of course, it was obvious. She must have seen Manus and me that day in the Bogside. I opened the door with a smile on my lips and hatred in my heart.

'Maureen.'

'You're surely not going out like that?' she asked, taking in the minidress, the bare legs, the high-heeled sandals. 'You'll catch your death, Mother.'

Mother. It was a joke: her attempt at frivolity, but it always felt like an admonition. The cloud of censure blew off her like dust: a reminder to live up to my responsibilities, to shorten my hair, lengthen my hemline and, most of all, not to cavort arm-in-arm around the Bogside with a man who wasn't my husband. Baring my teeth, I invited her in. Thankfully the children called her upstairs to read to them in bed and Kevin and I crept out before they knew we were gone.

As he drove, Kevin hummed tunelessly. I stared out the

window at the darkening hedgerows speeding past. Now that we were on our own, we had nothing to say to each other. This is marriage, I reminded myself. A married couple didn't need to talk and yet we had no shortage of things to talk about: work, children, family – an endless stream of commentary. Kevin drove the car with authority and, in the same way he did everything else, ponderously. Sometimes I wondered how we had come together. It seemed that an accident rather than fate had united us. I sank into the passenger seat and chewed on the inside of my cheek. Then his voice graduated into singing and I wanted to howl like a dog at the moon.

Laura and Cathal were sitting in the pub when we arrived, an awkward space between them. From the glasses on the table, I could see that she was on her second Bacardi and Coke and, already, her eyes had a vague, unfocused look. It didn't take much to get Laura drunk. The pub was one of the late-night joints that had sprung up on roads around the Border. The façade was a single-storey stretch of white plastered wall with black mock-Tudor boards and ugly brown-paned windows. At the back, a barnlike extension had been added to accommodate the customers who flooded over the Border to avail of the late-night licensing laws. Inside, the room was filling up with Sunday-night customers. Lined up at the bar already were the serious drinkers: men in small groups with half-drained pint glasses in front of them accompanied by whiskey chasers. The buzz of voices had a purposeful sound, a soft roar punctuated by laughter.

Because Kevin and I went out so rarely, a visit to the pub had a particular character for me, like a visit to a carnival or a circus. I was dazzled by the lights, the cigarette smoke curling up to the ceiling. On the table Laura's drink looked rich and inviting.

'I'll have the same,' I said to Kevin.

He went to the bar and ordered a round. When he returned with a tray of drinks Laura began to tell a rambling story about a next-door neighbour who had recently moved in.

'He'd remind you of a gorilla,' she said. 'Apparently he's a wrestler. For practice he has a sledgehammer and a truck tyre in his garden shed. When he works out it's like Big Ben in our kitchen. I gave him a right earful one day but he paid no heed. And Cathal won't stand up to him because he's yellow. So now I've taken to playing the radio real loud early in the morning but it only makes him worse. He's forever banging on and on and on.'

Cathal caught Kevin's eye, 'Do you ever notice how some girls can bang on and on?'

'Hey, four eyes, look at who's talking,' Laura said. 'You never shut up.'

Getting between Laura and her husband, Kevin had said once, was like trying to break up a fight between snarling dogs. He drank deeply from his glass and then, after he wiped his mouth with his hand, he turned to Cathal. 'That's a nice pint.'

'Aye.'

'Were you at the match?'

'Aye, we hammered them.' Cathal cheered up and the two men burrowed down together in their seats.

I looked at Laura. Slyly her eyelids drooped and she gave a deliberate yawn. I wondered what Manus was doing and where he was.

'What?' Laura was looking at me curiously. I shook my head and said nothing. She leant forward. 'Don't you wish now we could go out for a drink just once without it turning into a football match?'

I laughed. If we'd been alone, maybe I would have let

down my reserve and told her about Manus but Kevin's knee was warm beside mine under the table and his voice still sounded a warning in my head. I looked around. At the other end of the lounge a band was setting up. A woman was sitting alone at a table. She had peroxide blonde hair and was wearing a shiny, tightly fitted blouse and a pencil skirt. She was drinking a glass of vodka through a straw as she waited to be called up to stand at the microphone.

I nudged Laura. 'Why the straw?'

Laura shrugged and shook her head. She was wearing the dress with the rose pattern that she had worn that day we'd gone to Derry. A chiffon scarf was tied neatly around her neck.

I leant over to her and whispered, 'So how's the bakery business?'

'Oh, fresh,' she giggled, 'wild fresh.'

Pulling down the edge of the scarf, she leant forward, and surreptitiously showed me her neck. I could make out the dull red mark of a love bite.

'*Oh Laura!*' So loudly that the men looked up.

Laura took a ladylike sip from her glass and winked at me.

'So tell us,' she said brightly to the men, 'have we won the match yet?'

At that moment the band struck up. 'North to Alaska' pounded around the walls. Laura sat back and wriggled in her seat. The two men stood up, their glasses in their hands.

'We'll go down to the bar, get away from that noise,' Kevin said.

I went to stand up too but Laura pulled me back.

'You go on,' she mouthed at him over the music. 'We'll follow you.'

So we sat on together, swaying to the music. I disliked it when Laura got jarred. She reminded me of a dog the way she slobbered at my shoulder, shaking her head and singing out of tune.

'Country and Western, don't you love it, *bubububuuu . . .*' she crooned in my ear. '*I met my darling and . . .*' she changed the words as she sang, squeezing my arm fatly, '*he gave me a great big . . .*'

The rest was lost in the blare of music. The rum was doing its work: I felt happy at last. I drained my glass and was about to go over to ask Kevin to get me another one when he was there beside us with drinks. Carefully he placed them on the table and straightened up without smiling.

'Cheers, Kevin,' Laura said and, when she saw the expression on his face, 'Cheer up. It may never happen.' She raised her glass and, eyeing him coquettishly, took a sip from her glass. 'Yum,' she breathed. 'Yum. Yum.'

He moved away to the safety of the bar.

Now the woman was standing up at the microphone. Under the lights her blonde curls sprang up from her head, brassy and stiff, and her earrings sparkled. She stood as if to attention, her breasts jutting out and her short legs planted on the platform. The babble of conversation didn't wane when she turned to the band and signalled for them to begin. There was something brave about her, I thought, the way she stood her ground, alone and proud.

Even though the world ignored her, she blessed us all with a dazzling smile as a saxophone, wailing, led her into the first song. Smoky and deep, her voice told of sleepless nights, filled with yearning. A couple got up to dance, a small dapper man wheeling a large woman in front of him. Dreamily they circled the floor while, eyes closed, the woman on the stage, with a sob in her voice, sang of forbidden love. Amplified around the room, the notes of the saxophone piled in around her. When she had finished, the singer stood back from the microphone and the band took over, booming out across the dance floor, which was empty except for the small man and the big woman turning together in wide circles. Around and around they danced while, above their heads, a mirrored ball twirled slowly.

The woman at the microphone began to sing again. The roar of conversation subsided as people turned their faces towards her. At the tables, some drinkers began to sing along, as a wave of emotion washed out to meet them.

Laura and I joined in, swaying and singing, '*And, darling, when we're apart, I'll always belong to you . . .*' she was laughing into my face, her breath tangy with cigarettes, '*so don't forget that you belong to me.*'

I was carried on the notes as they soared and fell. Does anyone ever belong to someone else? The memory of Manus still hurt but I didn't love him. I was definite about that. In fact I didn't think I even liked him. I became aware of Kevin, looking at me across the dance floor. I could tell from the way his head was bent to one side that he was only half-listening to what Cathal was saying.

Who is that stranger staring at me, I found myself wondering.

When the band struck up again, Laura drained her glass and stood up.

'Come on, Rosy,' she said briskly, straightening her dress. 'If we want more drink, we're going to have to hunt it down.'

The singer had already finished up, to scattered applause, and had walked back to her table. The dance floor filled up as the band bounced relentlessly through 'The Hucklebuck'.

Laura wended her way through the dancers and I followed her until we found ourselves standing beside the woman who, minutes before, had silenced the crowd with her singing. Up close, her face was a mask of powder with scarlet lipstick smeared around her lips. She smelt of perspiration and talc, and her hands were shaking.

'Jesus, Lily, the state of you,' Laura said but the woman ignored her and instead crouched down over her drink, sucking greedily on the straw.

16

It was after eleven o'clock by the time Laura and I made our way into the bar. There were people still coming in and the place was heaving. We had to shout to be heard over the noise.

'Will you have another?' Laura asked.

I shook my head.

'Ah come on, Rosy! The night's still young.'

'No, Laura, I mean it,' I said firmly.

She pressed her way through the crowd to order one Bacardi and two Cokes.

'They're paying.' she said to the barman and nodded towards Kevin and Cathal who were seated at a table, deep in conversation.

While we waited, a big-bellied man pushed in beside us and shouted drunkenly at the barman. Up close his face was puce and dripping with sweat. When he saw Laura, he leered and reached a giant arm around her waist. Without flinching, she leant over to him and made a grab for his crotch. He staggered back, tripping over a stool, his glass flying out of his hand. Bellowing, he was a stallion rearing up before us, huge and dangerous. Suddenly I was fearful of everything: the man's rage, the roar of the pub, the loneliness of the peroxide blonde, the stranger who had stared across the dance floor at me . . . Kevin.

'Oh, Laura, be careful!'

She just laughed as the man backed away. Then, lifting the drinks from the counter, she set out through the crowd and I followed. When we got near the table where Kevin and Cathal were sitting, she waited for me to catch up.

'That'll teach the big shite to keep his hands to himself,' she said.

Then she looked hard at me.

'What?' I asked.

'Rosy, you're such a ninny. One of these days you're going to have to stand up for yourself.'

'Laura . . .'

It was impossible to have a conversation. The room was filling up fast, a thunder of voices drowning out the sound of music, so that only the pulse of drums made it through the noise.

When we had sat down at the table, Laura asked if we had heard the one about the man who wanted his wife to do it in the doggy position. Kevin and Cathal ignored her. Engrossed in conversation, they had no interest in her jokes.

Kevin was speaking in his calm, measured way. 'I'm not saying that their demands are wrong. Nobody could say that. One man, one vote – I mean, who in their right mind could argue with that? Of course there has to be justice and civil rights. The means, though, that people choose to express their grievances have to be commensurate with the ideals. I spend my life working to get buildings properly built and fitted out. To see them burnt down in a night is unforgivable. It is criminal. The way I see it, those people have nothing and they don't want anyone else to have anything either.'

'But you can't say that!' Cathal's face was pink with excitement and his mouth was distorted as he shouted over the roar. Spittle landed on the table. An empty glass at his elbow was swept onto the floor.

'Shite, Cathal!' Clutching her glass, Laura pulled away from him in mock terror. 'You'll have my drink destroyed.'

'The people are right,' Cathal continued undaunted. 'It's the only way. They're rising up against oppression and there's only one way out. You burn down the city and start again.'

Kevin shook his head. 'You can say whatever you like, but nothing will convince me. Look, the British government is involved now directly. Why not give them the time they need to bring in the reforms without causing further unrest?'

'No, no, no! British imperialism cannot be trusted *ever*!' Cathal was shouting now. 'Seize the time, that's what the Black Panthers say. It's how revolutions are made: at the point of the conflict is the point of struggle. Don't you *see*?' Cathal punched the table with his fist. 'It's happening here. The Revolution. Working-class people are rising up to seize their moment. We have to show our solidarity with them. We have to stand with them and not just fucking preach at them about reform.'

'The working class, my eye!' Kevin said hotly. 'It'd be different if any one of them *was* working. I mean, if they did work, they wouldn't have time to be out rioting in the streets.'

Cathal sat back and pushed his glasses up his nose. 'Whoa!'

'Non-violent protest is one thing. I can support that, but this is anarchy,' Kevin pressed on. 'People getting hurt. Violence. Hatred. That's all those people understand.'

'But, Kevin,' I said, 'it's not like that at all.'

He turned towards me. '*What?*'

His eyes were bloodshot, his skin blotched. I could tell he was drunk; in fact he was drunker than I'd ever seen him before.

'Well,' I mumbled, 'I don't think it's like that anyway.'

'And what do *you* know about it?' He was shouting now, his face contorted with rage. 'What the hell do you know about anything?'

'Kevin, please –'

'They are just feckless. No wonder they act like wild animals.'

I was the target of his rage, but Laura's eyes narrowed as if she'd been waiting for the moment and was ready for him.

'So, Kevin,' she leant forward and hissed across the table, 'is that what you think of us?'

'Oh Jesus wept,' he muttered.

'I'll tell you what animals are.' Laura was on a roll now. 'Animals are the RUC lifting people and taking them down to the station to give them a doing-over. Animals are the B Specials on a dark night stopping your car and pointing a gun in your mouth.'

'Calm down, Laura – I don't mean you,' Kevin said. He glanced in my direction.

No, he hadn't meant her but, with Laura beside me, I felt strong.

Laura was not to be mollified.

'I think you did,' she said.

188

Kevin threw up his hands in mock defeat.

'And, anyway,' Laura continued, 'Cathal is right and you are wrong.'

Behind his glasses her husband's eyes widened in surprise.

'Whoa!' Cathal said again. Then he sat back in his seat and grinned. It was obvious that Laura was only getting into her stride.

'What would you know, Mr Engineer? Never had a taste of an RUC baton or watched your father waste out his days for want of a job. *Never* been hungry. No indeed, I'd say. And you call *us* animals. You've some cheek. Tell you one thing,' Laura straightened up and folded her arms across her breasts, 'we know how to behave.'

Now there was a flicker of amusement in Kevin's face.

'Is that so?' he said.

'Aye, I can tell you. No Bogside woman ever horsewhipped her own father.'

Kevin rubbed his head, trying to make sense of what Laura was saying.

'No Bogside woman,' Laura said again, emphasizing each word, 'ever horsewhipped her own father.'

'What the hell's she talking about?' Kevin turned to Cathal, who shrugged and then ducked into the safety of his pint.

With relish, Laura said, 'Not like your Lady Muck.'

Now Kevin was asking me, 'What's she on about?'

I prayed that Laura wouldn't tell him but I couldn't stop her. Ignoring my warning look, she smiled at the two men and took a sip from her drink.

'How about another drink, pet?' she said.

Immediately Cathal got up and set off for the bar.

Laura turned to Kevin. 'I'd have thought Rosy would have told you.'

Kevin said nothing. I stayed quiet while Laura, her eyes full of mischief, told Kevin in detail about Clara Hall-Davidson and her father. As the story unfolded, Kevin recoiled. He didn't look at me but I could see his face close down, his mouth form an angry line. I reached out to touch him but he pulled away, a seepage of anger filling the space between us.

'Kevin . . .' I said miserably.

He ignored me and drank the dregs of his glass.

'I'm going home,' he said and stood up.

There was an inevitability about the scene: him marching through the crowd to the exit, me running after him, trying to keep up.

In the car park he rummaged for the car keys. The air was still and cold. Everything was hard: the glint of tarmac, the white barnlike building, stars piercing the night. And Kevin, his face grim, his body tense, ready for a fight.

'Do you want me to drive?' I tried to mollify him but it was no use. There was no way to reach him.

He didn't reply and, finding the keys at last, he wrenched open the car door and got in. I had to jump in to keep up with him. The wheels screamed as he turned the car around to face for home. A clear night. There was a multitude of stars in the sky and a silvery sheen on the distant lough. A touch of frost in the air. Houses along the roadside were drowned in sleep. Not a light to be seen. A fox shadowed across in front of the headlights, and narrowly missed being hit by the car.

'Kevin, please slow down.'

I watched his knuckles on the steering wheel. His breathing thickened in the interior of the car and the windscreen turned opaque.

'Look. I would have told you,' I said, 'but Aoife was so keen to have riding lessons, I didn't have the heart.'

He didn't reply. I sat back in a welter of self-justification. It wasn't a mortal sin. The children were always safe. I'd made sure of that.

Suddenly Kevin spoke. 'I don't understand you. I don't know how your mind works or what you're thinking.'

'Not an awful lot, most of the time,' I said gently and nudged him. He flinched and pulled away as if he'd been stung.

'I mean it.' His voice was flat, unforgiving.

As he turned the car off the main road, the headlights picked out the banks of whin bushes on each side. An ash tree bent sorrowfully over the road. I leant my forehead against the window. The road dropped down towards the lough, past Mundy's gate and the gateposts, rounded and mossy. Our house was a disconsolate mass hidden among the trees. The ditches were full of menace and creatures scuttling under the brambles.

'*It's not a ditch. Around here we'd call it a sheugh.*'

I remembered how Kevin had corrected me on the day we came to view the house, as we drove down a narrow road with ditches on either side until we came to the entrance to the house. It had been a day of pearly stillness, doors creaking open onto a palace of richness, shabby and rundown as it was. Out in the garden Aoife sleeping in her pram, a look of ecstasy on her face. I had gripped Kevin's hand as we moved through rooms full of light and darkness, a wave of joy surging through me. This was home and in the days and nights that followed it was our private world where we were safe from danger.

'How do you spell it?' I had asked.

'What?'

'What you call a ditch.'

'A *sheugh*? You can't write it down,' Kevin had answered. 'We had a teacher once who was from Dublin.

He kept asking us about local words and we used to say to him: you can't write those words down – you can only say them.'

Laughter rumbling in his throat, he had been at ease. And I thought he could have taken me there and then, even though the estate agent was rummaging around in the yard below. When we looked into each other's eyes, I saw him as if for the first time, and I wanted to tell him that I loved him. What stopped me, I don't know. For some reason Daddy's limp body on Mr Adjouti's arm came into my head. Too many secrets, Kevin had said. Yes, he was right but, that day, he had understood what I had been unable to say. I knew that he knew, from the flick of his shoulder, the smile in his eyes. We moved from room to room, our hands intertwined, and I remembered thinking, that day, that our hearts were intertwined too.

Maureen took one look at Kevin's face, packed away her spectacles and knitting, said her goodbyes quickly and melted out the door. As the sound of her car faded into the night, I sat down at the kitchen table. With the range banked up for the night, the kitchen was cold. I shivered. My red cardigan was hanging on the back of a chair and I pulled it on.

'You've changed so much,' Kevin said, his voice reverberating off the kitchen walls.

I shrugged. Head down.

'You never used to be like this.'

'I don't know what you mean.'

'You're like a stranger. Ever since you started that bloody job. We used to talk and now it's like you're somewhere else and you never tell me about anything.'

'Mostly we used to talk about you and your job. You always wanted to do the talking. I don't remember you paying much attention to what I did.'

It felt artificial the way our voices rose, full of anger, and battered off each other, exploding into scattered phrases that collided. *You did. You didn't. Why are you . . .? Why not . . .?*

This is a real row we're having said a voice inside my head.

'And you never support me.'

What was he talking about? My whole life was caught up in minding and caring, in feeding and cleaning and washing windows to let the light shine in. What else did I do only support him and the children?

'I don't know what you mean.'

'Exactly. That's the problem.'

I shook my head.

'I honestly don't know what you're talking about,' I said.

'When we're in company I do not expect my wife to speak out against me.'

The conversation in the pub. I looked at him in astonishment.

'Even when I don't agree with you?'

'Yes, for God's sake. Yes. Yes.'

His hand riddled through his hair. In his eyes there was no warmth, no anger.

Dread chilled me to the bone.

'But, Kevin, I can't always . . .'

Then, his face darkening with anger and hurt, he changed tack. 'And putting the children at risk, Rosy – what the hell were you thinking? I don't expect to be told by Laura Gillespie of all people.'

I was lost. I had lost. Tears came from nowhere, washing through me like rain. I rocked like a baby, my hands up to my face.

'Stop it,' said Kevin.

I only cried louder.

'*Stop*!' Quietly this time. His warning hand on my shoulder. '*Listen*!'

We both heard it. An indistinct rumbling. Then a delicate thud.

'What is it?' I whispered.

Kevin shook his head and muttered, 'Maybe the cat. I don't know.' He got up and went through the scullery to the back door.

Nothing.

Then I heard the sound of the back door splintering open. Shouts tumbling into the kitchen and Kevin, white-faced, backing into the room. Two shadowy, dark figures stampeding out of the night, their heads encased in black balaclavas, scarves around their mouths, eyes darting inside the woollen holes. They didn't look human. They were more like aliens lumbering around our kitchen. The blue glint of a hatchet in one man's hand. The bigger man brandishing a shotgun.

'*What the hell*!' Kevin's voice was loud, uncertain.

Immediately the bigger of the two went close to him as if he were about to embrace him.

My thoughts fragmented, my mouth arid with fear. Aoife. Conor. All I could think of.

'Don't say a word,' the man hissed, the gun in his hand rearing up like the snout of a dog at Kevin's chest. A thread of sweat drifted down Kevin's nose and his mouth contorted in fear. 'Do not move,' the man said, 'until I say so.' His voice was muffled in the wool around his mouth.

I stood up, caution to the winds, and screamed, '*Who are you? What do you want?*'

Immediately the smaller man grabbed me by the arms and thrust me back onto the chair. My wrists burnt as he tied them together with baling twine behind my back and pulled the knots tight. I moaned at the pain.

'Quit your gurning,' he said. Behind the woollen scarf his voice was high like a boy's. Almost playful.

The bigger man turned to Kevin. 'Show us where you keep your guns.'

For a moment Kevin stayed motionless but the shotgun dug deep into his shirt. He began to move like a man under water, heavily out of the kitchen, followed by the gunman. Aoife's hamster turned the wheel in its cage, making a soft whirr under the thump, thump of their shoes on the wooden stairs. The smaller man sat down beside me and touched the edge of the hatchet blade with his gloved finger. As he looked around the kitchen, a little giggle bubbled out from inside the scarf.

'And nary a cup of tea to be had,' he said.

I stared at him. *Guns, they want guns.* I thought stupidly, *Who are they?* Kevin kept three guns under our bed. What if Conor ever found them, I used to chide him. 'They're not loaded, Rosy,' he had said. 'I'm not a fool, you know.' I could hear the door of our bedroom being opened over our heads. Our bedroom, where even the children had to ask to be let in, was now being invaded by an armed hoodlum. I felt sick at the thought. As I sat on the edge of the chair and waited, I could feel my wrists going numb and my wedding ring tight on my swelling finger.

Then I heard the cry – a bird's call of danger – spirited high above the rafters of the old house. A young child's cry. *Conor.* I leapt up, the kitchen chair toppling backwards onto the floor as I ran, awkwardly, pounding up the stairs, falling from side to side until I reached the landing. Behind me, the man/boy was trying to keep up, his boots hammering on the stairs. I didn't care – the only anxiety coursing through me was for Conor.

At the top of the stairs I saw his little white face, evacuated by sleep, eyes drooping, mouth open. One brief sighting and then our bedroom door opened and the bulk of the bigger man blocked my view. I kept moving towards the man. He was so close I felt the heat of his body and a stale smell exuding from his shirt. I was maddened into recklessness, like a cow after her calf. I tried to push him aside with my shoulder.

'Not so fast,' he said and laughed, as if we had all the time in the world. One hand gripped my arm while the other kept the shotgun trained steadily on Kevin.

I reared up at him, adrenalin flooding through me. I was fearless, desperate. No one would stop me. They had no right. *This is my strength*.

'You cowards,' I spat out. 'We're a soft target, is that it?'

Filled with scorn, I wanted to challenge the black masked head in its coiled scarf. Startled, the man faced me, his head rising up involuntarily to meet my gaze.

I stopped.

Those eyes. Those cool, green, impenetrable eyes. I had seen them before. The panda holes in his balaclava showed nothing more but there was no doubt in my mind.

How's the bakery business?

Oh, fresh . . . wild fresh.

Was this to be our deliverance, I wondered, the fact that I recognised him? Despite the effort he had made to hide any giveaway features, I knew that inside those gloves were nicotine-stained fingers, a blackened thumbnail and a wedding ring. No disguise could hide the truth.

'*Haaaaah!*' I howled. 'I know who you are!'

Mine was a fleeting moment of triumph: the flicker of fear I engendered in him. Then everything was as before. The gun like a dog catching a scent. If a man ever gets you in a dark alley, Mammy used to say, be sure to make a lot of noise. I opened my mouth to scream out his name. Instantly, darkness enveloped me and something coarse and hairy pressed against my face. Blinded now, I was staggering around on the landing. I was panicked and there was a roar in my ears – Kevin's voice. Loud and then subdued to a gurgle.

What's happening?

Arms pressed hard around me until I was gasping for breath. Were they trying to suffocate me? Then the realization that I was struggling under a blanket, the same blanket that had been left out since that day Kevin and I had made love in the garden. Once there was light. Now there was only darkness. A voice that I recognized as mine wailed thin and high, as I tried to fight my way out of the woolly prison. I was helpless.

'Put her in the van.' That was him.

A boyish squeak. 'What for?'

'She knows.'

'What the fuck.'

'*Do it!*'

17

Every time the van hit a pothole, I was pitched violently against its metal side. A stabbing pain shot up my arm. My shoulders and elbows were sore and I wanted to cry out. Vainly I tried to keep upright as I half-sat, half-lay in the darkness. I could tell from the rocking sensation that the van had been driven off the main road and onto a track. As it lurched along, I wondered if it was being driven along a track at all or if we were moving out across open land.

Fear engulfed me. I was disoriented, unable to tell what direction we were heading in. I was lost. Would I ever be found?

When the smaller man had grabbed me and forced me out of the house, I had screamed as if my lungs would burst. Methodically the other man had carried on, placing Kevin's guns and boxes of ammunition on the floor of the front seat, then opening up the van doors. Meanwhile the smaller man had pulled the blanket off me and, after removing the scarf from around his mouth, tied it over mine. The acrid smell in my nostrils, the stale taste of cloth in my mouth. Nausea rose in my throat. I was afraid I would choke on my own vomit. He pulled a rope tight around my arms and body and then pushed me into the back of the van where I cowered, terror travelling through me like a poison.

A click of boots across the gravel. A long pause.

Then:

'Did you lock them in the bedroom?'

I recognized the voice. The breadman. Laura's friend.

'Aye.' The younger one, his voice barely audible.

The two men got into the front of the van and the engine roared into life.

In the darkness I couldn't see anything. The interior of the van was unlit and sour-smelling. As it shivered and rattled its way out through the gate, I fell against the side, my head crashing on metal. I was helpless, like a ball being thrown around in a box.

All my future was encapsulated into minutes in the back of a filthy van that was speeding along secret roads and turning off into a side-track leading deeper and deeper into the earth's centre for all I knew, lengthening the distance between me and the everything that made up my life: Kevin, our children, the house on the water's edge, the cat asleep on the windowsill. The argument between Kevin and me was a lifetime ago: an irrelevancey. He was locked up and helpless inside our bedroom. Even he could not protect me now.

I thought of the high walls of Derry and the skyline of buildings towering over the Bogside. The power of others had been the cause of Laura's nightmares: was it the reason now why the men had come looking for guns?

Was it? Any words that I framed were lost in the heavy material that gagged me. *It is not a dream.* My nose was itchy and I wanted to scratch it but I was trussed up like a chicken. A moan escaped through my pores, through the hair on my head, through the tears drying on my cheeks.

Suddenly I thought of Conor, his little white face at the top of the stairs and of Aoife asleep in her bed, her arm thrown out across the pillow, as she muttered faintly. Dreaming of puppies probably. She was safe; they were safe.

As my eyes got accustomed to the dark, I could make out, silhouetted against the windscreen, the two men. They continued to ignore me, as they had done from the moment they had bundled me into the van and locked the door. I did not exist. Maybe they would ignore me enough to leave me out on a hillside and hope I would never make it back. Maybe I still had a chance.

Every so often, the men talked to each other. At the start of the journey the young one had been loud, aggressive, his high-pitched voice rising above the engine's drone. '*You must,*' he kept saying, '*you must . . .*' The other one – the breadman – sounded agitated. He is afraid, I realized with surprise. Afraid of what? His responses were low and breathless, as if he were trapped. I strained to hear but I couldn't make out what he was saying.

'*Listen,*' the younger man said. '*Listen, you.*'

The other's reply was low, indistinct.

'No,' the younger man said, '*you don't have any choice.*'

Everyone has a choice, I wanted to cry out but my mouth was dry and sore inside its cloth cage. I was straining to catch the answer but there was none. Nothing except the sound of the engine.

Time was passing: minutes, hours maybe. I couldn't tell how many miles we had travelled. We could go on for ever, I thought, bumping along and me crashing against the wall every time the van hit a mound or a hollow, the night blanketing me against any chance of escape.

Abruptly the van stopped. I held my breath. The sound of

the engine died. For a long moment, nothing happened. Then I heard the sound of steps around to the back door and I was being pulled out, stumbling, between the two of them.

Listen, I tried to say to them, *listen to me* . . . but it was a whisper dying inside my mouth. Gagged and tied and bruised, I could barely move, my legs trembling so much I couldn't even stand. On each side of me the men gripped my arms and deliberately carried me forward. The air was a shock against my skin. It felt free and careless. I could see at last. Moonlight bathed the landscape in the luminous tones of a photographic negative but, after being locked inside the van for so long, I was blinded momentarily by the glare.

For a moment, it seemed as if no one had ever stood amidst the bracken and whin before this night and seen the curve and fall of the land, the black outline of a mountain above the valley of sleeping trees. Rocks scattered across the ground were white shoulders rising out of a carpet of vegetation. Below I could hear the roar of running water. A dab of spray spitting up from behind a rock was a clue to the hidden course of a river.

What river? Where was I?

The light came from high in the sky, a great silvery moon that smiled down on the scene. On me and the two men. Suddenly the air was full of promise and majesty. I resolved to run to the edge and drop down mindlessly into the valley below, to sink into the water's fall. With every muscle tensed, I made my attempt. Fast as I could, never looking back, running into the darkness and away.

When I tried to put one foot in front of the other I found that I could hardly walk. As I stumbled I wept and my tears blotted out everything: mountains and rocks and trees. Aoife and Conor inside my head. One had grown into a young man and the other a laughing woman. They were changed beyond recognition and yet they were still unmistakably my children. I wanted to call out to them and the woman, close by, who had her face turned away. Mamo, I wondered, or Mammy. Or me.

All emotion drained away. I had lost the ability to move, and now I was losing my ability to feel. Before me stood a young, dark-haired woman with smiling eyes and a streak of grey in her hair, and a pale thin man, dressed in tweed, looking thoughtfully past my shoulder. There was a dog at Aoife's side, an ebony walking stick in Conor's hand. The two of them did not see me but they were all I saw. All I wanted to see, the moonlight hardening around their images.

A cry of despair welled up from deep inside me. Johnny Doherty stood before me and loosened the gag around my mouth. I cried out but no sound came. My lips were too dry. My throat was dessiccated into dust. I could only mouth the words I wanted to say.

'Turn around,' he said.

Silence lengthened across the valley and up into the crowning sky and then, from behind me, came a rush of air in the boy's voice, high-pitched and anxious: 'Fuck's sake, hurry up! What are you waiting for? *Hurry up*!'

'Kneel down,' Johnny said.

A male cough, a discreet click – that was all I heard – and the night breeze whispering through the branches. In the moonlight a bird was opening its sleepy throat to sing when

WINTER 1970

Tom

18

His thoughts were like water cascading along a ravine and swirling around the hunched body caught in the rocks. There was no respite. No chance of rest. He hadn't bothered to close the curtains because night or day made no difference: he was always awake. Eventually, although it was dark, he got up and dressed himself by the light of the moon. Below the window, the dog yelped in the yard. After a rabbit, Tom thought, or maybe a rat.

Even when he was out of his bed, he knew that there was no peace to be had.

On the bedside table the framed photograph of his wife gleamed in the silvery light, her face frozen into a smile. Her eyes watching him as he laid out his good suit and the black tie he kept for funerals. He drew on his trousers and fixed the braces over his white shirt. Then, last of all, he put on his good shoes and stood before the dressing-table mirror and brushed his hair. When he had finished, he knelt down beside the bed to say his morning prayers but, even with his eyes closed and his face buried in his hands, he could find no relief. Still kneeling, he put out his hand and, turning towards the photograph, reached to pull it near to him. Her face was close now, more than a vague white smiling face above the neat collar of her dress. Her expression was so friendly and generous, his eyes filled with tears. He clutched the candlewick bedspread in his fists to smother the sound of his crying and, all the time, she was gazing at him as if nothing had changed, as if life was the way it had once been and that, somewhere out in the fields, she was picking a blackberry to place in his mouth.

He had never felt so alone.

In all the years of living on his own, he had managed to keep busy with the house, the farm and the Hunt. Now everything he had lived for had crumbled to dust. He sat back on his heels and said over and over, '*Marnie, Marnie, Marnie* . . .'

Ever smiling, she was blind to him. Silence filled the room as he wiped his eyes and stood up, easing out the stiffness in his legs. Deliberately he turned the framed photograph over and left it lying face-down on the bedspread.

The garden was lit by a grey pre-dawn light. Dew glistened on the grass. A ragged mist still clung to the trees as he stepped out into the chilly air. In his hand he carried a coil of rope which he measured out carefully: one length for the dog, six lengths for himself. He marked it with a knife and then placed the rope on the tree stump that he used for chopping wood. The axe cut through the rope cleanly on the mark that he had made and he picked up the short length and put it inside his coat. The longer length of rope he left coiled up on the kitchen table when he went back into the house to get his keys.

206

The car was slow to start. Then at last, to his relief, the engine kicked into life and he drove down the brightening driveway. Once he was out on the road, he turned the car towards Newtowncunningham. Behind him the dog stood up on the back seat, wagging her tail and panting at his shoulder.

Annie Dwyer was sixty-eight years old and had a pincushion face and untidy grey hair. She was a kind, slovenly woman who had tried to get close to Tom after Marnie died. She had brought him apple tarts and plates of wizened scones for which he had thanked her courteously before politely closing his door on her.

'Tom Mundy!' she said when she saw him. 'What has you about so early?'

She led him into the kitchen which was still cold from the night before. There were dishes in the sink and the floor was unswept. Hurriedly she pinned up her hair as, with a sigh, she caught sight of herself in the mirror on the shelf over the stove.

'Sit down, sit down, will you,' she said, pulling out a chair for him, but he remained standing. When she turned towards him and saw his clothes, she said, 'Ah, the poor wee lass. I hear two forestry men found her.'

Tom said nothing.

'But I could have sworn that the priest said the funeral was tomorrow. Or is someone else dead that I don't know about?'

He pretended not to hear and said, 'Annie, I need a favour.'

'You know you only have to ask.'

'Would you mind the dog for a wee while?'

Puzzled, she looked down at Liadh. The dog had lain down on the rag rug in front of the stove and gone to sleep. 'I will indeed. She'll be company.' She looked meaningfully at Tom. 'I get lonely too, you know.'

He looked past her towards the window where daylight was streaming in. At the back doorstep, he noticed there was a tin basin overflowing with potato peelings and cabbage leaves. He drew out the piece of rope that he had brought with him, tied a noose at one end of it and said, 'See, Annie, this is a lead for her if you take her out. You slip this part over her head and it'll tighten if she tries to run away.'

Annie took the rope and pulled it between her hands. 'Where would I be going with a dog, I wonder?' she chuckled. She looked up at him and noticed the pallor on his cheeks. 'Tom, you don't look well.'

'I'm all right.'

'Now that you're here,' she said, 'you'll surely have some tea and maybe a boiled egg?' At their age it was always better not to ask a body what ails them, she thought, for fear of what they might tell you.

But no, Tom would not stay. To her surprise, he shook her hand without speaking. Then he turned on his heel and left the house without saying another word. When she had closed the back door after him, the dog leapt up, whining and scraping at the window.

'*No no!*' the woman said, giving the dog a tip on its nose with the end of the rope.

The dog looked astonished and sat down abruptly. Annie laughed and eased herself into the armchair beside the stove. She stretched her arms above her head and opened her mouth in a yawn. Resigned now, the dog rested its head on the woman's knee and closed its eyes.

'There's only the two of us now,' Annie said aloud. Then it struck her that she hadn't asked Tom when he was coming back for his dog.

When he returned home, Tom boiled the kettle and took

down the last of the chocolate biscuits from a tin in the cupboard. He filled the pot with an extra spoonful of tea leaves so that when the tea was poured out it was black and sour-tasting, the way he liked it. By contrast, the chocolate was rich and sweet. He sat at the kitchen table. The sweet and sour tastes on his tongue filled him with an unholy joy. He felt free for the first time since the day when he had heard of the disappearance of Rosaleen McAvady.

When he looked up, he saw her face smiling at him in the photograph propped up on the dresser. His young neighbour. For a long time he sat at the table without moving, his hand resting on the coil of rope. At his elbow the last of the tea in the pot went cold and there was nothing left on the plate but a few crumbs. With a grunt, he stood up and carried the cup, saucer and plate over to the sink, washed them and left them to dry on the plate rack. As he did so, he thought of the two women who were in the house now: one above in the bedroom and the other one, with her laughing eyes, all around him. He imagined their spirits, free to roam without hindrance, through the house and out across the fields.

Tom Mundy picked up the rope and looped it over his shoulder. He looked around the kitchen: at the table and chairs, the window over the sink and then he walked out into the garden for the last time.

PART TWO

DUBLIN 1998

Aoife

19

Aoife McAvady is a serious young woman. She has a broad forehead and eyes set wide apart. She doesn't smile much but, when she does, the effect is startling: as if a veil has been torn aside to reveal a luminous flash. She has no illusions about her looks. If anyone compliments her on her appearance, she becomes embarrassed and shakes her head.

'Actually, I think I look like a cow,' she says quickly as if to choke off the words before they gain currency.

Aoife's friends laugh when they hear her response, but she has a point: there *is* a bovine quality to her face. Far from making her appear unattractive, people generally find the characteristic appealing. They feel comfortable in her presence and reassured by her air of placid unconcern. According to her curriculum vitae, Aoife is reliable, honest, hard-working and able to cope well in a crisis – and, in her case, the curriculum vitae is a true reflection of her capabilities. Her unruffled manner makes her seem young for her age. The fact that her thirty-sixth birthday is imminent and there is no sign of a boyfriend in her life is a cause of some concern to her friends.

'I am perfectly happy the way I am,' she insists.

Privately she wonders if she feels any emotion deeply. Happiness or sadness are words that she understands the meaning of and yet, somehow, neither describes her true feelings. Or the lack of them. Contentment, satisfaction, the satiation of desire: these states of mind she understands but she knows for some inexplicable reason they are inadequate when compared to the emotions that other people take for granted. Falling in love. Hate. Anger. Heartbreak. Secretly she considers such emotions to be messy and extreme.

Am I happy now? she wonders as she turns the key in the lock and opens the door of the veterinary clinic. Inside the air reeks of animals and disinfectant. She picks up a pile of letters from the floor and puts them on the reception counter. Daylight struggles through the venetian blinds as she pulls up the shutters and lets light into the rooms. As the clinic manager, Aoife makes it her business to be at work earlier than the others. The nurse always comes in shortly after her, followed usually by the receptionist and, by the time the veterinary surgeon arrives, everything is set up and ready for him. Aoife enjoys the period of calm that precedes the disturbances of the day. She walks along the narrow corridor that leads to the examination room and, when she flicks a switch, there is a cold fluorescent call to action. Beyond the examination room, in the back of the building, two dogs sleep in their cages. A shaggy mound opens a bleary eye and blinks. Aoife kneels down and puts her finger through the wire but the animal shrinks back.

'Idiot dog,' she says and stands up to leave.

She unlocks the door of her little office. The walls are plain and unadorned, the desktop cleared, the wastepaper basket emptied. It is the only room in the clinic that hasn't been colonised by the smell of animals. Yes, she thinks, it is a relief to be back and to find her office unchanged. The room is as clean as an egg, just the way she likes it. It doesn't suit Aoife to be away from her job. She prides herself on her reliability but the last few days she was so sick – vomiting, diarrhoea, the lot – that eventually she phoned for a doctor. Into her apartment arrived a small, coffee-coloured doctor who spoke with a cheery Bengali lilt. He sat on her bed and asked her questions. Then he closed up his medical bag and pronounced that she was suffering from an SKV.

'Madam,' he said, 'you have an SKV – some kind of virus – and the only treatment is to drink a lot of water and to have bed rest.'

Five minutes was all it took and the doctor, still chuckling, left her apartment with a cheque that she could ill-afford nestling in his breast pocket.

'Welcome back, Aoife.'

A helmet of greying hair over a bony face: the veterinary nurse stopping for a moment on her way towards the back room to hang up her coat.

'Thank you.'

'Everything is better?'

The nurse is older than Aoife: Justina, a middle-aged Polish woman who likes to disappear into the back room to smoke a cigarette when the waiting room is choking up with people and bad-tempered, sick animals.

Aoife nods.

'Jacob is on his way.'

Jacob. The nurse never fails to remind Aoife that she and the vet are on first-name terms. Unlike Aoife.

If she only knew . . . Aoife thinks, smiling a ghost of a smile, her head down over her work.

Outside the office window a car door bangs. Aoife looks up but she does not move from her desk. She slips her hand into her handbag and takes out a lipstick and a tiny mirror. For an instant, her full lips and tranquil eyes gaze back at her and then they disappear into the pocket of her jacket as the door to her office is opened.

Jacob Smith has the shoulders and thick neck of a rugby forward. His skin has a burnished look and his glossy black hair is speckled with grey. The impression is of a powerful presence, tense and muscular, inside his well-cut suit. On catching sight of Aoife he grins broadly. All's well in the world, he tells himself.

'Good morning, Aoife. Nice to see you back.'

'Good morning, Mr Smith.'

A fugitive moment: their eyes barely meeting before he vanishes down the corridor, calling out for the nurse in a cheery rasp.

The day passes unremarkably. The receptionist is on leave, so Aoife sits in the waiting room as it fills up with people and their pets. In the afternoon the nurse takes over and Aoife is glad to escape into the haven of her office. She is in the middle of sorting out tax returns when the door opens.

'Come into my office,' Jacob Smith says. 'I've something to show you.'

She stands up and follows him down the corridor. His office is even smaller than hers and when they sit down their knees collide. A whiff of sweat when he swivels around on his chair and raises his arm to lift a file down from a shelf. They sit, shoulder to shoulder, and everything about him is too close for comfort: the slight soapy smell of his hair, the vein throbbing at his temple. She shifts on her chair, and tries to concentrate as drawing after drawing is unfolded in front of her.

'Here is . . .' he jabs with a fingernail, '*That's where* . . .' He frowns, his lower lip jutting slightly, as he displays the contents of the file.

Aoife forms a vague outline of what he is showing her – a low, white building with a tall chimney, surrounded by grass and hedging – hills in the distance and a sleek aluminium sign in the foreground.

'So what d'you think?' He clasps his hands behind his head and, almost barking with delight, rocks back on his chair, away from her now. His face is flushed.

She says, 'Well, I . . .'

'I know what you're going to say.'

'Really?'

'Planning permission. I know.' He straightens up. 'Well, the answer is I haven't got it yet, but it's the only thing left for me to do. The final missing piece.'

'I wasn't going to say that.'

'I'm already working on it.'

'Actually,' she says, 'I was going to ask if you've thought this plan through.'

'Indeed I have. I'm going to call it The Jacob Smith Pet Crematorium.'

She pauses. For a moment laughter threatens in her throat.

'I mean about the implications,' she says.

'It's in a perfect location.'

Undeterred, she continues, 'I just wonder if you've worked out the financial implications. The costs of servicing the debt could crucify you. And your practice here could suffer if you're sidetracked into another venture, particularly a venture in the back of beyond. Where is it anyway?'

I don't need to hear this, he thinks, least of all from her.

'Aaaw, feck it, Aoife!' He hunches forward, glowering, gripping the arms of his chair.

She bites her lip. 'You did ask me for my opinion.'

Then she lowers her voice and rests her hand gently on his tensed fist.

'Jacob, you're the boss around here,' she says. 'So whatever you say goes.'

'It's in the midlands. Fantastic site. Just *wait* 'til you see it, Aoife.'

It's as if he hasn't heard her criticism, as if nothing she says matters compared to the rush of adrenalin that he's experiencing.

A small boy's grin brightens his face. 'I've got an option on the land. I'm almost there. It won't only be used by the clinic here. Every vet in the country has disposal problems. They'll all want to use it.'

In the cramped space of the office, his exuberance is suddenly overpowering. She looks down at his hands, the knobby joints, the fingers drumming on the desk.

'We'll talk about it later,' he says, his eyes full of excitement, 'you and me, when the time is right.'

She understands the secret sign he is giving her.

Aoife lives in a one-bedroomed apartment in Sandymount. It is in a newly built block, a restrained four-storey cube made out of brick and glass, occupying a corner site with a view – if she stands on a chair in the bathroom and looks out through the tiny frosted window – of the sea. She has bought the apartment with a bank loan that leaves her with hardly any spare cash after she has paid the mortage and household bills, but the sense of security that comes from owning her home fills her with satisfaction.

She has her father to thank for the apartment. He provided the deposit that enabled her to buy it. She feels guilty when she thinks about him and how tough it was to shoulder responsibility for them all and move to Dublin with two small children and their Auntie Maureen, who had agreed to leave her house in Letterkenny in order to mind them.

Once they were settled in the house in Ballinteer, their father drove off to work, every morning, leaving an uneasy trio behind.

Auntie Maureen believed in discipline, well-polished shoes and tidy bedrooms. By the time she was nine years old, Aoife had embarked on an underground campaign to thwart her aunt in every way she could. It was a war that neither one could win. *Wait 'til your father gets home*, her aunt's final resort.

Aoife can still see the tiredness in her father's face, his eyes emptying when he came in through the front door to be met by his sister's litany of complaint. In silence, he ushered Aoife into the living room and shut the door behind them. Once Aoife had been wary of her father but now she sensed something broken in him that made her fearless.

'Now, young lady, you're going to apologise to your aunt.'

'I won't.'

Father and daughter eyeballing each other. Both of them stockily built and flat-faced. A mirror-image, one in miniature.

'Come on, Aoife, you have to.'

She shook her head.

'Jesus Christ.' He glared at her.

She didn't flinch but when he turned away she felt suddenly bereft.

'Daddy . . .'

His back to her now. Shoulders hunched, he didn't speak, just shook his head. His attention was concentrated elsewhere. Without even knowing it, he had won.

'All right then,' she said so that he would come back to her.

He turned and smiled.

She looked up at him sternly. 'But I won't mean it.'

On the road where they lived there were no secrets. Mr Mallen at Number 14 wasn't working in England like his wife said. He was being dried out in St Patrick's hospital. Everyone knew about Mrs Agnew in Number 5 going manic and thwacking Simon Heavey on the head with a sweeping brush for no good reason and how he ran all the way home, his schoolbag bouncing on his back. On the road Conor and Aoife were '*the poor things*', the children without a mother, while the neighbours treated their father with a shy respect. Occasionally their father tried to get Conor to join the other fathers with their sons on the road in a game of football but Conor resisted. He didn't like sports. He preferred to stay in the bedroom he shared with Aoife, drawing fantastical monsters and making models of dinosaurs.

While Auntie Maureen slept in the front bedroom with the double bed, their father slept in the box-room. It wasn't right: the biggest person in the house occupying the smallest room. There was something about the cramped space, the unadorned walls, the worn carpet that put the idea into Aoife's mind that their father was planning his exit: that one day he would leave them without any fuss and disturbance.

Then, in 1976, without warning, he lost his job and began to take up two-month contracts in Saudi Arabia. The first time Aoife saw the suitcase open on his bed, she was paralysed with fear.

Even now the memory is vivid: of her father standing in the hallway in the house in Ballinteer. He was dressed in pale slacks and a linen jacket, everything about him suddenly new and unfamiliar.

'Promise me you'll be a good girl for your Auntie Maureen,' he said.

This Aoife found impossible to do. She clung to him, howling, until he prised her fingers off his arm, picked up his suitcase and went out to the taxi waiting outside.

'I'm telling you, we are going to be orphans,' she told her brother later. 'He'll die in the desert and then we'll have no mammy or daddy.'

At this news, Conor burst into tears. Instantly, she felt better and put her arm along his narrow shoulders to comfort him.

Around that time Conor took to sleeping on the floor. While Aoife slept in the top bunk, Conor had slept in the lower bunk until he chose to lie out on the floor, wrapped up in a duvet and with a pair of runners for a pillow.

'Why?' Aoife asked.

When she was on the point of drifting off to sleep, he muttered: 'My things.'

His things: the collection of objects he had suspended on lengths of thread from the webbed underside of her bunk. In pride of place was the skull of a bird he had found in the garden, so light that its beaked profile swung gently when the bedroom window was left open. Later he added a sea urchin, seedpods, dried thistle heads, a plastic dinosaur, a child's red handbag dredged out of the stream at the bottom of the road, a broken china cup from the dump, an old Hallowe'en mask. In the bunk-bed gloom, the array of suspended shapes and colours acquired a vague air of menace. He kept adding to the collection until there was no space left and his move out of bed and onto the floor became inevitable.

'They're jujus,' she said helpfully to Auntie Maureen who looked cross, as if it were Aoife's fault that her brother engaged in unnatural practices.

By this time Aoife had developed an interest in the

paranormal, voodoo in particular, along with a growing attachment to heavy metal bands.

With their father gone there was no protector, no intervening figure of authority. Auntie Maureen had sole control but, although she was only twelve years old, Aoife could sense the older woman's anxiety.

'*Bamboula, bodoum, bodoum!*' she said loudly just to watch Auntie Maureen jump.

Eventually life became easier for everyone. Aoife moved into the box-room and, when their father came home on his visits, he slept on a pull-out couch in the living room.

When Conor was seventeen, he went to Bolton Street to study architecture, while Aoife, with bad grace, went into her second year on a business course, having got abysmal marks in the Leaving Cert. Auntie Maureen went home to Letterkenny and there was no-one to care if the gutters choked with weeds or the manhole in the back garden blocked up and sewage seeped out over the overgrown lawn. Each time their father came back from Saudi Arabia he spent his days doing repairs before he headed off again but, despite his best efforts, he could not prevent the house's inexorable descent into decrepitude. At last he decided to put it out of its misery and, before long, a *For Sale* sign was poking up over the front-garden hedge.

'I've done my best for you both,' he said to Aoife and Conor. 'It's time you flew the coop – time we all flew the coop. There's nothing to keep us here any more.'

Then he told them he had moved in with a woman in Riyadh and that he intended to settle down with her. As he spoke he was smiling, and Aoife realized that in all the years they had lived in Ballinteer she had never seen her father look happy.

Evening is drawing in, darkening the car park below her

window where cars are lined up, sleek and wet, like a row of fish on a slab. She keeps returning to the window, only to find the scene unchanged. Then, at last, the arrival of a monster with chrome bull-bars and spotlights fixed to the roof: Jacob's jeep. Inside, she knows, it stinks of dogs and the back seat is full of boxes of veterinary products spilling out onto the floor. Among the Fiats and Ford Cortinas parked in front of the apartment block, the jeep looks enormous and out of place. She wonders, sometimes, what the neighbours think. But, since she is hardly aware of their existence, she imagines that her presence is as peripheral to their lives as theirs are to hers. Occasionally she sees the back of a woman pulling a baby buggy up the stairs, or a young man clutching a briefcase as he heads for the bus stop. She has lived in the apartment for three years and likes the anonymity that surrounds each resident. She could be dead for days and nobody would notice. Perversely, she takes comfort in the thought.

The intercom buzzes. Aoife lifts the receiver immediately. Damn, she thinks. Too eager. Not a good idea to show it.

'The door's open. Come on up,' she says, her voice higher than she would like.

A glance at the mirror in the little hall of her apartment. Shadowy eyes peer back at her, a fringe of black hair above the flat planes of her cheeks. On her face is a look of anticipation. Hanged for a sheep or a lamb. Or, in her case, hanged for a cow. When the doorbell rings, she smiles at her reflection.

Jacob is standing outside in the corridor. He's dressed as if he's setting out for a day's fishing. He has on the full outfit: Barbour waterproof jacket and trousers, a tweed hat with flies stuck into the brim, and a pair of waders.

She looks at him, astonished. 'Why are you –?'

Laughing loudly, he lumbers into the little hall and crushes her in his arms. The smell of rubberized cotton thickening in her nose, she feels momentarily smothered by his embrace. She pulls back – she is the same height as he is – and stares at him.

'Ha, I surprised you, eh?'

'Jacob, why on earth are you dressed like that?'

He chortles. 'Give me a drink first, Aoife.'

He sweeps into the living room, sits down heavily on the sofa and begins to remove his waders.

He may be fifty-seven years old but he's just an overgrown child, Aoife thinks, and picks up each wader before it lands on her cream wool carpet. Along with his hat and coat, she stuffs them into the tiny cupboard in the hall.

'A jolly good idea! I told her I was going night fishing on the river. Won't be home 'til all hours, I told her. Then I thought I'd dress up in my gear and give you a laugh.'

Her. His wife whom Aoife has seen occasionally in the clinic, coming out and nodding at Aoife before disappearing through a haze of expensive perfume, into the sports car that takes up two car spaces in the yard. She is fine-boned, his wife, with a high forehead and pale blonde hair that seems to spring out of the top of her head and curve in behind her ears into a discreet French knot. When she smiles, she reveals a row of little pointed teeth. There is something evanescent about Jacob's wife, Carol. The pearl necklace, the sleek black clothes, the Hermes scarves and camel-hair coat that she favours heighten her air of otherworldiness. Her face looks as if it's made of bone – delicate, cold and expressionless. The effect is fey and spookily dramatic at the same time. Dracula's Bride comes into Aoife's mind whenever she sees Mrs Jacob Smith.

Is it guilt that makes Aoife think that way about Jacob's wife? The truth is she hardly ever thinks about her, nor does she dwell on their two children: the teenage boys who attend Castleknock College and excel at rugby and whom Aoife has never met. Actually Aoife doesn't feel guilty about the affair. After all, she never sought out Jacob. She isn't one of those people who set out to ensnare a successful moneyed man in order to secure a comfortable old age. She has seen women like that in the foyers of expensive Dublin hotels, pretty young things clinging to ageing, grey-faced men – men whom, she notices, all have the same expression on their faces: a look of satisfied vanity mixed with bewilderment. Their eyes inquiring, how did this happen?

Aoife had sworn that she would never go out with a married man, no matter how tempted she was, and yet that is exactly what she has done. With a great, unquestioning swoop, Jacob Smith, husband and father, captured her. When she started working at the veterinary clinic, she was in awe of him and the truth is – not that she would ever show it – that she still is. To have ended up as the other woman was never her intention, but there is something irresistible about Jacob – his generosity, his boyish enthusiasm, his knowledge of the world – and he is the first man, the only man, who has ever been able to satisfy her sexually.

When he saunters past her into her little apartment, she feels a familiar sense of inadequacy. What does he see in her? He is too suave, too hearty, too rich for her and yet, without question, he has been the pursuer, she the pursued. Relentlessly he brought her down as if she were one of the deer that he likes to hunt in winter. He is the quintessential hunting, shooting, fishing type, he told her over their first dinner together. In the restaurant, the lights were turned down so low it seemed to her that everybody in the place must be having an illicit affair. Even so, as she peered in the half-light at a menu full of unfamiliar French dishes, she was terrified that someone might see them together. Jacob had laughed heartily and ordered a bottle of champagne to celebrate what, he said, was the start of a beautiful friendship.

'I'm an ordinary man, Aoife. What you see is what you get,' he said after the dessert plates had been cleared and he clasped her hand . . . and she understood that he could just as easily have added, *And what I see I get* . . .

His eyes were smiling but she could not say that she knew him.

Even now, he is a mystery to her, despite his protestations of simplicity.

'Night fishing?'

'On the river, at night, you can fool the fish.'

How did this happen, she asks herself yet again as she goes into the kitchen for two glasses. It has happened, she decides, because she finds their affair exciting: the secrecy and intrigue, the undertow of intimacy. It makes her feel alive.

Jacob has eased off his jacket and waterproof trousers. Underneath he is wearing a canary-coloured sweater and faded jeans.

'Come here to me, my darling girl.'

And she runs into the sunny embrace of his arms. He hums a tune as his lips touch her hair. *Bumdidibumdidibum* . . . she recognises the William Tell Overture.

'*The Lone Ranger*,' he says when he sees her puzzlement. 'The television series, remember?'

She shakes her head. She probably wasn't born, she tells him.

'God, I forgot. Of course not,' he says. 'Hero of my youth. *Bumbumbumbaah!*' He traces his finger down her cheek. 'I'll be the Lone Ranger and you can be Tonto.'

'I'd rather be the Lone Ranger, thank you very much.' She speaks more sharply than she intended but he doesn't take offence.

He grins with delight and then draws her head nearer until his mouth is close to her ear.

'Oh, Aoife, don't think you can fool me,' he whispers. 'You are hard on the outside but I know that you are soft inside.'

In reply, she whispers into his neck, 'Oh Jacob, I hate to disappoint you but in my case it's the other way round: I'm soft on the outside and hard on the inside.'

Jacob throws back his head and laughs. *Honk, honk, honk,* like a parched sea lion. His lips crushed on hers, his arm strung around her shoulders, they stagger into the bedroom.

In bed it seems to her that they are fighting, so fiercely passionate is their lovemaking, butting each other, biting and licking and stroking skin, ear, mouth, buttock.

Afterwards they fall back into the pillows, panting and sweaty.

'It's like animals rutting,' she mutters into the pillow.

Jacob agrees. 'Most people don't understand how closely humans resemble animals.'

He turns to look at her, his dark eyes liquid and pleading, his curly speckled black hair. A cocker spaniel, she decides.

'Tell me you love me,' he says.

'I'm not sure that I even like you,' she says.

He grips her arms and draws them above her head on the pillow and lies on top of her. '*Tell me.*'

'Get off me, you gorilla!' she shouts, laughing.

'Say it!'

'Believe me, Jacob, I'd love a drink more.'

Immediately he rolls off her and pads out of the room. She hears the suck of the cork and the gurgle of liquid first into one glass, then into the other. She lies back and gazes at the ceiling. So, she wonders, am I happy now?

They stay in bed, drinking wine and watching television, until it is time for him to go.

Aoife likes the way he is unfazed by her bluntness. Unlike other men who have wanted to change her, Jacob glories in her as she is. Other men may find her independence a threat but, she realizes, nothing could possibly dent Jacob's supreme self-confidence. It is a by-product, no doubt, of being raised in a family of a doting mother and sisters. Not that he talks much about his background, but Aoife imagines a large south Dublin house with a maid and cars in the driveway behind high wrought-iron gates. Once he told her that his mother was determined to have a lawyer for a son and that his decision to become a vet caused ructions. His wife, too, would have preferred a lawyer – or, better still, a judge – he intimates, but he doesn't talk about his home life. And Aoife doesn't ask. She likes the nature of their lovemaking: unquestioning, instinctual, mindless. It excites her, the animal coupling, all intensity without emotion, and the way Jacob, when he's coming to an orgasm, opens his throat and howls with pleasure. In her work at the clinic she has learnt more about human nature than she ever expected: how people can be more demonstrative with their pets than with their own children; how human cruelty can be magnified when unleashed on animals; how grief can be as heartfelt over a lost pet as for a dead spouse – sometimes more; how quickly, if let, dogs learn to dominate their owners; how you can end up resembling your dog but no one ever ends up looking like their cat. And to prove the point, jowly, droopy-eyed men come trundling into the clinic with their basset hounds or on one occasion, a young woman, pert and snub-nosed, arrives with a poodle on her arm.

'But,' Aoife wonders aloud to Jacob, 'why dogs? I mean married couples don't end up looking like each other.'

'I suppose it's the lesser of two evils.'

Deep in thought, Aoife doesn't laugh.

'Here's a test,' Jacob says. 'If you put your dog and your wife in the boot of your car and come back two hours later . . .'

Aoife looks at him.

'Which one of them will be glad to see you?' Jacob laughs loud enough for the two of them.

She will never own a pet, Aoife decides, in case she ends up looking like it. Then she thinks of Jacob. Maybe she feels that way because he fills a gap in her life the way a pet would. In between their bouts of lovemaking, there are times that are devoid of any real connection between them. When they meet secretly they are two people with one purpose in mind and, when that purpose is satisfied, she is impatient to see the back of him.

At midnight he slings the waders and waterproofs jauntily over his back and turns to kiss her again before opening the apartment door.

'Don't you have to put those on?' she asks, pointing to the waders.

'Naah. Only did that to give you a laugh.'

'But won't she . . . your wife . . . won't she wonder? I mean, you've no fish to bring home after your night on the river.'

'Listen, if I brought home a fish and told her I'd caught it, she'd know something was up.'

And yet, Aoife thinks, you caught me.

At the door he stops and looks into her eyes. 'Listen, about that planning permission . . .'

His voice is low as if they are joined in some new conspiracy. His eyebrows, she notices, have white hairs among the black. He seems older, suddenly, now that there is less of the bombast about him and he is looking at her almost plaintively.

'Yes?'

Of course she will go with him to the meeting. Gently she strokes his neck while he stands, eyes closed, a look of ecstasy on his face. At times like this she understands instinctively how, without any effort, she is able to reach out and encompass the very edges of his personality.

20

Driving through the rain across the midland tracts of bog, Jacob almost misses the turn for Carnshaugh. Swearing, he swings the car around to turn down a road that runs through the fields. This whole thing, he is convinced, is a test set by malcontents and bureaucrats. His pet incinerator is state of the art and Carnfuckingshaugh is lucky to get it but, he has been advised, before he gets planning permission, the local people have to have their say.

'Well, once they've had their say,' he mutters to Aoife, 'then I'll have my way.'

The road is narrow and winding and it takes them a long time to get to the parish hall. Jacob and Aoife know they've arrived at the right place when they are met by long lines of cars, jeeps and trucks parked up on either side of the roadway.

'It looks like a country funeral,' Aoife says to him.

'Well,' he says, 'it better not be mine.'

Three people stand huddled at the gates of the parish hall. Jacob growls under his breath. 'Fuck me, it's a welcoming committee.'

He drives the Mercedes up to the gates, stops the car and rolls down the window. The woman in the group comes forward and bends in to speak to him. She is of slight build and indeterminate age, with mouse-coloured hair.

'I'm Mrs May Condell.'

'Aha, I see.'

Then she giggles, 'I'm the troublemaker who organised the meeting.'

Up close, Mrs Condell has the look of a neglected cat, in her shapeless, salt-and-pepper tweed coat. There are traces of prettiness in her heart-shaped face and melancholy eyes. She introduces the man beside her. A local farmer, she tells them. Sam Cowen is impressively taciturn and stands rooted to the spot, a giant of a man who towers over the other two. The caretaker of the hall makes up the last member of the group. A wiry little man with burnt black eyes, he runs to open up the gates and waves them onto the gravel area in front of the hall.

When they get out of the car, Jacob introduces Aoife as his office manager – and to her surprise – his project co-ordinator. On hearing this, three sets of eyes swivel in her direction. Polite, guarded expressions on their faces. Gravely, hands are shaken all around.

The caretaker bends apologetically towards Jacob: 'Sir, if you wouldn't mind putting the car around the back, please, sir?'

Jacob gets back into the driving seat, wrapping his coat around his knees while Aoife jumps in beside him. He starts up the engine and slowly edges the Mercedes across the gravelled area to swing it around to the car park behind the hall. After turning off the engine, he leans across to open the glove compartment, takes out a hip flask, unscrews the silver top and has a swig.

'Want some?'

She shakes her head.

He takes another drink. The flask disappears into his pocket.

'So far we've met the obnoxious, the obtuse and the obsequious.' He slaps her knee playfully. 'Things can only get worse.'

'If it's all right with you, we'll have the meeting now and you can have a cup of tea after,' Mrs Condell says.

'Oh, I'm ready if you are,' Jacob says, all false bonhomie.

He strides ahead. The others follow him through the door. The parish hall is full and thrumming with people. Under the fluorescent lights, they sit in rows of plastic chairs or stand, leaning against the pea-coloured walls. Everything is bathed in a warm protective haze of cigarette smoke, floor polish, manure, traces of cooked cabbage and a faint steam rising from wet overcoats.

At one end of the hall there is a stage with steps up to it. Mrs Condell walks up onto the stage and sits down at the table to face the crowd. Sam Cowen lumbers up the steps and takes his place beside her. She beckons Jacob to join them. As he steps up to the stage, the conversation in the hall suddenly dies. Aoife takes her seat in the front row. As she waits for the meeting to begin, she turns discreetly to look behind her and is confronted by a phalanx of expressionless stares.

The meeting begins with a rambling explanation from Mrs Condell as to why a pet crematorium is not wanted in the village of Carnshaugh.

'Carnshaugh is a community and we want to keep it that

way. For our children and our children's children. We've nothing against the proposers and I'm sure they know what they're doing . . . I'm not technically minded myself . . .' She bends in the direction of Jacob. 'We've nothing at all against development but the environmental hazard is our main cause of concern.'

By the time she is finished she must have said it twenty times like a mantra: *environmental hazard*. Jacob listens to her patiently, although Aoife can tell, by the way he shifts around on his chair and keeps criss-crossing his legs, that he is fit to be tied. Eventually Mrs Condell turns to him.

'Now, ladies and gentlemen,' she says breathlessly, 'we have invited a distinguished guest. Mr Smith. To explain. Everything.'

She sits down and clasps her hands to her heaving breast. Silence greets Jacob when he stands up, an easy smile on his lips. His air of authority is underlined by the broad shoulders under his camel-hair coat, the pale blue shirt and matching tie, the thick wedding ring, the polished black shoes.

'Before I begin, I would like to ask you all a question.' He pauses, as if he has forgotten what he is about to say. Then, as if he has just remembered, he looks around at the audience. 'Tell me, how many of you here own a pet?'

A hand goes up. One after the other until almost everyone in the room has their hand up.

'So many,' he muses. 'Now think of that figure multiplied by thousands more in every community across the country. We love our pets and want the best for them, don't we? These days it just isn't good enough that we keep burying our pets any old way when they die. For one thing we run the risk of polluting our water courses. Being country people you know better than I do that when it comes to environmental hazard, water pollution is the biggest threat to our future. This enterprise – *our* enterprise – provides for a form of disposal that is state of the art. Believe me, it is *clean – clean – clean*.' Each time he says the word he punches the table softly with his fist. As he gazes around the hall, he continues to speak in a seductive, reassuring tone. He seems to grow and fill the space, in the way he reaches out to the audience and tells them that they live in this lovely place and that he understands their concerns. Indeed, that he would have the same concerns himself if he didn't know better and can assure them that he wants to keep Carnshaugh the way it is. Just like they do. And he wants to see progress that is well ordered and well managed. Just like they do. And there is something else, he reminds them almost apologetically: it would mean some employment for local people. And Carnshaugh would benefit from the visitors. Spending money on petrol, food, that kind of thing. The facility would be for the public good. 'For the good,' he emphasises slowly and delicately, 'of the *community*.'

The atmosphere in the hall is expectant now. Hushed.

When he has finished speaking, Jacob sits down and looks modestly at his hands. Now that he has netted his prize, he thinks, it's better not to be seen to gloat. From the audience comes the sound of scattered applause. Gracefully, he leans across and smiles at Mrs Condell, saying audibly, 'Thank you, Madam Chairman, I've taken up too much of your time.'

Blushing pinkly, Mrs Condell shuffles her papers and pats her hair.

What now? Aoife wonders.

Jacob catches her eye. Imperceptibly one eyelid droops.

Aoife bites her lip. Can it really be that simple?

Mrs Condell stands up and stammers out her thanks to everyone who has come, to the caretaker, to the parish priest and, most of all, to their distinguished guest who has taken the time.

Suddenly there is a squealing sound of a chair being pushed back on the floor. In the middle of the crowd a woman in a shabby white mackintosh is standing up and waving her arms to attract the attention of Mrs Condell.

'*Dammit, May*! Stop wittering on and give the rest of us a chance to speak.'

A rush of laughter bellies up from the floor. The woman's face is the colour of lard. A scarf patterned with horses' heads is draped over her shoulders. She waits for silence.

Then:

'Now I want to say something.'

Around her people lean back in their chairs in anticipation.

The woman straightens up. Her arms look as if they're double-jointed, the way she waves them about, to accentuate each point she makes.

'I'd like to welcome Mr Smith here to Carnshaugh parish hall. I hope he had a pleasant journey down from Dublin and I hope that his journey home is just as pleasant,' she pauses, 'and just as quick.'

A ripple of laughter runs through the audience.

'Mr Smith, maybe you think we're a bit simple now, being country folk like,' she continues, 'but from what I know of this parish, you could learn a thing or two from the people around here and what they think of this plan of yours.'

Stonily Jacob stares ahead.

'And just in case any of you here don't know who I am,' she swings around to address the crowd, 'I'll introduce myself. Bridget Wall, county councillor, at your service.'

A ragged cheer from the back of the hall.

She gazes around, waiting for silence and then continues, 'And I was elected by you good people to represent *your* interests. Not the interests of big business.'

An ancient man with a ravaged face, sitting beside Aoife, promptly drops his walking stick on the floor and begins to clap. Noisily the audience join in.

The woman lifts her hand to quieten them. 'And I was not elected to let an outsider come in here and pollute our homes and destroy our environment.'

The audience holds its collective breath as she pulls a document out of her coat pocket. She is in no hurry to proceed.

When she speaks again, her tone is silken. 'I have in my hand here a report that everyone is welcome to read. In particular, I invite Mr Smith to read it carefully.' With a flourish she riffles through the pages. 'This report has been prepared by experts who know all about incineration. And their findings prove, beyond doubt, something about incineration that the rest of us have always suspected.'

She holds up the report for all to see.

Then, with steely exactness, she says, 'This proves that incineration produces dioxins.'

Suddenly agitated, Jacob rises to speak, but he is ignored. The woman has grabbed all the audience's attention.

'Personally speaking, until yesterday I didn't even know what dioxins are. But I do now. I know and everyone in this hall needs to know that we are talking cancer here. Yes, the big C. That's what an incinerator in Carnshaugh would mean.'

The hall resounds with applause and the sound of feet drumming on the floor. Bridget Wall bows slightly and sits down. A sea of hands shoots up.

'That all went rather well, I think,' May Condell says after the meeting ends at ten o'clock and she is ushering Jacob down the steps. Immediately he is surrounded as people mill around the trestle tables where tea is being poured out and plates of sandwiches stripped of their silver-foil coverings. Near the door a child falls over a bucket that has been placed on the floor to catch drips from an angry brown stain in the ceiling.

A cup teetering on a mismatched saucer appears in Aoife's hand. She leans against a warm radiator and munches on a digestive biscuit. Somehow the setting feels vaguely familiar: the run-down parish hall, the timber-boarded ceiling, the leaking roof and the country warmth of steaming kettles. It is as if she has been here before, she thinks. At her shoulder, on a high windowsill, a bunch of artificial flowers is stuffed into a vase. As she stretches up to touch a dusty petal, she becomes aware that she is under scrutiny.

'So tell me now and who would you be?'

It is the woman who had spoken from the floor: Bridget Wall, the county councillor.

'My name is Aoife McAvady.'

The woman reminds Aoife of a horse, the way she makes a slow chewing motion with her mouth as if she is digesting the information by eating it.

'I am Mr Smith's assistant.'

The woman leans closer as if to examine her. Aoife draws back uneasily.

'You're poor Rosaleen's daughter.'

It's not a question.

Aoife recoils, her consciousness acknowledging that this stranger has slipped through a fault-line of her life and, without warning, has split it open. *Here it is*, Aoife thinks, her heart beating wildly. Here is the weight of memory cascading in on top of her when she least expected it, its immensity threatening to overpower her. She can hardly see; she can hardly breathe. Trembling, she places her teacup on the windowsill and turns towards the window. She would give anything to be out in the dark fields at this very minute. Instead she is cornered. There is no escape.

'You're the spit of her.' The woman's voice has lost its roughness. It sounds far away, almost unintelligible because it is so subdued.

Aoife thinks: *This woman knew my mother well and I didn't know her at all.* She knew the flesh and blood version of her mother, while Aoife has nothing except whispers, fleeting images, a few photos – memories as tenuous as snowflakes melting in her hand.

Dumbly she searches for clues in the face before her.

'The poor crathur,' the woman says. 'I was very sorry when I read in the papers what happened to her.'

Aoife strains to hear, aware of time rushing away into the thundering crowd. *Tell me*, she wants to say, *tell me everything*. And yet it is impossible: the words do not come.

'We were in college together. Your mother was good to me.' A fleeting smile crosses Bridget Wall's face. 'There were days I would have starved only for your mother.'

Islanded in thought, the two women stand together while, around them, the roar of conversation swells. *When will this turmoil end?* Aoife wonders. Her skin is clammy, her mouth dry. Although the air in the hall is oppressively warm and thick with a mixture of smells, she is shivering.

Suddenly the woman digs her elbow into Aoife's side, 'I'll tell you what. Seeing as you are Rosaleen's daughter.'

Aoife looked at her without comprehending.

'You listen to me now.' Bridget Wall is speaking urgently, under her breath. 'You can tell your boss that his burner's a washout if he tries to build on that site.'

This is business as usual. This Aoife can handle. She takes a deep breath and answers crisply, 'But the whole point is to have it away from any houses.'

The woman shakes her head.

'That way no one will lodge a complaint,' Aoife continues.

'I'm telling you as clear as I can. That site is a non-runner.'

'I don't understand.'

'There's too many farmers around here.'

'I still don't understand.'

'And as for the blow-ins, they're even worse. Once they get their planning permission, they pull up the ladder behind them. They won't let anyone build for miles around.'

'So are you saying that it can't happen?'

'Oh, never say die, dear,' the woman replies. Immediately she clamps a hand over her mouth. 'I'm sorry, that was thoughtless of me.'

Aoife looks at her icily. From now on, she decides, no matter what this woman says to her, she will not answer. She yearns for Jacob. She can see him, standing at the far side of the hall, deep in conversation with the parish priest. Will he stay with her tonight or go home to his wife? Either way she must not care. She is a match for him but as she gazes at him, engrossed in conversation, his head cocked, appearing to listen intently as he is set on charming the old priest, Aoife knows that if she ever weakens Jacob will break her.

The woman is trying to get her attention, gripping her arm and beginning to gabble with excitement. 'What I'm saying is you need to relocate. Move the incinerator up to behind the council housing estate and you will get your permission, I can promise you that. The council has industrial land idle at the back, so it will go through. I'll see to it. We could do with a bit of development in this village.'

Despite her resolve, Aoife can't resist asking, 'But what about the dioxins?'

Bridget Wall purses her lips. 'Never you mind about them.'

If my mother had lived, Aoife wonders, would she have ended up looking like this woman standing before her: thick-waisted and jowly, a scheming glint in her eye?

'But you said . . .' Aoife persists. 'I mean, what about the people who live on that estate?'

'Come election time, the people living up in that estate won't even bother their arses to go out and vote.'

Puzzled, Aoife looks at her.

The woman jerks her head towards the crowd. 'See the people here in this hall tonight? They are different. They'll be out. On polling day they'll be queuing up.'

Silken horseshoes and horses' heads slide across her shoulders as she adjusts her scarf. 'And I wouldn't mind but I grew up on that council estate. I know every one of them. I know their children's names. Come to think of it, I even know the names of their poxy dogs.'

Her eyes are pale discs embedded in the pudgy drag of her cheeks. Under her chin a dewlap wobbles. She taps a conspiratorial finger against the side of her nose.

'Mind you,' she whispers, 'I've said nothing.'

Sheets of rain swing across the windscreen. A gorse bush, ghostlike, rises up at the side of the road and disappears as the car plunges into the night.

'What a bitch!' Jacob bangs his fist on the driving wheel. 'What an unmitigated, tight-arsed, scaremongering, egotistical, lying whale of a bitch!'

'Mmmm,' Aoife murmurs, snuggling into the seat. The interior of the car whispers to her of luxury: of old leather, shiny chrome, warmth, safety.

Jacob fumes, 'I mean what the hell is in it for her?'

Aoife doesn't reply. She debates with herself whether or not to tell him about the conversation she had with Bridget Wall.

'What's her angle?'

'Jacob?'

'What?'

'What did she mean? Why was she talking about dioxins?'

He explodes. 'Godsake, Aoife, don't you start! There is no risk. It's baloney. I mean, fucking *cancer*.'

Aoife closes her eyes and presses her hand against the nape of his neck. His anger towers over any chance of conversation. It columns and spreads through the confined space of the car that carries the two of them back to Dublin: to the kind of life they both know and understand. His rage is prodigious and yet – and the knowledge gives her satisfaction – she holds the key to its dissipation. It is a power that she can choose to use or not. She isn't sure why she chooses not to. Maybe the mention of her mother is the reason: an intrusion as unexpected as feathered dandelion seeds floating out of a night sky. Anyway, people in council houses shouldn't throw stones, she thinks, her brain befuddled by tiredness.

Through the wind and rain they travel on and the farther the distance lengthens from Carnshaugh, the less inclined she is to tell him anything. She has an ability to lock awkward memories into a compartment in her head and she does so now, shutting away the memory of the evening.

She turns on the radio and, as orchestral music pours out, she asks casually, 'Are you staying tonight?'

To her surprise he nods. 'Carol's away at her sister's.'

'I'm glad.' She massages his neck as the rain beats steadily against the windscreen.

Her thoughts and Jacob's merge into one thought: a wish

to drown the memory of the meeting and its aftermath in the depths of their lovemaking. To wipe the slate clean.

Jacob sleeps fitfully, tossing and muttering in his sleep. Beside him she stretches out, wide-awake. She toys with the idea of waking him up and telling him what Bridget Wall said. She visualizes his sudden joy, his yelp of victory. She has no good reason not to tell him. He has a right to know, but then, she thinks, she has a right not to tell him. She tries to forget the events of the evening but, for once, finds herself unable to control the way her mind keeps running back to Bridget Wall. Their conversation makes for a sleepless night and she is all too conscious of the warmth of Jacob's body next to hers. Usually she revels in it but now she wants to escape. She slides away to the edge of the bed, rerunning the events of the evening in her head, and regretting that she hadn't questioned Bridget Wall about her mother. There is so little to go on – fragments of memories, stories retold over and over by Conor and herself: desiccated leaves whirling in an autumn wind. She is helpless.

Then, as Jacob shifts in his sleep, she remembers how she has power over him and, even now, how she refuses to relinquish it.

She curls up close to the edge of the bed and thinks of the argument they had, a few months after they had made love for the first time and the mysterious, dangerous flame between them had sprung into life. It was an argument about money. Jacob wanted to give her what he described as 'a gift of money'. Enraged and hurt, she turned on him.

'I'm your office manager,' she spat out, 'not your whore!'

He was chastened and so apologetic that she forgave him. She saw the relief in his eyes and realized that an obstacle between them had been removed. It made her feel unsure of herself: the thought that a barrier had fallen away. As if she was losing her balance.

Later, he chucked her gently under her chin. 'A penny for them.'

She shook her head and said nothing. The disagreement made her wary. She vowed never to make demands on him, never to try and change things. It was a matter of her pride.

'How about a trip away together? Would you agree to that?'

When he asked her, a sudden spurt of joy surprised her.

'I'll think about it,' she said.

Now, as Jacob tosses and turns beside her in the bed, she thinks about that argument and wonders if he was afraid, all along, that she was only after his money. It is a reminder that she has no right to him. In the darkened bedroom she feels that he has slipped away, that there is no one there lying beside her and that soon she will fall asleep alone.

In her dreams a crowd of people are storming the veterinary clinic and Bridget Wall, roaring like a bull, is at the head of the mob and brandishing a lasso. With a start, Aoife wakes up to find Jacob close up and snoring in her ear.

'*Jacob!*'

His hand moves down between her legs, eager as a puppy.

'Lover, lover, lover,' he croons sleepily, easing himself around the contours of her body.

'Jacob?'

'Mmmmm?' He is massaging her breasts and she can feel her nipples harden.

She whispers in his ear, 'Remember that idea you had about us having a trip away?'

'God, you smell good,' he says, rolling onto his back, and she feels herself being lifted up onto his body, his heart beating and his arms tight now around her, making her tremble.

'Well, let's do it.'

'Okaaay,' he echoes. 'Let's do it.'

And, with an almighty push, he enters her.

21

'So how are you today?'

Such a precise, solicitous voice on the phone!

'Conor!' Aoife says. 'How did you know I've been sick?'

'I didn't know but, since you tell me so, I think it's a good excuse for you to come over for dinner.' His voice becomes suddenly animated. 'You haven't seen the house since the builders left.'

'I'd like that.'

They agree on a time and date and when she puts down the receiver she smiles at the thought of seeing him.

Her brother, architect and young fogey, will never change. Conor is younger than Aoife and yet, up close, he has the look of a thin, long-fingered, walnut-coloured ancient. He is given to wearing immaculate mohair suits. He is happiest on a sun lounger by a swimming pool and spends a month, each winter, in the Canaries: hence the permanent tan. He lives alone and is not only to his sister but to everyone who knows him something of an enigma.

Aoife has often wondered about his personal life. She asked him once if he preferred men to women. It seems to her to be the only rational explanation for the absence of any female companionship in his life. He looked at her pityingly from behind his Dior spectacles, gave a polite laugh and said, 'On that subject I am agnostic.'

This gnomic reply did not enlighten Aoife. She decided that he was one of the people who didn't need other people.

For all his self-containment, his Zen-like calm, he is the only person whom Aoife feels really close to. Sometimes they don't talk for weeks but, when they do talk, they can pick up on their conversation without missing a beat. She loves her brother and she has no doubt that he, in his own oddball way, loves her.

Conor is the only person Aoife has confided in about her affair with Jacob. Her friends, even her closest friends, the two girls from college who make up an important part of her life, have not been told.

To her dismay, Conor took her news badly.

'It's my life,' Aoife said hotly but it turned out that Conor was not disturbed by the fact that Jacob was married nor that he was twenty-two years older than her.

'So what then?'

'Work and pleasure don't mix. You're working for him and you're screwing him. If you ever stop screwing him, then you will, sooner or later, end up not working for him. And, no matter what, there'll always be the mortgage to pay.' He shook his head solemnly. 'He is trouble, my dear.'

'God, for a man with such a refined aesthetic sense, you can be awfully crude.'

'Yes, I know.' He leant across to pick a hair from the

collar of her jacket, changing the subject without a second thought. 'All that work with animals. Aoife, I don't know how you do it.' Then he laughed. 'Come to think of it, a different job might suit you after all.'

She began to argue but Conor wasn't listening.

'Look, Aoife,' he shook a strand of her hair between his graceful fingers, 'you're beginning to moult.'

An outdoor light suddenly blazes and the security gate purrs open. Conor designed the house on a tiny mews site and has managed to create magic out of the cramped space. A two-storey glittering glass box rises up before her. Through the window Conor is revealed, lifting himself from a huge suede sofa and waving to her. He disappears from view. Then the oak door opens wide and he stands in the doorway, silhouetted against the light, his arms outstretched as if he is about to embrace her. He is wearing cream slacks, a seersucker shirt and loafers. With his close-cut hair and trim body he could be a male model in an American magazine. She steps onto the parquet floor and Conor, his arms still outstretched, turns around and leads her into the bright living area.

'What do you think?' he breathes. 'Isn't it just wonderful?'

Aoife looks around at the length of white wall on one side of the room, upon which is hung a large, unframed abstract painting. On the other, a full-height vista through a wall of glass, of giant ferns rising out of vegetation crammed into a tiny garden. Inside: the vivid red sofa, the Barcelona chair in the corner, clusters of spindly arched lamps and two glass tables appearing to float in the tall, airy emptiness.

'Wow!' she says.

Her response sounds weak and ineffectual to her but it is

enough to satisfy Conor and he invites her to sit, to have a drink, to tell him all her news.

There really are only the two of us now, she thinks as she sips wine from a tall wineglass.

By the time she and Conor were in college their father had got a permanent job in Riyadh and had moved in with a short, busty American divorcée, who had no children of her own. On one of his trips back to Ireland she accompanied him. Over *sole bonne femme* in the Shelbourne Hotel she had talked non-stop in a southern drawl, like a crazed, wound-up Dolly Parton without the witticisms. When the meal was over she stood up to go to the ladies' room. Then she paused for a moment.

'I just want to warn you two beautiful young people,' she said, 'you mustn't ever call me mommy. That'd make me feel *so* old.'

Aoife was afraid to catch Conor's eye in case one of them started to laugh. But it was not a laughing matter for their father.

'I really want you to like her and respect her,' he confided, looking anxiously into their faces.

For a moment the two of them were small children again, nodding their heads in unison. Their father's glance skipped away to the passing traffic beyond the hotel window while the three of them sat in silence and waited for the woman to return.

With a sigh Aoife leans back into the plump cushions. Conor sits on a stool and listens and talks. Outside, the lush greenery glows in the smouldering evening light.

Yes, it is just the two of them now.

'Conor?'

'What?'

She turns towards him, leaning on her elbow. 'Do you remember her at all?'

Silence. Conor stretches out his legs and then clasps his hands under one knee, lifting one foot off the floor.

'I don't know,' he says eventually.

They've had this conversation before. Sometimes his reply is different.

'You were too young, I suppose.'

'Aoife, I was four. A four-year-old child remembers things but it is all a blank to me. Although sometimes I think I do and then at other times . . .' He pushes his glasses up his nose and smiles enigmatically. 'Aoife,' he asks as he pours her another glass of wine, 'what's on your mind?'

She looks at him quizzically.

'I mean why that question now?'

'Jacob wants me to go away with him for a break. It's his idea. Some vets' conference in Coleraine and I can go along as his assistant.'

'How convenient.'

Aoife frowns at him and says, 'I don't know what you mean by that. I thought I might visit the old house on the lough while we were up there.'

'Tax-deductible sex,' he smiles faintly, 'is what I mean by that.'

'Oh Conor, give over!' She throws a cushion at him.

Adroitly he catches it with one hand and stands up to prop it up again on the scarlet sofa.

He sits back on his stool. Hunched over and quiet, he seems lost in thought.

Did he hear me, she wonders.

'I said –'

'I heard you,' he says and looks away.

Like snow, a pause lands in the room. She sees a tiny version of herself gazing out a window, the waters of the lough in the distance. She feels the run of a brush through her hair. Her mother's disembodied voice counting the brushstrokes as the bristles course down the back of her head. *Twenty-three . . . twenty-four . . .* Scraps of memories are all she has. They emerge without warning, floating in the air and then spinning away out of reach.

22

They came to Glendalough, the three of them: Aoife, Conor and their father. They were too old for family picnics – Aoife was sixteen, Conor fourteen – but their father insisted. Having carried their bags as far as the little sandy beach at the edge of the Upper Lake they were not keen to move again but, since the egg sandwiches were eaten and the flask of sugary tea drained, it was hard to see what they could do to relieve the boredom.

Conor was stamping around in the stream that ran into the lake, searching among the rocks for tiddlers. Aoife was lying face down, on the sand, close to her father who sat up awkwardly and emptied a stone out of his sandal. He banged the sandal off a rock and then slipped it on his socked foot again. High above the valley, the sun chased out of a cloud and, all of a sudden, bathed the scene around them with light.

I've lived more years without Mammy than with her,

Aoife thought, and I am beginning to forget what she was like . . .

'Like *her*, I suppose,' their father said in answer when Aoife asked: 'What was she like?'

On the path beside the lake, a short black-haired woman struggled to get her rucksack back on her shoulders. She was wearing khaki shorts and heavy walking boots. Her face was shiny with exertion as she hurried after a group of hill-walkers who had gone ahead.

In dismay Aoife looked at the woman and turned back to her father, her attention distracted momentarily by the sight of the angled mountains, their reflections ice-sharp in the depths of the Upper Lake. On the grass, families were picnicking and, above them, a line of hill-walkers, bearing rucksacks and walking poles, zig-zagged up the mountainside.

'D'you really mean her?' Her tone was incredulous. Her cheek pressed against the damp sand, she watched the dark-haired woman move resolutely along by the lake, her rucksack bouncing on her back.

Her father turned to look again at the woman.

'Not really, no . . .' He ran his hand across his forehead.

She waited.

'But I do see her sometimes in the street or in the supermarket. Someone so like her that, until I get close, it's got to be her.'

The sun was warm on Aoife's back. She stretched out and closed her eyes.

'But what was she like?' she said again.

This time there was no answer. Her father's head was bent down over his folded arms, his bald pate glistening with tiny drops of sweat. In the quiet air, his sobs sounded like the hawking of an old gate: a sound so terrible that she had to turn away. She curled up on the sand, her hands over her ears until he stood up, blew his nose hard and walked away along by the edge of the lake.

23

In the hotel dining room Jacob throws down his napkin and pushes his chair back from the table.

'Well, I'll be damned,' he says, 'if that isn't Henry Smithwick!'

I must say hullo, he thinks, find out how he's doing. Not so good from the look of him. Jesus, Henry has aged. Heart trouble, I heard, or is it something worse? Jacob can't remember, even as he saunters across the room and stops at a table where a number of men are sitting.

'Henry,' he says loudly, 'it's been so long I thought you'd died.'

At the sound of his voice, the men look up. One of them beckons him to join them. Bursts of rich, rounded laughter rise up in the high-ceilinged room to tease Aoife as she sits and waits for him to return. The pattern in the carpet zigzags across the floor in a mismatch of colours: brown

and grey and orange and red. Linen tablecloths fall in folds
to the floor. They remind Aoife of white-sheeted bodies in
a morgue. She is aware of the murmur of conversation of
the other hotel guests: the slurps and crunches of breakfast
sounds. Ulster fries. Marmalade and toast. Cornflakes. Tea
in silver teapots. She catches sight of a woman, across the
dining-room, staring at her. Quickly Aoife lifts her cup to
her mouth and drinks the dregs. She replaces the cup on its
saucer and examines the cutlery. Then she studies the plate
in front of her on the table: its navy and gold crest and the
words *The Royal Hotel, London*. This china, she thinks,
belongs somewhere else. Inexplicably it has ended up in a
hotel in Coleraine, as out of place as she is.

When Jacob returns, he is ebullient.

'Haven't seen that fellow for years. Old Henry always
sat beside me at lectures for roll call. It was alphabetical,
you know. Smith. Smithwick. We went through college
together and now look at him. He's my age and he's half-
dead. I don't want to be old like him. He looks like a
corpse.' He eyes her anxiously, 'God, Aoife, do I look old?'

Laughing, she shakes her head.

'Come on, tell me the truth.'

'You look half his age,' she says, knowing how pleased it
will make him.

When they go up to the bedroom to pack their bags before
leaving, the bed is still unmade, the rumpled sheets a
reminder: the two of them in the darkness, lying in each
other's arms. When he fell asleep beside her, his breathing
soft and comforting, she even dared to wonder if their lives
could be different.

'I won't leave my wife for you,' Jacob had said the first
time they made love in her tiny bedroom, a street-light
peering through the curtains.

'If I were you, I wouldn't leave your wife for me either.'

'Aw, Aoife, lighten up.'

'I mean it. This is just an adventure,' she said firmly. 'For both of us.'

Now, as she stands beside an untidy bed in a hotel on a Northern coast, she has a yearning desire to go to sleep, every night, curled up close to somebody else. I can dream, she thinks, safe in the knowledge that a dreamer always wakes up. What she feels for Jacob is difficult to define. In a way, it is deep and instinctual. Yes, but what else is it? Aoife sighs and cannot answer. When it comes to having an affair with a married man, she isn't proud of herself. They are both grown-ups, she would have said if anyone had challenged her – not that anyone knew or cared enough to do so. Not in this hotel full of men and women intent on enjoying themselves and getting tanked up in the bar until four o'clock in the morning.

'We might as well stop in Derry on the way,' Jacob says.

His hand on her arm, he ushers her towards the car and she is content to let him take control. After all, it was he who suggested coming on a trip to the conference which, he pointed out, would provide them both with the necessary cover.

'Nobody in their right mind ever goes over the Border these days. We won't know a soul. And if you want, you can go back to find your roots.'

He knows her story. He cajoled it out of her early on in their relationship but, by tacit agreement, it was rarely mentioned again. His optimistic outlook is based on an avoidance of thinking about the past. He prefers to live in the present.

So, he was eager to know, what did she think?

'Yes,' she had whispered, 'I'd like that.'

Stroking her hair lightly as he spoke. He was like a father reassuring a child, she thought. A sudden rush of emotion had her reaching up to grasp his hand in hers and bring his fingers to her mouth to kiss, one by one.

'Just remember where those fingers have been,' he said and she imagined him cradling a bloodied bird, or plunging his fist into a cow's vagina.

'Ugh, I know.' And she leant against him to kiss him on the mouth.

In the car park along the Derry quay, Jacob parks the car and gets out. He walks to the railing that runs beside the river, grips the handrail, and proceeds to stretch his legs, one at a time, bouncing gently like a runner getting ready for a marathon. Reluctantly, Aoife emerges from the car. A cold wind is whipped up from the River Foyle. The city exudes an air of fatigue, the buildings staggering uphill, the church steeples a faint grey colour against the sky. With its dank walls and sombre buildings, the city looks miserable.

'So here we are.' The sound of his voice is too boisterous for comfort.

In the streets are a few desultory passersby. Aoife and Jacob go into a florist's to buy a bunch of flowers. When they come out into the street again, she notices the street sign and stops in her tracks.

'I think my mother worked in an office here, as an architect. Strand Road. Yes, I'm sure I'm right.'

'An architect,' Jacob echoes, clearly impressed.

Aoife walks quickly along the pavement, looking for some sign of the office. What the practice was called? She can't remember. McDonald and something? Would she even know it if she saw it? Past shops, a cinema, and then as they draw nearer to the Guildhall, they come across bombsites, cavernous and dark, like missing teeth in an ancient mouth. The gunmetal sky reaching down to the hoardings. The scrawled graffiti: WAR OR PEACE. UP THE PIRA. BRITS OUT. MAN UTD FOR EVER.

Hope dies inside her. A veil of rain is dragged across the street and she and Jacob end up huddling in a doorway.

'I don't think I've ever been in a more depressing place in my life,' she says.

'Oh, I don't know. Clones on a Sunday afternoon comes close. That's suicide territory, believe me,' says Jacob, who spent a summer as a student working on a pig farm in County Monaghan. Shoving his hat down over his eyes, he grips her arm and they run to the car without waiting for the rain to stop.

To Aoife, the day is like a series of snapshots or a film running on fast forward. Once over the Border, they stop at a hotel overlooking Lough Swilly, order sandwiches in the lounge and sit in creaking leather chairs, listening to the radio for news about the latest settlement in Northern Ireland.

'Will it work though?' Jacob asks.

'What?'

'The agreement, the settlement, whatever is going to come out of these talks. Thirty years of violence. I just can't see it coming to an end.'

A lifetime. Thirty years. Nearly my lifetime, she thinks.

'Please God,' she said, although she didn't believe in God.

'I think it might be better if they kept God out of it.'

When they finish eating, he reaches into his wallet.

'Please let me pay for this,' she says but he won't. This is on him, he insists.

Earlier, in the hotel foyer in Coleraine, she remembers, she felt a frisson of unease when he took out his credit card and put it on the reception desk. I'm a kept woman, she wanted to say to him, lightly, as if to share as a joke, but he turned to greet Henry Smithwick, wizened and stooped, coming towards them out of the crowd, his knowing glance sliding over Aoife and away before he turned and muttered, 'Son of a bitch, Jacob, you haven't changed.'

Now, in the bar of another hotel, she reaches for her handbag, saying, 'But I want to pay.'

'*No.*' The weight of his hand on hers silences her.

He drives fast through a countryside that is blurry with rain. It doesn't take long to arrive at the graveyard. Everything looks neat and trim, with a newly painted railing and yew trees, dense and dark, sheltering the graves laid out in straight rows. The rain stops.

'Are you sure you don't mind waiting?'

'Darling, it's your mother. Of course not. Take your time.'

Darling. Always the gentleman. The expensive car, the big jeep, the camel-hair coat. Is it all for show, she wonders. How long can the two of them go on together? Some day it will have to come to an end.

She rests her hand on the headstone but cannot bring herself to pray. She examines the dedication cut into bare, unadorned limestone: *Rosaleen McAvady RIP – 1941-1969. Beloved Wife and Mother.* The last time she was in the graveyard Conor was there too. They had travelled up together, with their father and Auntie Maureen on the twentieth anniversary of their mother's death. Nine years ago since, together, they stood around the grave. It seems like only yesterday.

'There are just the two of us, Conor and me,' she tells her mother. 'Now that Daddy's run away with Dolly Parton.'

Below her, Jacob is standing by the car, his hair ruffled in the wind, his arms crossed over his chest. Do I look old? he had asked her at breakfast. The way he is hunched into the wind, bare-headed and whey-faced, at the graveyard gate, he certainly looks his age and more. What possessed her to get involved with him? It is a madness of sorts, a diversion from reality.

This is a part of my life, Aoife thinks, this grave covered in marble chips within its stone surround. This is reality. She kneels to lay the bunch of flowers at the base of the headstone.

Mother, she says silently, meet Jacob.

A blast of cold Northern air flattens the grass. There is nothing more she can do there. On the rare occasion that she visits the grave of her mother, she experiences a feeling of failure. As if there is something more to be done, something to be brought to completion, which she cannot fathom.

When she comes down to join Jacob at the graveyard gate, he opens his arms and says, 'My poor darling.'

She presses against him, gratefully, so that he feels the coldness of her body.

'Are you sure you want to keep going?' he asks. She looks shrunken suddenly, her mouth drawn into a bitter line. 'Are you all right?'

'Of course I'm all right,' she snaps. Then, instantly contrite, 'Oh Jacob, I'm sorry.'

'No, no, you're upset, of course, my poor darling.'

If he says that again, she promises herself as she gets back into the car, she is going to scream.

Jacob starts up the engine. 'So where to next?'

'Just follow the road until you see a sign.'

But there is no sign to lead them onto the road to the old house. She keeps peering down side roads until she loses faith in her own sense of direction.

'Oh, turn down here. I think this might be it.'

The car dips and rises on the uneven surface of the lane as it descends towards the lough but all they find is a tumbledown ruin of a church, its gable wall intact, stark and lonely, rising above the hedgerow.

'Sorry, we must have taken the wrong turn.'

'Let's take a look, anyway, now that we're here,' Jacob says.

He parks the Mercedes up tight to the hedge. She slides across the seat and follows him out. His coat swings around his knees as he ducks through the entrance and into the ruined church. Inside there are headstones and nettles in abundance.

She holds back as he moves between the headstones, trying to read a name here, a dedication there.

With his finger, he traces the letters on a mossy stone and reads aloud, '*Underneath this Stone rests the dust of the Rev Robert Reed and the remains of his wife, Sara Cunningham.*'

She looks up at the trees, waving madly in the wind.

'There's more,' he says. 'Don't you want to see?'

Aoife shakes her head and turns to walk towards the car. When she is about to open the car door, she catches sight of the puppy. Rough-coated and smiling, the young dog dances along the road towards her, wagging its tail in a delirium of delight. She stoops to pat it but the puppy runs past her and cowers under the hedge.

Then she hears the noise that has frightened it: a heavy, mechanical roar in her ears. She turns to see a tractor bearing down and suddenly Jacob is beside her, making a lunge for the puppy to hold it tightly in his arms. He and Aoife stand together in the gateway to the ruined church as the tractor trundles towards them. As it inches close to the parked Mercedes, the dark figure in the tractor's cabin raises a hand in salute.

Agonized, Jacob stands and watches, his hat in one hand, the other holding on tightly to the puppy.

Aw, Jesus, he thinks helplessly, don't scrape my car.

Aoife holds her breath as the tractor squeezes past. The puppy looks up at her. When she meets the animal's soft brown gaze, something rattles under her skin – a recognition. There was an old man, she remembers, and her heart lifts.

Daylight is fading off the lough as the tractor disappears around a corner. Jacob is laughing now with relief. He lets the puppy go and the animal bounds down the lane and vanishes from view.

As Aoife climbs into the car, she tries desperately to remember any details.

'I remember him,' she says. 'I just can't think of his name.'

Jacob isn't listening.

'I thought the Merc was for it.' He rubs his hands, turns the key and, when the engine springs into life, begins to manoeuvre the car around in the laneway. Back and forwards the car is shunted while patiently he manages the gears.

Aoife stays silent as he concentrates on the task, although she wants to hear her voice above the sound of the engine, to extract the memory that is dancing tantalizingly beyond her consciousness.

Jacob is the first to break the silence.

'Do you want to keep looking?' he asks.

She shakes her head. He is relieved. When she told him that she wanted to see the old house on the Inishowen peninsula he told her he understood, although privately he couldn't understand why anyone in their right mind would want to rake up the past.

'Right-oh! Hot whiskeys in the first pub we come across.'

It feels all wrong to her. The day is ragged and unfinished, but she is enervated by the warm smells of leather and aftershave, the wipers whispering back and forth and the engine throbbing as the car trundles up the lane and then glides out across the main road.

There is a fire in the hotel lobby and mahogany doors with etched panes and brass handles. Jacob rubs his hands and makes for the bar.

'How about dinner? I'm starving.' His mouth looks huge as he reads the menu. 'Mixed grill with chips. Steak and onions with chips. Roast chicken with chips,' he reads aloud. 'Give me the lot!' His cheerful laugh clatters around the bar.

Aoife smiles indulgently and, digging her hands into her coat pockets, sits back in her seat. The bar is quiet. It is early evening and they drink their hot whiskeys and chat aimlessly.

'Much better to have a night's sleep than driving all the way to Dublin tonight. We'll make an early start in the morning,' he says and goes out to the hotel reception to book a room.

Aoife relaxes in an armchair and waits for him to return. It feels good, she discovers, not to care. Whatever hunt she was on, it is now over. The spoor has grown cold. Warm air creeps between her shoulder blades and brings the smell of onions.

In the hotel restaurant, a few diners are already in place and eating. The waitress is grey-haired, stout and jolly and wants to know everything: where they're from and where they're going. Jacob needs no invitation to engage in conversation. He talks to everyone: bank clerks, waiters, delivery men. His curiosity is insatiable and yet, once he has left whomever he's talking to, he forgets all about them.

'Why do you do that?' Aoife asked him once, with a mixture of interest and irritation.

'Do what?'

'Talk to everyone you meet as if you know them.'

'Doesn't everyone? It's what we Irish do.' His air of practised innocence hid a lot, she knew, but on this matter he seemed genuinely puzzled by her question.

She shook her head and said nothing.

'Are you telling me so?' The waitress has put away her notebook and is standing there as if there isn't another customer in the place.

Jacob waves at Aoife and says, 'Her now, she used to live around here – isn't that right?' He turns to her for corroboration. Aoife glares at him and he wonders at how unappealing she can make herself look on occasion. With those wide-apart eyes and stubborn frown she looks, Jacob thinks, like a spoilt child. Fleetingly he remembers Henry Smithwick inviting him to join a golf outing to Portstewart and how he had passed up the offer. He'd have given his eye-teeth to play on that course. Instead, he is trailing around Donegal wasting his precious time when he should be sinking a few at the nineteenth hole after a game with old Smithwick and maybe a bet on the side. Here he is, stuck in a second-grade hotel with little Miss Sulky. Jacob sighs. Why does life have to be so *complicated*?

'McAvady,' Aoife says when asked.

The waitress's expression does not change. Her non-committal 'Really?' gives nothing away and yet Aoife feels a tremor in the air. Something, she is certain, has been left unspoken. She waits for the waitress to speak but she says nothing.

Aoife orders chicken and Jacob orders steak. With a contented sigh, the waitress takes out her notebook again and writes down the order.

When the plates arrive, each dish is drowned in thick gravy. Wadges of mashed potatos, peas and sliced carrots and a plate of chips piled high.

They eat without speaking until Jacob says, 'This steak is surprisingly good.'

The waitress overhears him and comes pattering over to the table, crowing with delight. 'Ah now, you can't beat a bit of good steak.'

'Actually a steak is something you *can* beat,' he grins up at her, 'It's a woman you can't beat any more.'

The waitress joins in his laughter. Aoife puts her knife and fork together carefully on the plate and dabs her mouth with her napkin.

The name comes to her out of nowhere. Since the waitress is back, she thinks, I might as well ask.

'I remember an old man with a dog. I think his name was Mundy.'

The woman shakes her head.

'Before my time, I guess,' she says. 'Will you have some dessert? There's apple tart with cream, Black Forest Gâteau with cream, ice cream.'

'With cream?' Jacob asks.

'Oh, aye,' the waitress answers solemnly. 'The ice cream always comes with cream.'

Aoife gives Jacob a secret, artful smile and he feels himself getting hard. Jesus, he thinks, she is a witch. He reaches his hand under the table as if he's dropped his napkin but, instead he touches her knee and then, slides his hand up, as far as he can, inside her thigh. She colours.

He withdraws his hand and says lightly, 'How about dessert, darling?'

'Mmm, yes, but I'll have some apple tart first.'

Oblivious, the waitress waits until he decides on ice

cream and then she disappears out through the kitchen door.

They are sitting over their empty plates, drinking cups of coffee, when the waitress circles the table again, lifting their plates and fussing over them. Did they get enough to eat now and was everything all right?

Then she turns to Aoife. 'The chef says his father knew the Mundys. He says Mrs Mundy now was a lovely woman.'

'Oh really?' On getting this information, Aoife is uncertain what to do with it. Had there been a wife, somewhere, hidden in the house among the trees? Now that she has his name, she remembers the man clearly – his narrow eyes and long rangy legs – a scarecrow in a long black coat and the dog always at his heels, a collie with a long, sharp snout.

'And Mr Mundy?'

The waitress hesitates. She leans against the table, resting the plates on her hip.

'Mr Mundy, och aye,' she says.

'Whatever happened to him?'

'I'm not from around here. I'm from Letterkenny.' The waitress's shoulders droop as she shakes her head.

Aoife senses some deep, submerged commotion. It isn't healthy, she thinks, to be rummaging around in the past like this. It's so long ago. And yet the idea of her mother persists. It never goes away. It is like a limb, jerking and twitching, long after amputation. Rest in peace for never.

'Penny for them?' Jacob's face is leaning close to hers, beads of sweat at his temple, his hand hot on her knee. In the depths between them, shadowed forms swerve and collide.

'Let's go to bed,' Aoife says because she can't think of anything else to say.

24

In the shopping centre the café is located near the gym. On Saturdays the three young women meet there, feeling virtuous, showered and loose-limbed after their morning work-out. Each one has a sports bag at her feet and a cup of cappuccino in her hand.

'First we exercise to get the weight off,' Aoife says, 'then we come in here to put it back on.'

'Delicious coffee though, isn't it?' Claire licks the creamy foam on her lip.

'Sex on a stick,' agrees Valerie.

Valerie and Claire are Aoife's oldest friends. They were at business college together and have kept in touch ever since. Sometimes she thinks of them as her only real friends. Cheerfully Valerie dunks a chocolate biscuit into her cup and pops the gooey mess into her mouth. Valerie works in a cosmetic-surgery clinic located in an industrial estate in west Dublin. She has full red lips, coral skin and rich brown hair tumbling onto her shoulders. She is big-boned and voluptuous. It is only when she stands up that her girth becomes obvious: the sway of thighs inside her dress, and her buttocks, startling in their grandeur. There is a splendour about Valerie that is irresistible to a certain kind of man. She often has a man in tow, but not necessarily the same one. Sometimes it's difficult – because the men are so alike, withdrawn and diffident – to tell one from the other. Valerie maintains that she loves the company of women more than that of men and it is true that she revels in female friendship. It is the deepest, most important emotional tie, Valerie claims, that she will ever know.

Now Valerie is having fun at Aoife's expense.

'*Come on!*' she says. 'Why don't you pull the other one?'

With her spoon, Aoife scoops a last mouthful of froth from her cup and shrugs.

Valerie peers at her, 'Four days away together and *nothing* happened?'

Aoife does not dare look up to meet her gaze. She feels herself blush.

'Ha!' Valerie pounces. 'I knew it.'

'Oh Aoife!' Claire, who has been listening, turns a sorrowful face towards Aoife. 'He's married.'

'I know he is,' Aoife snaps, 'but *I'm* not.'

Claire looks pained and twines her hands together. In business college Claire was a star pupil, speeding ahead of Aoife and Valerie academically, with the promise of a great career ahead of her. Now she looks as if life has flung her up against a wall and beaten the stuffing out of her. She wears a grey sweater and trousers, her face is pallid, her hair pulled severely back off her face. She looks anaemic and older than her thirty-six years. By the time her first and only baby was a year old, Claire's husband had died in a car accident. Although she does not complain outright, her air of perpetual disappointment speaks for itself. Eight years on and nothing, except the subject of her son Robert, seems to hold any joy for Claire. There are times when Aoife finds herself being irritated beyond the limits of endurance by the other woman's aura of unspoken suffering. Without being conscious of anything other than her own internal sense of grievance, Claire has the ability to make others feel bad about themselves.

Valerie is childishly jubilant. 'I *knew* you were getting laid. You're far too smug to be celibate.'

Claire meanwhile, continues to look troubled. 'And I was worried about you going up to the North,' she says. 'I mean there could have been bombs in Belfast and I was afraid you might get hurt.'

'Oh Claire!' Aoife touches her hand gratefully. 'Anyway I was in Coleraine. It's a long way from Belfast.'

She remembers the British Army checkpoint they passed on the way into Aughnacloy, a grim fortress on the Border, bristling with barbed wire and, beyond it, the Union Jacks fluttering in an icy wind. Past a burnt-out hall – Catholic, Protestant, she had no idea which – the desolate fields, the shuttered villages and empty streets.

'I was watching the *News* just in case,' Claire says.

'And did you see Gerry Adams talking?' Valerie leans forward, her breasts billowing against the edge of the table. 'Isn't he to die for?'

Aoife says nothing. It is not that she is unfeeling but she refuses to feel. What happened belongs to her and to no one else. And to Conor, of course. It is impossible to bring it out into everyday conversation. *Let me introduce my mother: the corpse in the river.* There are so many people that she can't remember their names and can't keep count of their number: that RUC woman, this child in Ardoyne, yet

271

another young soldier. Sometimes a name is snagged in her memory but, before long, a fresh atrocity wipes it away. All of them disappearing, like leaves whirling downstream. *Instead of killing each other, isn't it better that people are in rooms and talking?* While this is being repeated in the newspapers and on television all the time these days, Aoife turns inwards. She welcomes the familiar cloud that descends on her. It absorbs whatever emotion she might otherwise feel. It mummifies every part of her. She sits and watches the crowd of shoppers walking past outside the café, as if they represent some argument that she is duty-bound to accept.

'How can you be so passive?' she asked Conor once. He looked at her with his cool dispassionate gaze. 'Because I choose to be,' he replied. Now she is adopting the same course.

'So,' Valerie is saying, 'tell us about your Mr Smith. Is he good to you?'

'Well, yes, I suppose so.'

'For heaven's sake,' Valerie's brilliant eyes are fixed on hers, 'I mean financially.'

Aoife shakes her head.

Valerie leans towards her. Her voice is throaty and languid, her crimson fingernails tapping on the tabletop. 'Always think of the rainy day.'

Aoife demurs, 'I don't need –'

'You must have heard the old song.'

'What are you getting at?'

Valerie smiles seductively and begins to sing. Her voice is sweet and true.

'*When those louses go back to their spouses,*' she croons, '*diamonds are a girl's best friend.*'

'Give us a break.' Aoife is laughing, in spite of herself.

Valerie shakes her hair off her shoulders and sits back.

'I'm not going to talk about him any more,' Aoife says firmly.

'Perfectly right.' Claire agrees. 'It's none of our business. Let's talk about something else.'

'All the same, it must be serious.' Valerie winks at Claire.

'Why?' Claire wonders.

'I mean, going all the way to Coleraine,' says Valerie, 'just for a shag.'

Claire yelps in dismay.

'I'm not after his money,' Aoife interrupts, 'if that's what you're trying to make out.'

Valerie is irrepressible. 'And there'd be nothing wrong if you were. One day you might be glad of it. I mean, look at Claire here. You could do with a Sugar Daddy, couldn't you, Claire?'

Claire shakes her head. 'I'm just happy to be here. Since Robert's started at the Scouts, I don't know myself. Simple things like going to the gym and sitting here with both of you is such a treat.'

Valerie isn't listening. She concentrates on Aoife.

'You just be careful.'

'Oh, I'm on the pill, so you needn't worry.'

'No, Aoife, you be careful,' Valerie says again. 'I mean, don't let your heart rule your head.'

Aoife gives a bitter caw. 'Sometimes I don't think I have a heart.'

Valerie looks furtively at Aoife as if she wants to share a secret with her alone. 'One day, believe me, you could find yourself falling for him.'

'Well now, there's a surprise!' says Aoife. 'I never took you to be a romantic, Valerie.'

Claire glances at her watch. 'I'd better go,' she says but she doesn't move.

Unwilling to part company, the three women sit and talk

as the waitress clears the table and wipes it clean with a cloth. Eventually Claire stands up.

She sighs wistfully. 'I *really* have to go.'

25

On the phone the receptionist's voice is faint. Hungover.

'Sorry I can't be in today. My granny died. Sorry.'

How many grannies does that girl have? Aoife growls with frustration as she puts the receiver back in its cradle. Monday morning. She hasn't had time to get the clinic ready for the day and already there's trouble.

It's getting beyond a joke, Aoife and the Polish nurse agree. Something will have to be done.

When talking to Aoife, the nurse stands too close for comfort. She blows cigarette smoke in her face and has no sense of humour, but there is a bond between people who work alongside each other when they unite against a malingerer.

Aoife sits down at the desk in the waiting room. Oh, what she wouldn't give to be in the haven of her office.

In the corner of the waiting room a fat girl sits, her face

framed by a mass of hair. She's wearing an oversized T-shirt and has a tiny, canvas bag on her lap. Just what I need, thinks Aoife when she realizes that, inside the bag, a black rat lurks, conjuring up images of plague and pestilence. At the sight of the pointed face inside the bag, the furry ears and black whiskers, the long naked tail, she feels queasy.

'His name is Reggie White,' the fat girl says when she comes up to the desk.

Aoife concentrates on inputting the rat's details into the computer and then tells its owner to sit down and wait.

A swell of nausea hits Aoife. Abruptly she leaves the desk and goes out of the waiting room into the corridor. As she stands there, taking deep breaths and trying to stay calm, she sees the nurse approaching.

'Are you sick?' The nurse looks at her suspiciously as if Aoife is putting on an act.

Aoife shakes her head, goes back into the waiting room and sits down at the desk.

The fat girl is winding a strand of hair around her finger. Among the waves of hair cascading onto her shoulders, something, close to her neck, is moving. A little whiskery face peeps out. The girl smiles and reaches up to stroke its furry back. Aoife gets up and, this time, runs to the toilet but, even after vomiting into the bowl, she still doesn't feel any better.

After work she drags herself home to the apartment and falls into a bed that rocks her around on a sea of nausea. What is it, she asks the ceiling, what is wrong with me? The evening light wrings a last gasp out of the bedroom and then the night closes in, a merciful blanket.

When she wakes up, the bedroom is pitch black. The dial on the clock beside her bed tells her it is four o'clock. The witching hour. Silence. In the street a car slips by. She is wide awake and relaxed now. A shopping list, a dental appointment, she must remember to collect dry cleaning: all the things she hasn't even thought of during the day. Now she feels sure that she is better. It must have been something I ate, she tells herself, nothing more than that, and she falls back again into a delicious sleep.

The next morning she can hardly stand.

Her head aches as she sits on the edge of the bed retching into a basin she holds on her lap. Oh Mother, she gives a strangled cry, what's wrong with me? *Oh Mother*. From somewhere deep inside her come tears that she can't control and the sound is like that made by a child wailing in its sleep. But she isn't a child and she is awake. What is happening to her?

The tide rises again and her head is down into the basin, tears and vomit streaming. And she knows, even though it's impossible. Even though it is impossible, she knows.

Oh Mother.

Terror seeps into her veins and her head burns. She tries to grapple with what is happening but it makes no sense. She always takes precautions. Every morning, without fail, she swallows the pill she leaves out on her bedside locker. Like a knight donning armour before he faces into battle. So that nothing can go wrong. When was her last period? She can't remember. No, it must be cancer, she tells herself. Yes, cancer is better, even if it means she's going to die all alone.

In the end she phones the veterinary clinic to tell them she is sick. The nurse doesn't even try to disguise her disgust.

'Jacob will be so mad.'

Maybe it isn't cancer. Perhaps she's going mad, Aoife thinks as she attempts to make an appointment with the little Indian doctor. A foreigner, she thinks, would be easier to talk to at a time like this.

The voice on the phone giggles, 'No Indians here and no cowboys either.' Then, 'Ooops, I beg your pardon. You want an *Indian* doctor?'

'He came out to me when I was sick weeks ago.'

'I'd say that was one of the doctors on call. They're all foreigners.'

The doctor she ends up with is an Irishwoman, not much older than herself, who leaves the room with a little sample of her urine. Aoife is cold and sweating. Her hands clasp and unclasp as if of their own accord until the doctor returns.

'But I can't be.'

'Well, the contraceptive pill is 99.9% effective when used correctly. Unfortunately vomiting and diarrhoea can reduce its effectiveness, so additional precautions need to be taken.' The doctor's tone is neutral. She pauses and then, 'I'm sure you would have been told this already.'

Dumbly Aoife shakes her head.

'Be that as it may, you are, I would say, about seven weeks gone.'

'But I *can't* be.'

She begins to sob, burrowing down into her arms. The doctor glances, surreptitiously, at the clock above Aoife's head.

'It's a shock of course,' the doctor says, more gently this time, 'but you're still young enough for everything to go to plan. And you're very early. You have months to prepare. It is a natural experience.'

Aoife is not listening. 'No, I can't be.'

She stands up, wipes her eyes with the back of her hand.

The doctor smiles a slight smile. 'Believe me, once you get accustomed to the idea that you're expecting a baby . . .'

Aoife feels the ground give way. She gropes for the chair and sits down, weeping uncontrollably, grabbing tissues out of the box on the doctor's desk.

The doctor says nothing until her cries weaken, then, 'I know it is hard to accept.'

Aoife looks at her hopefully but all the doctor says is, 'This is something to help with the morning sickness,' and she hands Aoife a prescription.

Without another word, the doctor stands up smartly and goes to the door to let her out.

The rail carriage is empty apart from one old man in the corner, clutching his free travel pass. As the train moves forward, there are flashes of light and shadow through the windows and the wheels on the tracks are thudding, heavy and light, like the sound of a heart beating.

White foam races across Dublin Bay. A flock of dunlins peck in a pool of green slime. In the distance are the seaside stripes of the twin towers of Poolbeg. Cranes and gantries sprawl along the waterline. Cars stream along Merrion Road. At Booterstown Station a man embarks, carrying on a conversation into his mobile phone. There is nothing untoward here, Aoife thinks, except that somewhere deep inside her, something is growing.

She had intended to go home but when the train stops at Sandymount Station she doesn't move. It is immaterial where she ends up. She can't even take care of herself and yet everything in her life has attained a new significance. Her freedom, most of all. She wants to start again: to go somewhere far away from her double life, the deceit that once excited her and now fills her with revulsion. To escape to somewhere new and exotic: to Borneo or the Arctic Circle. She wants to begin again. To be born again. To find redemption.

The train moves on, rocking like a cradle pushed by an invisible hand. The backlands of the city appear at Lansdowne Road and the rugby stadium looming above.

Jacob, a Leinster man to his core. *Jacob* . . . how is she going to break the news? The backsides of buildings flash by, untidy gardens, detritus, collapsing windows, flat roofs with water tanks, aerials, asbestos panels, vent pipes with little pointed caps. Brand-new office blocks rear up, glassy-green and casting long shadows.

What is she afraid of? All over the world, other women have endured what she is going through, shared the same slipping-down sense of panic. More than anything, she wants to be alone and rid of whatever it is that has taken up lodging inside her.

The train slows to make its entrance into Pearse Station. Orange brick and pigeons cooing in the cast-iron, skeletal roof girders. Glass roofs arch over the line. Reminders of other places: Liverpool Street Station, Euston Station where countless Irish girls, carrying their cardboard suitcases, alight from a train and disappear into nowhere.

The train is up high now, over the city streets and the River Liffey. Double-decker buses pass below her and she has a bird's-eye view of attic windows, the North Star Hotel, a group of boys carrying cans of beer disappearing under the railway bridge. At Fairview Park, there are banks of trees. Then Harmonstown, Kilbarrack: metal gates chained up, CCTV, houses crammed close together and useless areas of weeds and gravel guarded by security fencing. For me to go away, she thinks, would be like going to the northside of Dublin. The same: only different.

At the end of the line she gets out and walks from of the little station. There are cruisers moored at the yacht club and shops and restaurants lining the harbour. It's foolish to think she can run away. Sooner or later she has to confront what is staring her in the face. For the moment, she is content to walk along the harbour to the road that rises towards Howth Head. On each side, large houses with spectacular views of the sea are armoured by high walls and electric gates. Everything is hidden. A crime could be committed behind those walls, she thinks, and no one need ever know.

The sight of an apartment block overlooking the sea jogs her memory.

She visited a young man who lived there once, years ago, when the apartment block was new and modern and desirable. He and she sat in his living room and watched the sea crashing up against the harbour wall. After dinner they went up to the Abbey Tavern for a drink and sang rebel songs and the English tourists sang the loudest of all. It didn't mean anything. Meanwhile, in a Belfast street, a car was sliding to a halt and somebody walking along the pavement was asked his religion and, sooner or later, the wrong answer was given and a bullet put through somebody's head. Later, in his apartment, the man told Aoife that he was gay. It was like Confession, she thought, the way he whispered to her in the darkness, his voice full of shame. It didn't mean anything. They remained friends afterwards until he moved away and she began working for Jacob Smith.

The apartment block, she notices, has worn badly over the years. It looks shabby and unloved; the brickwork is stained and the gutters full of weeds.

The man went away to England because he was afraid of being found out. Most of all, he told Aoife, he was afraid of his mother. At the rate we export our problems to England, she thinks, one day we could have no problems left. She can escape. She can disappear into nowhere. It doesn't mean anything.

26

'You're making the right decision, you know,' Valerie says.

'I know.'

'I mean, it's for the best.'

'I *know*.'

'Better not tell Claire though.'

'I don't intend to. The fewer who know, the better.'

'You wouldn't want to end up being known as the girl who's had an abortion.'

Aoife winces.

'Are you going to tell Jacob?'

'No. Yes.'

Valerie looks quizzical. 'Which is it?'

'I have to. I can't afford to pay for it. It costs hundreds.'

'Jesus, what a bloody mess.'

'Literally.'

The two women look at each other and then suddenly, in

the silent room, the sound of their laughter breaks like glass. A sob swells in Aoife's throat and Valerie puts her arm around her.

'Be strong,' she says.

Aoife stiffens. *Mother*, she thinks, where are you now that I need you?

Telling Jacob proves to be harder than she expected. When he phones and invites himself around to her apartment, she is relieved. At least I can break the news to him away from the clinic, she thinks.

'If you're hungry, I'm afraid there's nothing in the fridge.' She is amazed at how easy it is to talk to him on the phone. As if there is nothing wrong. As if nothing has changed.

'Not to worry. I'll look after it. I want to celebrate,' he chortles. 'Have I got news for you!'

You're not the only one, she thinks.

Jacob replaces the phone and grins at nothing in particular. He can't stop grinning. When his contact in the County Council phoned him that afternoon with news about the incinerator project, it was like a weight lifted off his back. Yes, yes, yes, he heard himself saying. Yes, he would have agreed to anything once the man said, '*We can give you planning permission as long as you . . .*'

'Not a problem,' Jacob said. 'Not a problem. Believe me.'

It's only now he can admit to himself the stress he's been living under. No one understands what it's like to be a risk-taker, he thinks, but I've pulled it off. Hah, I've won. Wait 'til Aoife hears the news. We'll celebrate tonight like we've never done before.

Like a puppy, he bounds into the apartment, carrying a supermarket bag full of groceries.

'So how is the patient?' He wraps his arms around her and nuzzles into her neck. 'I need you to get better, darling. Me and my animal kingdom need you.'

She takes the bag and silently removes its contents. A bottle of champagne, a baguette, two sirloin steaks and a monster bag of potato crisps. As she flattens out the meat on the counter, the sight of the blood is nauseating but she bites her lip and takes a deep breath.

Jacob, meanwhile, is brimming with excitement. Just when he thought his dream was over, he says, a man from the County Council phoned him.

'I'd just about given up. I thought the project had gone down the toilet, but you won't believe what happened. He said if I moved the location of the incinerator, I'll get my planning permission. There's a site zoned industrial that the Council own and they want me to put the incinerator there. No problem. Can you believe it?'

Aoife gazes at him. Gleefully he punches the air with his fist.

'Aoife, I've won! The locals can object all they like, but it won't make a blind bit of difference. That mad bitch Bridget Wall will be fit to be tied.'

The less said the better, Aoife thinks as she sets out plates and glasses on the table. Jacob paces the room, talking so excitedly that she has to interrupt the flow of words to get him to sit down at the table.

'Jacob, dinner's ready.'

Eyes dancing, he smiles at her. Touches her hair.

'God, Aoife,' he says hoarsely, 'you're the best.'

He devours the steak she has cooked for him and he eats most of the steak she leaves on her plate. Between mouthfuls, he regales her with stories about the clinic. As he does so, she realizes that this is a familiar pattern. She cooks. He eats. He talks. She listens.

'Jacob,' she says.

The flow of words continues without him stopping for breath.

'Jacob,' she says again. Louder this time.

She has never seen him so angry before. Jacob being cranky, grumpy, short-tempered and even, on occasion, angry, she is familiar with but, this time, the scope of his rage is terrifying. Shouting and screaming at her. She cringes and, at one point, wonders, when he stands up and his chair clatters onto the floor, if he is going to hit her.

'Jacob!' she tries to pacify him but he's in full throttle.

'You planned it, didn't you? Don't tell me. I'll never leave my wife for you if that's what you're after. Never, you bitch, never, you –'

'*Stop that, Jacob, and sit down!*'

She stands up to him – looks him straight in the eye – even directs him to straighten up the chair and to sit down on it. To her relief, he obeys without protest. For a moment there is a silence. The squall has passed over.

'I'm going to England.'

He looks at her with suspicion. 'What?'

'I'm going to England to have –'

'I heard you the first time.' A sullen expression settles in his face. His fists look enormous on the table.

She holds her breath but, instead of shouting, his voice drops into a hurt mode.

'So you think you can make that decision by yourself,' he says. 'Did you never consider that it is mine too?'

'What?'

'Well, it *is* mine, isn't it?'

Suddenly she feels an immense weariness. Her arms are like ton weights and she wants to rest her head on her hands, close her eyes and fall asleep.

'I'm going to go. Whatever you say, I'm still going.'

He looks abashed now. His face folds into a look of concern and his hand creeps across the table to hers. 'Christ, Aoife, I'm so sorry.'

She shakes her head and turns away. The sight of him contrite fills her with revulsion.

'What can I do to help?' he says, holding her hand tightly now. His eyes glisten.

Oh no, she thinks, he had better not cry. She shrugs and, without looking at him, says, 'I need money, that's all.'

'Yes, of course. Do you want me to go with you?'

She shakes her head vehemently.

A sense of relief is growing stronger in him; she can tell by the way his face relaxes and his arms extend out to touch her. She recoils and he shrugs, drains the last of his wine and stands up, a hangdog expression on his face.

'Oh you poor, poor darling,' he says.

So, she thinks, I'm no longer *his* darling.

'I have to go. Carol's arranged for us to go out with the boys.'

Oh yes, the boys, his precious brood.

'I'm really sorry,' he says.

He is pathetic, she thinks, as she waits for him to stumble out, one arm in a sleeve while he struggles to put on his coat. His steps, quick and eager to be out the door and gone.

The only other person she tells is Conor. When she phones him, he suggests meeting for lunch at a new Japanese restaurant which he says has the best sushi in Dublin. He is sitting up at the counter when she arrives. Behind his blue-rimmed spectacles his eyes are like polished stones. She sits down beside him and dolefully eyes the pale rings of fish and balls of seaweed and wonders if she will ever eat again.

When he hears her news, Conor says nothing for a moment. His expression is inscrutable. He stretches a hand to a plate of *sashimi* and begins to pick at it with his chopsticks. He munches slowly and deliberately in silence.

Then he asks, 'What do *you* want, Aoife?'

For a moment she is silenced. It is the first time she's been asked the question and she is unprepared. What does she want? To be unpregnant. That would help.

She frowns and shakes her head. 'I have to go away.'

'No,' he says flatly, 'you don't have to do anything, Aoife . . .'

'I feel that I'm trapped.'

Conor continues as if he hasn't heard her, '. . . except what you choose to do.'

She shakes her head and grimaces.

'Are you sure this is what you *want* to do?'

'What do you mean?'

'Well, you know,' he says. Behind his spectacles his expression is that of a concerned old man.

He has a kindly face, she thinks. Yes, Conor is nothing if not kind.

He touches her arm and murmurs, 'Maybe your biological clock is ticking?'

'Conor, please!'

His gaze does not falter. Then he grins at her. 'Well, I know mine is.'

'Can you imagine me as an unmarried mother? Christ, Conor, I can hardly look after myself.'

'You wouldn't be alone.'

'What do you mean?'

He smiles gently. 'There's just the two of us now.'

A burning sensation in her eyes. No, she must not cry. No, not again, so she says nothing.

'Neither of us knows anything about babies,' Conor

pops a tube of seaweed filled with rice into his mouth and munches energetically, 'but we could learn.'

'You're joking.'

'You know I don't make jokes.'

It is true: neither of them is properly equipped to deal with life. No surprise really, she thinks, considering how the two of them were reared. Poor Auntie Maureen: her knowledge of children was so limited. All that effort gone into getting them to polish their shoes and keep their bedrooms tidy and have their hair partings straight and, when adolescence loomed, Maureen simply hadn't a clue. Granny O'Sullivan, Aoife's maternal grandmother, tried to help out but, by the time Aoife was fourteen years old, no one was capable of controlling her. Even after she was expelled from school for smoking and drinking and was sent to a cramming college, there were phone calls home. Increasingly, their father worked abroad and it was left to Auntie Maureen to try and manage one surly teenager and her eccentric younger brother. In the end, when they were old enough to sort out their own problems, Maureen, with a sigh of relief, headed home. She went on to become the first lady captain in the local golf club to be elected for three years in a row. After dealing with the two of them, Maureen told Aoife, keeping the peace between the feuding lady members of Gortlea Golf Club was a piece of cake.

There is a wistfulness in Conor's eyes now. 'No reason why not. Brother and sister. After all, Dad and Maureen reared the two of us.'

'They didn't exactly do a great job.'

'Well, we didn't turn out to be axe murderers.' He shrugs. 'We've done okay. You know what they say, good enough is good enough.'

Aoife shakes her head. With surprise she realizes she's hungry. On the moving belt beside her elbow a stream of little dishes passes her by and she wonders if she should try the *okra* or the *teriyaki* roll. She opts for both and takes them down and begins to eat.

'You're familiar with the phrase *"the right to choose"*?' he says.

God, who isn't? All those endless arguments beating backwards and forwards. Closed minds, angry words. Pro-life. Pro-choice. When they come on the television, she always zaps them immediately.

Fastidiously Conor touches his mouth with a napkin before speaking. 'Well, Aoife, you have the right to choose *not to*, as well as *to*.'

Shaking her head, she tries to imagine Conor changing a nappy. For her, any future other than the one she has mapped out for herself is simply unimaginable. 'It's all arranged.'

'Are you going on your own?'

'Valerie said she'd take me to the airport.'

He looks down at his plate, his eyes hidden. She wonders what he is thinking but is afraid to ask.

They talk about other things until they get up to leave. Her brother drops his credit card onto the silver tray at the cash desk and as they stand, waiting for the payment to be processed, she stares into the shelves full of Japanese take-away dishes. Such bloodless food, chilled and delicate, with white plastic chopsticks sealed in their cellophane wrappings. They remind her of surgical dressings and hygienically packed instruments. For some reason she finds the sight of them reassuring.

'This is my final word on the matter, I promise,' Conor says. He opens the door for her to pass through. A soft, gingery breath on her cheek when he leans towards her. 'Do whatever you think is best for *you*, Aoife,' he says, slowly and distinctly, 'and not what you feel is expedient.'

Outside, the street is busy with people rushing back to work after their lunch break. They stand on the pavement for a moment. Aoife gives him a quick hug and they say goodbye. When she walks away, her heart feels light for the first time in days and she turns back to catch sight of him. Suddenly she has an urge to wave to him or even to blow him a kiss before he rounds the corner but, when she turns to look, her brother has already gone.

In a playground at the edge of the park Filipino child-minders and a few mothers sit on benches while the children career among the swings and slides, screaming with excitement. As Aoife passes the railings, a frowning monkey face pokes through and sticks out a tongue at her. They're a different species, children, Aoife thinks. They are wild and ungovernable and yet, to be married and to have children: that dream is always there, nestling among the complications of growing up, lit up and reinforced by everything she sees and hears. Because no one ever asked me, she says whenever anyone asks why she isn't married. There were men – a few – who came near but, these days, she has nobody apart from Jacob, of course, but he hardly counts.

Like Conor and Valerie, she is travelling light, although she knows that Claire worries about her being on her own. There was a conversation over coffee and cakes where Claire asked her, 'Aoife, aren't you afraid, when you're old, that you will die alone?'

'Everyone dies alone,' Aoife had replied with certainty.

Now she isn't so sure.

27

As she makes her preparations, the way ahead has the characteristics of a pilgrimage that is organized and ritualized. Preordained. Days have a dreamlike quality and she feels she has no control over what is happening to her.

'Have you any regrets?' the doctor in the family planning clinic asks her. 'Have you had any second thoughts?'

She asks herself the same question.

Each time the answer is the same: she intends to fly over on a Thursday and fly back the next day. She will go alone. Although Valerie offered to go with her, she refused the offer. No, thank you, she said, I don't want company.

Jacob slips into her office. He closes the door behind him and then he places a fat envelope on her desk. He stands there, waiting for her to open it. She would have preferred to be on her own when she opens it but it is obvious that he wants approbation, maybe even gratitude.

'How very generous,' she says dryly, after counting out the notes.

'Ah, Aoife, don't be bitter.'

She gives him a look of such loathing that he colours and leaves without another word. Conor is right. It will be impossible for her to stay in this job. One step at a time. First she has to get through the next few days. Then her life can start again. Concentrate on the future, she tells herself, after it is over. *It . . .* It's not even an operation, she learns, it is a procedure. *It . . . it . . . it . . .* It doesn't mean anything: it is papery crackling skin falling apart as she wriggles her way out. Freedom, at last, from the unease that accompanies her from the moment of waking, the shadow dragging at her side, the other life.

Too much.

Now she has made her plans, the future is settled and she feels calm. Even the morning sickness fades into a grumbling disquiet. Aoife wonders if the veterinary nurse notices any change in her but she is interested only in using Aoife's phone to make long-distance calls to Krakow without Jacob finding out.

Raindrops patter on the window. The sound is restful as Aoife concentrates on her work. Then the phone rings: a harsh jangle of sound.

It is Valerie. Full of concern, compassion and plans for a night out together.

Aoife is doubtful. 'A night out?'

'Look, you have a choice: you can stay at home and mope or you can come out with us. Claire said she'll come too and she hasn't been out for years. We'll get wasted and the next day I'll drive you out to the airport and you'll be back before you know it.'

Aoife can't think of any reason to say no. She wonders if she should be suffering pangs of guilt and hiding away until the dark deed is done, but Valerie has holed any possibility of self-pity. Valerie is on a crusade.

'I know how to blow your mind, Aoife. A night in Temple Bar and you will forget all your troubles. No shitty prick of a boss, no –'

'Jesus, stop.' Aoife is laughing despite herself. 'He might hear you.'

'So that's a yes then,' Valerie says, satisfied.

Out on the town: it's not a bad idea. She's getting fed up with Jacob padding around her at work, his spaniel eyes looking mournfully at her. '*How are you feeling today?*' each morning when he arrives in – trying to figure out if she has changed her mind during the night. How he must hate her!

Sometimes the thought of travelling to England overwhelms her. It is a step into the unknown. Nobody before her has ever taken that step, because nobody she knows has ever admitted to taking it. One more day, she thinks, and then her life can start again. And this will be *over*. She wraps her dressing gown around her and rummages through the clothes in the wardrobe. Something bright, silly even, irresponsible, yes. Something red to match the brittleness in the air. Something suitable for a scarlet woman. The Devil take the high road. That is what Granny O'Sullivan used to say when Aoife was a child. *What would she think . . .*

Better not think what Granny O'Sullivan would think.

An unearthly glow suffuses her reflection in the mirror. I look remarkably well, she notices with surprise.

Valerie thinks so too. It is obvious from her awestruck expression when Aoife stands at the door of the restaurant, dressed in her red dress, bright-eyed and radiant. In some ways, Valerie is a romantic: she wants her friends to enjoy great rushes of passion and secret trysts to fire up her imagination but, at heart, she is as level-headed as they come. She has no intention of ever settling down with a man, she insists. 'No way. Not even if he came bedecked in diamonds.'

Now Valerie's expression is tinged with respect. She is subdued by the thought of pregnancy, its power to upend expectations and shatter dreams. Carefully she notes the changes, even at this early stage, in Aoife's physiognomy and says almost enviously, 'God, Aoife, you look fabulous.'

As usual, Claire is late. When she arrives, she is flustered. Child-minder problems, she says and slips in beside Aoife, her eyes averted.

She knows. Valerie must have told her, Aoife realizes. So much for keeping it quiet. She grimaces at Valerie, who shrugs and flattens out her hands.

'So how are you feeling?' Claire asks solicitously.

'Jesus! I'm fine. I'm grand. I'm fecking ecstatic.'

To her surprise, Claire does not try to dissuade her from going. Her voice is quiet, matter-of-fact. 'I suppose it's for the best, although I can't imagine. You are doing the right thing, you know. Otherwise your life would be . . .'

'I know,' says Aoife, 'but please, just don't go on about it.'

'Gin and tonics all around?' Valerie says as she waves at a hovering waiter.

The restaurant begins to fill up with people. In the background modern jazz music fizzles and swoops. Lights go on. Suddenly the place is alive and exciting to Aoife. She looks at her friends and they are transformed too; she can see it in their eyes, and the way they splay their arms on the table and giggle into their drinks. Everything tastes better than it has done for weeks. Greedily Aoife eats and, after the main course, they compete to see who can order the most extravagant, most calorific dessert. A great gooey slab of chocolate cake is placed in front of her. Deliberately Aoife lifts a spoonful to her lips and swallows the confection down as if her life depends on it.

'I don't know about you,' she says when she clears the plate, 'but I'm stuffed.'

Valerie pours the last of her drink into a tall glass full of cream and meringue and strawberries and then plunges her spoon in. She is only getting started. 'Come on, girls, another round while we're still in the mood. You know what they say: one gin and tonic is all right. Two is too many but three is not enough. And we've only had three.'

Claire leans across the table. Her eyes are unfocused. There is a blob of cream at the corner of her mouth. She grasps Aoife's hand and says thickly, 'I think you're being very brave.'

'Do you?' Aoife looks at her interestedly. 'I thought you'd be dead set against what I'm doing.'

'No, no, no.'

'I'm surprised.'

Claire whispers, 'I just don't like the word.'

'I know. The A-word.'

'Yes, but I understand – I mean, why you think it's for the best.'

'Do *you* think it's for the best?'

Claire does not reply. Even Claire, who has wrapped her entire life around her son, does not judge her. Aoife sighs. When it comes down to it, apart from the Rosary brigade, is there anybody in this country, she wonders, who is actually against abortion? A cardinal sin is committed on a daily basis and yet, as far as she can see, it is accommodated with ease. She phoned the number she found in the *Yellow Pages* and the arrangements were made immediately. She could have been planning a trip to a musical in London, it seemed so effortless. Just as long as no one actually *talks* about it, as Claire would say. As long as the A-word is never mentioned, everything will be all right.

She tries to imagine the reaction if she told her father or, even worse, her Auntie Maureen. Ha! She shrinks at the thought. Then there would be fireworks for sure. She would never hear the end of it. Aoife doesn't feel brave at the thought of being found out, but she doesn't feel frightened either. She just feels numb.

In the street, crowds of young people press around them through the darkness. A stag party of Englishmen, shirt-tails hanging out of their trousers, mouths slack and roaring. One of them bumps against Aoife. He straightens up the leprechaun hat on his head and staggers on. A slurred apology wafts back.

When will I begin to feel again, she wonders.

'Mind the sick!' Valerie assiduously sidesteps a heap of vomit oozing across the pavement, and leads the way into The Norseman pub.

A blast of heat, fumes, noise and cigarette-smoke envelops them. No time to think. It's all a challenge: a struggle to get served at the bar, to have oneself heard in conversation, to stay upright in the crowd. It is intoxicating, overwhelming, mind-deadening. Valerie fights her way to the bar and comes back gripping three gin and tonics.

Then they lose each other in the crush of people. Aoife is drinking deeply from her glass when a man falls against her and the drink slips out of her hand. She swings around to look at him.

'Sorry,' he mumbles.

Despite her protestations, he insists on buying her a drink. As he advances towards her, carrying the drinks through the crowd, she notes that he looks younger than she is. He is wearing a T-shirt and skin-tight jeans. As he comes close, she sees the cropped hair, the tattooed neck, the narrow waist. The silver buckle on his belt that spells out the word *Mother.*

'That's an interesting belt.' Aoife feels duty-bound to make conversation with a boy who has bought her a drink and who loves his mother.

'Yeah.'

'What do you do?'

'I work on a ship.'

He's even younger than she thought but there is something fresh and open about him that she likes.

'Really?'

'I've been away four years and after we docked yesterday I went home to Pearse Square but me mam and all the family was gone.'

'Gone! What do you mean?'

'Away. None of them been seen for over a year by the neighbours. They could be in Tallaght, for all I know.' His cheerfulness is incongruous. 'They left no forwarding address.'

'Oh, I'm sorry.'

'Do you live nearby?'

She gives him a wary look. 'Maybe.'

'I'm back on ship tomorrow.'

He moves up close to her, his breath warm on her neck. Muscular hands. Taut stomach. Clean. He's not bad-looking, she thinks as she takes a sip from her glass.

'You remind me of something,' he says.

'A cow. Don't tell me, I know.'

'Naah, you're too pretty.' He reaches out to touch her hair.

A wave of tenderness pulls through her, an inexplicable tug.

'I'm pregnant,' she says aloud just to see him jump but he can't hear her above the noise.

'You're who?' he asks, the light of hope still in his eyes.

'On the other hand,' she says, 'maybe not.'

28

At the back of the pub, in mirrored walls there are myriad reflections of Claire putting on her coat.

'I've got to get my bus!' she screams to Aoife above the din.

Valerie waves a languorous hand and, lolling back, looks up at Aoife and smiles. Her hair is mussed, her lipstick is smeared and her bra straps are slipping down her fleshy arms. The man on whose knees she is sitting has his eyes closed. He is singing to himself.

'Come on, Aoife.' Valerie pats the seat beside her. Her skin is shiny with sweat. 'Join the party.'

Aoife hesitates.

Suddenly the man throws back his head, opens his eyes and roars at the ceiling, '*Come on, Eeeefeee!*'

She can't take any more.

More in hope than anticipation, she scans the pub for a

receding coated figure. The room is swinging around and the heat is sweltering as she pushes her way through the crowd. Once she is out on the street, the air feels easy on her skin. It brims with exotic smells, wafting up from the van parked on the corner: mutton grease, kebab spices, the vinegary whiff of chips. Claire has vanished up ahead and, for a moment, Aoife is uncertain what to do. To go back into the pub or to go home: neither option is appealing. Wobbling on her high heels, she struggles along the cobbled street until a bench materializes and invites her to sit down.

I am dizzy and directionless . . . the thought rattles around in her head in a way that she finds hilarious. 'Directionless and dizzy,' she sings softly as she sits down on the bench and sways to the rhythm of the words. 'Yes, I am dizzy and directionless.'

Nobody pays the slightest attention to her. Two buskers start up a discordant 'Whiskey in the Jar', battering their guitars as if they want to crack them open. A drunk leaning up against a derelict wall tries to join in the chorus. Without missing a beat, the nearest busker reaches over and punches him in the ribs. The drunk slides down the wall like an old sack and lies slumped in the gutter.

Time to go, Aoife decides.

As she passes the crumpled figure on the ground, he is crooning quietly to himself, 'Whiskey in the jar O . . .'

When she gets to the entrance of Temple Bar Square, she stops and removes her shoes. Crowds of drinkers, disgorged from pubs, push past her but she ignores them. The relief is sudden, intense, wonderful: now she can walk for ever, dangling her shoes from her fingers as she goes. Life is good, she thinks, even if she is stuck in this spewed-out, drunken maelstrom. Her stomach growls. How can she be hungry again? I'm famished, she realizes; I could eat enough for two.

Jesus, no! Perish the thought.

Clumsily she opens her handbag, removes her purse and jams it into her jacket pocket. She isn't so drunk that she can't find somewhere open that is serving food. Any food. She moistens her lips at the thought. Curry especially.

She crosses the square and turns up a side street. Narrow, cobbled and dark. Shuttered windows wait for their morning deliverance. Quiet pools of light she steps into, then onwards, past a public house festooned with beer ads, painted shillelaghs and shamrocks. Then she is in darkness again.

At the top of the street, a tiny restaurant is lit up. It has a sign over the door in swirling pink and purple colours: *Nirvana* in handwritten letters with flowers painted through them. A row of beads hangs along the top of the window, twined through a garland of artificial flowers. Through the window she can see plastic tables and chairs. The place is empty except for a little Chinese man, who is bent over a sink in the kitchen at the back of the restaurant. Above his head an embroidered dragon glowers in a wall hanging. A Chinese restaurant pretending to be an Indian one, Aoife wonders, or maybe the other way around. Anyway, she doesn't care: any food is better than no food. Nirvana is for hippies, she decides.

Hare Krishna, here I come.

She rattles the door handle to no avail. She knuckles the glass. Unaware, the Chinese man continues to work at the sink. Aoife's fist grows louder now and more insistent, hammering on the window.

Then she sees it.

With its edges torn and curled, the large poster is pinned up on the rear wall of the room. The colours are gaudy and bright. A background of white foam scudding across a wild sea and white clouds above. The foreground is taken up by the figure of a tall woman dressed in thin, diaphanous garments, flattened against her body by a fierce wind. In her mighty arms she carries a white fringed bundle. Her black hair flows over her shoulders and onto her breasts. Waves of hair and waves of water curl and fall around her.

Aoife feels dizzy. She put her hand up against the glass door to steady herself. The image swims before her eyes, tellingly, as if it is a vision of something unimaginable and hidden.

What is it?

Not a hallucination, she knows that much. It is nothing more than some garish poster of a woman standing erect and gazing out across a sea. Aoife presses her forehead against the glass. She has no idea how, or what it means, but she knows that if she can get near enough, she will see what is wrapped in the white shawl that the woman is carrying. She is drawn towards it as if it holds some meaning, solves some mystery that she was not even aware of.

Aoife's breath catches in her throat. She bangs on the window, desperate now to be let in. Some instinct has taken over. It makes no sense but she knows as well as she knows her own name that she *has to get inside*.

The man working in the kitchen is oblivious of her presence. Although he is standing with his back to her, Aoife is sure that he is Chinese. There is something unmistakeable about the stiff black hair, the tiny gestures he makes as he washes and stacks dishes, the black cotton jacket and the way he toils while the boiler's roar masks the sound of Aoife's drumming on the glass.

'Let me in!' She is crying now. There is no response.

The man finishes his tasks, wipes his hands on a cloth and disappears out of sight. With a howl of frustration, Aoife turns away and leans her back against the window to look up to the night sky. Tears dribble down her face as she slowly, deliberately, beats her head against the window.

Without warning her foot slips on the footpath.

In that instant, slivers of glass shower around her. An ice storm of sparkling lights and razored edges through which she is falling. Senselessly spinning out of control. The scream she hears comes from her own mouth and she knows she's toppling backwards through a broken stream of light. She is outside and now she is inside. The room tipping crazily around her. The glare of the ceiling light hurts her eyes, so she closes them. In the darkness, she feels suddenly disembodied. Weightless. She is ready to float away and yet, in another part of her mind, she knows that she is lying flat on her back on the floor of a hippie restaurant and asking herself one, simple, concentrated question: *Where are my shoes?*

For a moment she hears only silence. Then there is the sound of running feet and voices. She opens her eyes. The Chinese man is kneeling at her side and gazing down at her. Clasping and unclasping his hands. His mouth is open and he is saying words she doesn't understand. She feels nothing now except the heaviness of a body that refuses to move.

'I'm all right.' she keeps saying. 'I'm all right.'

The room waltzes around her as strangers peer into her face.

'There is blood. It's coming from her head.'

It is an Indian woman speaking this time, her face up close, creamy-brown skin and a scent of sandalwood. She slips a towel under Aoife's head. Aoife smiles faintly and struggles to sit up.

'Lie still.'

The woman's order brooks no argument so Aoife lies motionless on the floor and gazes up for a while at the swinging ceiling light. Then, closing her eyes again, she hears footsteps, a phone and the man's sing-song voice.

'Here soon. They will be here soon.'

The two of them are as delicate as birds, Aoife thinks, one Chinese and the other Indian, the man and the woman fluttering around her, their voices true as larks. She could fall asleep to the sounds they make: sweet, fragile music that can capture secrets and keep them safe until they are ready to fly.

Then, suddenly, the sounds change register. There is a thundering roar, the whine of an ambulance, a door crashing open, men in the doorway, a muttered gibe – 'Another drunk' . . . 'Miracle they don't all end up dead.'

There are two of them. Men in uniforms with walkie-talkies. Their questions keep coming and she has to answer each one. Yes. Yes. No. A bit here. They make a cradle of their arms to lift her onto a stretcher. Resolute and strong.

'I'm all right,' she insists but they ignore her.

Out on the street a blue light is circling, noises, hi-vis jackets, revving sounds. From across the street a garda looks on with a bored expression. The ambulance doors yawn wide to receive her and inside everything is bright and absolute. No quarter given. As she is lifted into the ambulance on the stretcher, she whispers between parched lips, *I'm all right.*

There are no stars in the sky. A vague orange cloud hanging low on the eaves of a roof: that is all she can see. Then the ambulance doors are slammed shut.

29

Aoife is brought into a cubicle swathed in plastic curtains and a nurse with a clipboard asks her questions.

'So how many drinks did you have?

'I don't know, six or seven . . .' She pauses. 'God, too many.'

'Did you go unconscious?'

'No.'

'Do you feel sick or nauseous?'

'No.'

'Any health problems?'

'No.'

'Are you pregnant?

'Yes, I am,' she whispers.

After the nurse leaves, she lies back on the bed in the cubicle.

As the hours pass, the physical pain becomes almost a

relief compared to the interminable waiting. She is trapped in a state of suspended animation in a world of sickly lights, hard seats and cold, bleak walls. The only diversion is the criss-cross of the walking wounded through the Accident and Emergency Department.

When the doctor swishes through the cubicle curtains, he is fresh-faced and merry. He moves fast, his stethoscope aslant on his shoulders, and sets to work.

She does what she is told. Goes here into this room and there into that one. Machines hum and click. Now she is sitting on a chair, holding her shoes in her lap while nurses pass, files in their arms, without looking at her. By the time another nurse comes and examines Aoife's head, there is nothing left to be done. Her head has been stitched, her wrist has been X-rayed. Nothing is broken. The nurse's fingers explore Aoife's head. She is like a monkey searching for fleas: the way she folds back the strands of hair at the nape of the neck.

'Well,' the nurse says brightly, 'aren't you the lucky one?'

Aoife is silent. Only the Irish can think it is lucky to fall through a plate-glass window and split your head open.

The fingers continue to probe. 'Five stitches. I'd say it hurt.'

Aoife grunts. She is a lucky one.

The young nurse says admiringly, 'Doctor's done a lovely job on you.'

Easy to say, Aoife thinks, since I can't see the back of my head.

The nurse says, 'Have you a brush or a comb, darling?'

Aoife rummages in her handbag and finds a hairbrush. For a moment the brush rests in the palm of her hand and she stares at it. So small it could be made for a doll. Why was she so anxious to get inside that restaurant? She can remember her feeling of desperation but she has no idea what caused it. When the nurse begins to brush Aoife's hair, the utilitarian world of trolleys and bedpans, of walls shiny as metal, chilly plastic curtains, blood and mucus mopped clean and soiled sheets bundled away: all of it disappears.

She stands behind me. I can't see her but I can feel her presence, the steady pressure of her hand on the hairbrush as she counts aloud. Nineteen, twenty, twenty-one . . . The tug on my scalp. I'm seated at her dressing-table, looking at the view through the window. A sweet, blowy day outside and the heavy branches of a chestnut tree are swaying. The light is dappled and agile. In the distance little waves shiver across Lough Swilly towards Letterkenny. A swan rises from the water, its wings wide and beating. Another swan follows and the great birds wheel around before heading out to sea. Eventually my mother will reach fifty strokes and the memory will be over – but, on this occasion, she is not in a hurry. There is time to lean towards me and squeeze my shoulders gently. In the mirror our reflections meet and we smile at one another.

I am six years old. She is twenty-eight.

'I should have been a hairdresser,' the nurse says. She has a round face and brown plaits bouncing around her ears. She looks like a cheery peasant girl in a book of fairy tales. Aoife can't help smiling.

'Thank you,' she says when the nurse has finished.

The nurse puts out a plastic cup with two pills. Without thinking, Aoife pushes it away and says, 'I should tell you I'm pregnant.'

A shocked look and a quick check on the clipboard. Then, 'Well, dear heart, aren't you the lucky one?'

Aoife says nothing.

'They're painkillers. These won't do any harm.' Again the nurse puts the plastic cup beside Aoife. There is a look of wonder mixed with disapproval in her eyes. 'You could have lost the baby.' She is serious now. Unsmiling.

'But I didn't,' Aoife says, meaning it as a question.

The nurse's plaits tremble as she shakes her head.

She hands Aoife the hairbrush. 'Now, you mind yourself, darling.'

When Conor arrives, he is dressed in a suit and tie and looks as if he's going to a business meeting instead of collecting his errant sister after a night on the tear. At the sight of his neat, unquestioning demeanour, Aoife is overcome by a wave of shame.

'I'm sorry,' she whispers, crying on his shoulder. 'I'm very, very sorry.'

Embarrassed, he holds her arm as they move out through the doors. Beyond the hospital gates, even at the late hour, taxis hurry by and an ambulance arrives and offloads another casualty to be stretchered in past them.

In the car they do not speak. The night speeds past as they travel along Dorset Street. A cavern of shuttered shopfronts, blank upper windows, grimy net curtains. When, finally, she does speak, her voice is slurred, although inside her head she is already stone cold sober.

'Valerie's taking me to the airport tomorrow, so I'll be all right.'

Conor slides a glance at her.

'Today, I mean,' she corrects herself, reading the clock on the dashboard.

His expression says everything. His reticence is a reproach. Even though he has not uttered a word of criticism, she feels stupid, self-indulgent and utterly incapable of getting things right. Miserably she leans her forehead against the window.

Crossing the Liffey they move south, into a different part of the city. A grey, elephantine church stands behind railings. Rows of detached, redbrick houses hunker in shrubbery, their upper windows banked by curtains. Behind the curtains people are asleep in their beds. How many of them, Aoife wonders, are actually wide-awake and haunted by night-time disturbances, by unhappy whispers, by confessions and tears?

She leans back and closes her eyes but she cannot rest. The wind has risen. Branches bending across streetlights create giant shadows as she gazes out into the flickering dark.

At Sandymount, the sea is churning madly, white spume splattered along the edge of the strand. In the sky, great ridges of cloud swallow up a shrunken moon.

'Do you ever think of her?' she cannot stop herself from asking.

Conor keeps his eyes on the road, his hands resting on the driving wheel.

'Now and again.'

She crouches away from him, her forehead pressed against the car window. The pavement streams past dead gardens and grieving trees.

Then:

'Every day,' he says.

Conor insists on unlocking the front door for her and accompanying her up in the lift. Once she has reassured him that she intends to go straight to bed, he says goodnight, or, as he says, should he say good morning?

After he has gone, the apartment reverts to a watchful gloom. She moves around the living room, picking up a magazine from the floor, tidying a vase on the table.

Outside the wind beats against the walls, a window creaks. In the bedroom an overnight bag is still open on her bed. Everything is in order and she zips the bag closed and puts it down on the floor beside her bed. Has she forgotten anything? A crooked picture on the wall is straightened, the pillows on the bed rearranged. Even though she is exhausted, she is crackling with anxiety.

How will she ever sleep?

She need not have worried. In the embrace of the duvet, she closes her eyes and instantly finds herself slipping away into a dreamless rest *that knits up the ravelled sleeve of care* – her last thought.

Imperceptibly the gloom is waning when, hours later, she wakes to a noisy room. The wind against the window is a vibrating sheet of metal. She imagines that someone is beside her and, instinctively, she stretches her hand across the empty expanse of her bed.

To be alone is not a hardship, she thinks. The storm outside concurs. *Yessssss* . . . When she closes her eyes again, the image of the woman in the poster floats in the air: her great stature and kohl-ringed eyes, the glossy black hair around her shoulders, the wild sea. The folds of cloth against her body, her steady gaze and the white fringed bundle in her arms.

Aoife's head aches. She must have been terribly drunk. Tentatively she touches the back of her head and feels the weal behind her ear, the edge of a plaster. She checks the pillow for bloodstains. Reassured when she finds none, she stretches out in the bed and pulls the duvet up under her chin and clasps her hands. Now she has the time to think about the events that have led her to this point. Getting pissed on the night before she goes to England to have an abortion. Jesus! What would her mother have thought? Is there even the remotest chance, she wonders, that her mother would have understood what she is going through now?

'I think she might have understood,' Aoife says aloud. Deliberately, as if she is addressing the room. 'Not because I know her, which clearly isn't the case, but because I know that acceptance is at the core of everything we do.'

Ruefully she thinks that it is all too easy to imagine others as a reflection of ourselves, particularly when they are dead. She has no way of being certain and no firm grasp on reality. Everything is conjecture. She sighs. It is not beyond the bounds of possibility that her mother could have turned out like that woman in Offaly. Had her mother lived, she could have been like her friend Bridget Wall: a sly, scheming woman who enjoyed pretending to be someone she wasn't.

As the light builds in the room, Aoife listens to the wind's roar. Her eyelids droop and in the shadows and hollow spaces behind her eyes she discovers fragments: a flickering light, a tug of a brush through her hair, a horse rearing up on his hind legs whinnying, an escape from the surge of hooves, the panicked eyes.

Her hand safe in her mother's hand: the remembrance of being loved.

Suddenly a loud buzzing invades the room. For a moment Aoife is confused by the sound. Then she realizes it is the intercom: a peremptory bellowing that demands a response. *Valerie*. Downstairs her friend is waiting to be let in. Yes, Valerie who leaves nothing to chance, who is here early so that the two of them can get to the airport in plenty of time. Aoife visualizes her turning restlessly on the step outside the apartment block and tapping her fingers against the doorjamb as she waits.

Aoife sits up in the bed and pulls the duvet around her

shoulders. Without moving, she waits while the noise continues. When it stops, she does not trust the silence. It is only a temporary lull, she reckons, and sure enough the buzzing starts up again. She waits until it stops but Valerie is not a woman to give up easily. The buzzer is activated again. This time it falters as if the finger pressing it has grown weary and discouraged. When the room goes quiet, Aoife is relieved that Valerie has given up at last.

She slides down in the bed and listens as the wind turns and falls. She even imagines that she can hear the distant sound of the sea, steady as breathing. Sighing, she closes her eyes. Nothing can bring her relief from the past. She shares the same flesh and bone with a mother she can barely remember. Theirs is a common DNA and that is the promise of immortality.

From a void the words emerge.

What?

She opens her eyes and, without understanding, says aloud the words issuing from her mouth, '*This is my strength*.'

Below her window a car engine coughs into life. Around her the room brightens. A new day is beginning. She can see the outline of the dressing table at the curtained window. Once that dressing table belonged to her mother: now it belongs to her. As she waits on the edge of consciousness, Aoife can hear the wind abating. Although her head still throbs, her mind is clear and untroubled. She understands that the past can be imagined only as ephemera: she can no more know her mother than she can fly to the moon.

And yet, in the same way that a language is learnt by speaking it, she can discover what it means to be a mother by becoming one herself.

When it comes to the future, she is free to choose.

Interview with the Author

Why write this novel?

It is over twenty years since my first novel, *Acts of Subversion,* was published. The world has changed dramatically since then. Social and cultural change, and political upheaval, is central to my second novel *A Shadow in the Yard*. The characters are fictional, creatures of my imagination, but the background is of a changing society in which recognizable historical events take place. Writing, I suspect, is a way to meet the challenge of living in a world that refuses to stand still.

As a former politician, do you see yourself as a political writer?

Not in the sense that the term is usually applied. The South African writer Nadine Gordimer once said:

'The novel is what happens when the riot is over; it's what happens when people go home.' The riot is seen as political and gets media coverage. The aftermath never does. And yet it is in this space that fiction thrives. The media bring us news of terrible events. They impinge on our consciousness for a moment before being overtaken by the next atrocity. When I worked as a TD, I was aware that a rapid absorption of information was required because I was dealing with many diverse political issues. More often than not the exigencies of the job demanded a rush to judgement, rather than a deeper understanding of events. How many of us living at one remove, for example, can remember the names of five people killed during the Troubles in Northern Ireland? Or even two? How many of us can fully appreciate the emotional damage caused?

You open the novel with the finding of a body. Why?

The death of Rosaleen – had it actually happened – would have only got brief media attention. The novel, on the other hand, tells of the circumstances that led up to her death and the effects it had afterwards. She is an innocent: she is, in John Hewitt's words, the young woman who strayed into the line of fire. In his poem 'Mosaic' Hewitt makes the point that to judge a period we need to have the whole story – *the tesserae* – in order to come to a conclusion. In Rosaleen's case, I wanted to tell the whole story.

It is a novel in two parts. Why?

A writer doesn't always know why a novel takes on a certain form. As this novel developed the characters took over and directed the story to an extent that was quite unnerving. Norman Mailer called writing the Spooky Art and he has a point. I tell myself the novel has this form because I decided to take the longer view, to explore the effects of loss over time and to understand how generations can make unconscious connections with each other, but the truth is that instinct – rather than intelligence – took me along the pathway that leads to the end of the novel.

You've led a busy and productive life since you wrote your last novel. Did you hanker after fiction-writing in the meantime?

After my first novel was published I tried – and failed – to write a second one. I had a bad case of writer's block. Meanwhile my life was taking a new trajectory: in 1992 I was elected to Dáil Éireann and that ended the possibility of writing anything longer than a shopping list. I didn't get time to hanker after fiction-writing: there just weren't enough hours in the day.

Are you working on another novel at present? Can you say a little about its themes and subject?

The novel I'm working on at present extends over a longer time span than my first two novels. I'm interested in exploring the Dissenter tradition in

Ireland and, fortunately, I have access to papers that belonged to my mother's family who were Unitarians from County Antrim. The papers are a rich source of inspiration but the novel is a work of the imagination – or will be, when I've written it. It's still early days.

How disciplined are you when it comes to a writing schedule? Do you write according to a planned schedule, or in bursts as inspiration moves you, or does the novel take possession of you and claim your full attention until it's done?

It takes me a long time to start a novel but, once it takes on a life of its own, I become a bit of a recluse and will work flat out until it's finished. Although writing a novel is a solitary activity, I find having contact with other writers to be stimulating. As a member of the Web group I am fortunate to be able to meet up with other writers and we critique our work on a monthly basis. We don't necessarily take each other's advice but I find it helpful to put my work out to be tested by writers whose judgement I trust.

It could be argued that the central theme of *A Shadow in the Yard* is motherhood and the profound importance of that role in society and our emotional lives. To what extent is that assessment true?

It is certainly *one* central theme in the novel. During my lifetime the lives of women have improved dramatically. Nowadays we take for granted the right to contraception, to work, to equal pay, to be able borrow money from a bank or to sit on juries. These rights were hard-won and are now embedded in our society. Yet some things don't change: having a baby can be as transformative an experience for women today as it was for their mothers. Maybe it always will be.

ACKNOWLEDGEMENTS

Thanks to my agent, the indomitable Jonathan Williams, my publisher Paula Campbell, production manager David Prendergast of Ward River Press, and editor Gaye Shortland – professionals all who guided me through the process of publication. I am grateful to Professor Gerald Dawe, Deirdre Madden, Lilian Foley, Paul Murray, Philip Davison and my fellow students at the Oscar Wilde Centre at TCD who provided the critical and constructive environment for this writer to find her voice again after so many years. I am grateful for my time at the Heinrich Böll Cottage on Achill Island, where solitude and the natural beauty of the landscape are so conducive to writing. Thanks to my good friends in the Web Writing Group who patiently travelled with me on my journey to the end of the novel; to Catherine Curran and Emily McManus who read the novel in draft form and gave me the gift of their advice; to Peg Longmore who was by my side and, most of all, to my children, Luke, Ronan, Sam and Emily, my partner Sean Lenihan and my extended family for surrounding me with love and joy.

Lastly I want to thank the swan from Bray harbour for flying into my back yard and thus becoming the inspiration for the first meeting of Rosaleen McAvady and Tom Mundy.